WICKED IMPULSE

Publisher © Chelle Bliss December 13th 2016
Editors Lisa A. Hollett
Proofreader Fiona's Dreaming
Cover Design © Chelle Bliss
Formatted by Chelle Bliss

ISBN: 9781682305133

BOOKS BY CHELLE BLISS

~MEN OF INKED SERIES~

THROTTLE ME (CITY & SUZY) Book 1, 2014

HOOK ME (MIKE & MIA) Book 2, 2014

RESIST ME (JAMES & IZZY) Book 3, 2014

UNCOVER ME (THOMAS & ANGEL) Book 4, 2015

WITHOUT ME (ANTHONY & MAX) Book 5, 2015

HONOR ME (CITY & SUZY) Book 6, 2016

~ALFA PI SERIES~

SINFUL INTENT, Book 1, 2015

UNLAWFUL DESIRE, Book 2, 2016

WICKED IMPULSE, Book 3, 2016 (COMING IN FALL)

~STANDALONE BOOKS~

REBOUND NOVELLA (FLASH AKA SAM), 2015

ENSHRINE (BRUNO & CALLIE), 2016

TOP BOTTOM SWITCH (RET & ALESE), 2016

DIRTY WORK (JUDE & REAGAN), 2016

MANEUVER, 2016

To learn more about Chelle's book visit chellebliss.com

For my biggest fan – my brother.
I'll always love you, Kevin.

BEAR

I fucked up.

It was a fact I could never deny.

My life had been a never-ending string of bad decisions and complications. Molly was just the latest—but not the greatest by any means.

The only thing I did right was marry the love of my life, Jackie. She was the most beautiful thing in the world and sweeter than any honey a bee could make.

When we found out we were going to have our second baby, we were over the moon excited. That was where my fucked-up journey began. Jackie didn't make it through childbirth; she hemorrhaged, and the doctors couldn't stop the bleeding.

Losing her altered me forever.

Not only was she taken from me too soon, I had a newborn baby boy to raise, along with a one-year-old daughter. I knew a little about kids, having two younger sisters, but I wasn't ready to do it alone.

Most of their life I was absent, in and out of jail for petty charges—things like stealing cars and being in possession of stolen property. My crimes never hurt anyone, except for my kids. They paid the price by not having me around and being left in the hands of my sisters.

It took me years to clean up my act.

Hell, decades, if I was being honest. Eventually, I pulled my head out of my ass and surrounded myself with true friends. City, Tank, and Frisco became my family, pulling me off the path of self-destruction.

If Jackie had made it…everything would've been different. We would've been a family, I would've stayed clean, and I wouldn't have been here with freakin' Molly.

I swatted her hand away when she reached for me. "Molly, doll, I appreciate the pussy, but you know this is nothing more than a simple fuck. Yeah?" I was bent over, pulling on my boots. If I put my ass on the bed, she would try to touch me again—and that shit was not happening. "So let's not make this a habit."

Pulling the sheet over her tits, she glared at me. "Bear," she whispered in a gravelly, smoked-too-long tone.

I cut her off, nipping that shit before she started with her bullshit tears to guilt me into giving her my cock once more. "Nope. I never had planned for anything more than what this was—a dirty, sweaty fuckfest."

"You're a bigger asshole than I thought, Bear." She crouched against the headboard with her arms crossed.

"Babe." I laughed at the stupidity of the situation. "When I said 'Wanna fuck?' I wasn't asking you to be my ol' lady. A fuck is a fuck—cock, cunt, and hopefully an orgasm or two. It doesn't make you mine."

She scooted forward and let the sheet drop from her chest. "I didn't even get one, you bastard," she seethed.

I didn't even bother glancing down at her tits, even though she wanted me to look. "Your greedy cunt latched on to me three times, sweetheart. Don't give me shit that you didn't come. You moaned my name like a bitch in heat every time too."

"Get the fuck out!" she yelled as I yanked the shirt over my head.

Using the palm of my hand, I smoothed down my shirt and smiled. "Thought you'd never ask." I waved on my way out, leaving the door open before I headed down the hallway.

She cursed me something awful, and it sounded like something out of a horror movie, but I kept on walking and paid her no mind.

When I walked outside and the wind blew, I caught a whiff of her cheap perfume mingled with cigarettes and sex. Usually, the stench of my sexual exploits didn't bother me, but for some reason, this time was different.

I'd been thinking a lot about Jackie lately. All the things I'd lost the day she left me. I hadn't opened my heart to anyone since then. People in love surrounded me, and it gutted me—knowing I missed that in my life.

Even though I'd had an ol' lady or two in the last twenty-something years, they didn't compare to Jackie. I was sure I'd never given them a chance, but it was hard for them to overshadow the perfection of my wife in my memories.

My phone beeped as I was about to climb onto my bike.

Tank: Get your dick out of her and come to the Cowboy.

I wanted to go home and wash away her scent, but Tank came before ridding myself of Molly's stench.

Me: On my way—be there in 10.

When he asked for a favor, I didn't question him. If Tank wanted me to drive into hell with him at four a.m., I'd show up to fuck shit up with him in a heartbeat.

***

When I walked through the doors of the Neon Cowboy, Tank was seated at our usual table and surrounded by the crew—Frisco, City, Morgan, Thomas, James, Mike, Anthony, and Sam.

They were deep in conversation from the looks of it, leaning across the table in close formation. I didn't even need to hear a word to know that something major was going on.

"Yo," City called out when I was only a few feet away. "Sit your ass down, we have a lot to talk about."

Joseph "City" Gallo had been the other part of our trio. Tank, City, and I had grown close over the years and become more like brothers than just friends. City was younger by ten years, but he was wise beyond his years When he flashed his perfectly straight, toothy smile, people responded. It didn't hurt that he had a pretty-boy face either.

I pulled out the chair, turning it backward and straddling it. "What's up?"

"It's Johnny," Morgan replied with his hand in a tight fist on top of the table. "I'm going to kill him if I ever find him." He slammed his fist down on the table, making all the drinks bounce and come down with a loud clatter. Morgan looked frazzled. His dark brown hair was all over the place and hanging into eyes.

I'd never liked that prick, Johnny. Since the day I met him at Race's track, there'd just been something about him that seemed off. Race raved about how helpful he was, but I just had a feeling about him. After Race bought the track from him, she hired him to stay on and help her get everything up and running in tip-top shape. He quickly cozied up to Fran, Morgan's mom, and the rest was history.

"He stole fifty thousand from the track's account and disappeared." Tank placed his hand on Morgan's shoulder and gave it a firm squeeze.

I was surprised by his balls but not shocked by the audacity. "When?"

"When he didn't show up at work today, Race knew something was fishy. Then the bank called because some checks she wrote bounced."

"Terrible," I muttered and shook my head. This wasn't the time for an "I told ya so."

"We're working this one off the books," Thomas told me with a raised eyebrow. "I'm sure you have no problem with that."

As the owner of ALFA PI, Thomas was my boss. He was also City's brother and ex-DEA. Thomas was the first person in decades who gave me a chance at real employment. I'd finally felt like I'd found a home with him and the guys.

"None," I said firmly. "But if I find him, I get to beat his ass first."

"He's all yours, buddy," James said before he looked around the table. "We're going to gather information and try to find a few leads, then we'll plan our attack." James, the co-owner of ALFA PI, liked to go rogue—that was what I loved most about these guys. No one wanted to call the cops or pussyfoot around a problem. Johnny was going to wish he had never been born by the time we were through with him.

Thomas leaned back in his chair and crossed his arms in front of his chest. "I know tomorrow is Saturday, but we need everyone at the office and working on this."

I grabbed the pitcher of beer and poured myself a glass.

Molly was still lingering in my mouth, and it wasn't pleasant. She was like a bad pill, and her aftertaste was stuck in the back of my throat. "I got nothing else to do."

"I'll be there too," Sam finally piped up in the conversation. "I'm always there when you guys need me."

Sam had changed since I'd first met him. He was still a cocky fucker at times, but I'd learned to deal with it. In the past, there wasn't a day I didn't want to punch him in the face, but he'd grown on me. He'd grown up a lot, and he'd always had our backs. Tough fucker even took a bullet without whining like a little bitch. I even dared to say he'd earned my respect—which wasn't easy to do, especially after you'd already been classified as a shithead.

City glanced at his watch. "I know it's late, but let's be there by noon. We don't want to give this guy too much time to get very far."

"There isn't a place in the world he could hide from us for long, brother," Mike said, rubbing his chin with the biggest smile on his face.

Mike was an interesting character. When he wasn't piercing people, he had spent time in the ring. He'd become a UFC champion before finding the love of his life and retiring. Or as I said…becoming pussy-whipped and quitting.

"How's Fran?"

"She's devastated and pissed off. My mom is downright scary when she's mad. Johnny better hope you find him first and not my mother," Morgan replied and grimaced. "We can't let her get involved. She's going to try, but it's a no-go, fellas."

"Understood," James replied.

"I have no problem telling her to butt out," I said and shrugged. "Want me to handle her?"

Morgan's blue eyes sliced to mine. "You will not handle my

mother."

I couldn't help but laugh. "Kid, you don't have to worry about me. I'm just sayin' she and I are equals. She'd listen to me."

"Bear," Tank whispered at my side and elbowed me in the ribs.

"What? I'd never touch the woman. Jesus. What the fuck do you guys think I am?"

"Seriously," Morgan said through gritted teeth. "You can never keep your shit in your pants. You're getting nowhere near my mom, Bear. Don't even think about helping."

I laughed it off, but I'd be lying if I didn't admit it bothered me a little. Fran was a fine piece of ass, but never had I thought about bangin' her silly. Wait. That was a lie. I did imagine it… more than once. I'd just never act on it.

"I'm a perfect gentleman," I told the table, and they all burst into laughter. "Bros before hoes." I shrugged.

"Dude." Morgan dragged his hand through his already messy hair, and he was struggling to stay in his seat.

I shook my head and set shit straight. "I'm referring to anything with a pussy, my friend. You guys—" I glanced around the table "—always come first."

Morgan continued to mumble under his breath, but he dropped the bullshit. Everyone agreed we'd meet at ALFA PI at noon, and then they slowly disappeared until there was only Tank and me left.

"Another?" I asked and grabbed the pitcher that was almost empty.

"I'm good." He waved me off. "You better watch what you say about Fran around Morgan."

"Come on," I groaned before I topped off my glass. "You know me better than that."

He glared at me when he stood up, hovering over me. "That's exactly what I'm afraid of, Bear. She's off-limits. Got it?"

I threw my hands up in the air and pushed back from the table with the pitcher still in my hand. "Fuckin' A. I'm not tapping that shit, Tank. Get the fuck off my back already."

"I've seen the way you look at her, dumb fuck. You're lucky Morgan hasn't caught on."

I slammed the pitcher against the table and narrowed my eyes. "Shut the fuck up already about this shit. I'm not going to fuck Fran."

"Uh-huh," Tank muttered before he left too.

Fuckers.

I might be an asshole, but I had morals. Didn't I?

BEAR

Thomas tapped a stack of papers against the conference table, peering around the room. "Good, everyone's here. What do we have on Johnny?"

We had been at it for three hours—making phone calls, tracking down leads, monitoring his digital footprint, and any other information we could get our hands on about John McDougal.

"McDougal isn't his real name," Sam spoke first and pushed a sheet of paper toward Thomas. "It's O'Sullivan, and he could be using either name."

"What about his cell phone?" James asked.

"It's been turned off," Morgan told us as he rubbed his temples.

"Have your buddy keep on it in case he turns it back on. We

just need a few seconds to find his location," James replied like we were all new to the game.

"Already done," Morgan said.

"Bank accounts?" Thomas asked, raising an eyebrow.

"Empty," I told him.

Thomas tapped his pen against the table and leaned back in the chair. "Can someone interview Fran and see what she knows about Johnny? She may think a detail isn't important, but it might give us a lead."

Morgan dragged his fingers down his face. "I'll do it."

"I got it," I told him because his mom might not open up as much to him as she would to someone else…someone like me.

Everyone at the table turned to me with weird looks on their faces. "What?"

"You want to do it?" Morgan stared at me with narrowed eyes.

"Well, yeah." I shrugged.

"Why?"

"She may not tell you everything you need to know. Parents don't like to be as open with their kids as they would be with a friend."

He gawked at me. "You're my mom's friend?"

I hid my snarl and talked to cover up my annoyance. "I'm your friend, asshole, and by extension, your mother's too."

"Fine," Thomas interrupted before Morgan could say something else. "Bear will interview Fran."

Morgan's glare didn't leave me as the meeting continued. I ignored the stink eye he gave me and listened to everything I could about Johnny. He was a slippery motherfucker. He hid in plain sight, underneath our noses, and we were never the wiser. I knew every man around this table felt like me—a complete fool.

"Where's the last place he used his credit card?" Frisco asked, making a new bullet point on his fancy legal pad.

Kids. They wrote stupid shit down or put it in their notes in their fancy-ass cell phones. I only wrote down the most important information.

I was old-school and used my memory with most shit. I didn't have time to flip through pages when I was working a case or trying to track someone down. I swear technology had dumbed them down about ten pegs in the evolutionary chain.

"Yesterday, just outside of Gainesville," Sam answered.

"Morgan?" James called out.

I glanced out of the corner of my eye and realized he was still staring at me. "Morgan," I said, finally turning to look at him with a serious face.

"What?" Morgan replied, his eyes growing narrower.

"Are you listening or giving Bear the evil eye over there?" James laughed, and I couldn't help but join in.

Morgan's face didn't change. "I think someone else should interview my mom."

Thomas cleared his throat before speaking. "It's already decided. Bear will do it."

"Come on, kid," I said with a smile on my face. "I promise to be a complete gentleman. You're like family to me."

His upper lip snarled, and I was about to say "Down, boy" when his face finally softened a bit. "Fine, Bear. I'm trusting you with this."

I nodded, and guilt gnawed at me because I did want Fran. I'd always pictured her naked underneath that tracksuit. She was an enigma to me. I could tell she had a smokin' body, but for some reason, she wanted to hide it like she was a Golden Girl. I didn't know what happened to some women when they matured; they felt the need to hide what they had when they should have been showing it to the world.

"Bear, can you meet with her tonight?" James asked.

"On it," I said as I nodded, trying to hide my excitement. "Let me go call her now." I stood and excused myself, feeling Morgan's eyes on me as I walked out of the room and closed the door quietly.

Instead of calling her from my cell phone, I decided to use the office line so it was more official. I sat for a moment and collected my thoughts before I dialed her number that I had scribbled on a tiny scrap of paper I'd hidden underneath my desk calendar.

It rang twice before Fran picked up. "Hello."

"Hey, Fran." I cleared my throat, suddenly feeling nervous. "It's Bear."

"Hey, hot stuff." Her voice was cheerful under the circumstances. "I thought you were Morgan."

"Sorry to disappoint you, sweetheart."

She giggled softly. "You're never a disappointment, Bear."

"I wanted to know if we could sit down tonight and talk about Johnny."

"That fucker. I have a lot to say. Come by tonight, and I'll cook you dinner."

"Franny, you don't have to do that. It's too much work. Why don't you meet me at the bar for a drink?"

"Nope," she said quickly. "I feel like cooking. It keeps my mind busy. Be here at six."

She hung up the phone before I could answer, and I was left staring at the phone, shocked. It'd been ages since anyone had cooked me a meal. I couldn't show up empty-handed. I knew the guys thought I was an animal, but there was a time when I'd had manners.

I stalked back into the room, keeping my eyes down and away from Morgan as I took my seat. The guys were talking more about Johnny and where his next move would be. There was very little we knew about the man, but I figured in the next twenty-four hours we'd have a clearer picture of who the pissant really was.

"Did you get in touch with Aunt Fran?" Thomas asked from the head of the table.

Fuck. Franny was related to almost everyone at the table and so far off-limits that I might as well not even have a dick. To put a beautiful morsel like that in front of me, dangling her like a piece of meat, and not to allow me to touch her was just plain cruel. "Yeah. I'm meeting her at six to talk about Johnny."

Morgan's eyebrow rose. "At the bar?"

"No." I shook my head while I crossed my arms. "She wanted me to come to her place."

"Uh-huh. Maybe I'll drop by." Morgan mimicked me and crossed his arms.

I turned to face him. "Let's get one thing straight, kid. Your mom isn't going to want to talk in front of you. Keep your ass away."

He leaned forward and invaded my space. "Why wouldn't she talk in front of me? She tells me everything."

"Has she called you to tell you everything she knows?"

His lips twisted. “No.”

“That’s my point. She’s embarrassed she didn’t realize he was a lying scumbag. Let me talk with Fran. She’ll be more comfortable.”

He exhaled loudly before leaning back in his chair. “Fine. Don’t get too comfortable.”

“Oh, shut up already. We’ve known each other for years. Have a little trust, will ya?”

“That’s the problem, Bear. I know too much about you.”

He did too. He’d been around for far too many escapades and antics than I’d like to admit. But Morgan didn’t know the real me. No one did. I shut him away a long time ago, putting up a steel fortress around my heart to protect myself. They all saw the wild, careless me but not the real man underneath.

I paid his comment no attention and turned back to the conversation at hand. “Let’s go over the information one more time so it’s fresh in my head.”

After another rundown of the information we had on Johnny, the conference room started to look more like a war room. Phones were ringing off the hook, people were jotting down notes, and we used the whiteboard to draw connections to important leads we needed to follow up on to catch the thieving bastard.

By the time I walked out of the office, I had just enough time to head to the little Italian bakery to grab some dessert. Fran probably worked her ass off on the meal, and it was the least I could do—plus, I wanted to make her smile.

BEAR

I pushed the empty plate away and rubbed my belly. “That was so damn good, Franny. I don’t remember the last time I had a meal this great.”

She beamed at me with the biggest smile. I couldn’t recall when I’d seen her so happy. “I like spoiling you.” The woman could cook like any of those fancy-ass chefs on the television. She didn’t just make a dinner, she made an entire meal. Course after course, she carried out of the kitchen, dishing it out onto my plate before I could protest.

“Spoil me anytime, babe.” I caught myself and didn’t say anything else because I was already verging on flirting, and Morgan would have my balls.

“Cooking relaxes me, but you know I’m really no good at it. Right? I mean, I’m no Maria.”

"Well, you must really be stressed." I glanced around the table filled with dish after dish of different foods. "As for being a good cook, I don't remember the last home-cooked meal I ate, so it tasted delicious."

She burst into a fit of laughter. "No one likes my cooking, not even Morgan. Want a drink?" She stood quickly and headed to the tiny cabinet against the wall. "I need something strong to get through this."

"I'm sorry," I said, feeling guilty about putting her out. "We could do this another time."

"Sit down," she commanded me without a thought. "I want you here. I need to talk about it. Alcohol helps. Want one or not?" Her bossiness was definitely a turn-on.

"Yeah, I'll take a gin and tonic."

Her dark, shoulder-length hair parted as she reached into the cabinet and grabbed three bottles. The tiniest patch of exposed skin on the back of her neck peeked out, and my cock started to stir. Off-limits, Cujo. Don't even think about it.

"Ice?" she asked with her back to me.

"Two cubes, please." My eyes traveled down her body, focusing on her ass and trying to see the outline through the flimsy material of her blue tracksuit. Why couldn't the woman wear jeans like other people? Her outfit did nothing for her body and made it so hard for my imagination to run wild. I couldn't even tell if she had on panties, but in my mind I pictured her without.

She set the drink down in front of me and caught me off guard. "Are you feeling okay? You look flushed."

I chuckled softly and hoped she hadn't caught me staring at her ass. "I'm fine. Just a bit warm," I lied my ass off.

"Want me to turn on the air?" she asked and started to move her track jacket away from her skin. "It is a bit warm in here." She stood quickly, removing her jacket and placing it on the chair before heading to the hallway.

My eyes zoomed in on her chest instantly. The white T-shirt was partially see-through, and all I could focus on was the outline of her black lace bra. Why did it have to be black? It didn't match the tracksuit. I highly doubted that the ladies in the Golden Girls wore black lingerie underneath their clothing.

"You should feel better soon. I turned it down a bit." She sat, moving the umbrella around in her pink drink. "Sex on the Beach," she said innocently.

I started to choke on my drink at the mention. "What?" I asked in a strangled voice.

"My drink. It's a Sex on the Beach."

My mouth formed an "O" before I started to cough again. All of a sudden, I pictured Fran running around in the sand with beads of water dripping off her while she was clad in a string bikini. What the fuck was wrong with me?

"Where do you want to start?" she asked before bringing the drink to her lips and staring at me over the rim.

What I wanted to say and what I needed to say were so opposite, but I went with work. "So today we learned that McDougal isn't Johnny's real name. It's O'Sullivan. Other than that, we don't have a ton to go on, but you may be able to give us some clues."

"O'Sullivan?" she asked, setting down her drink on the table in slow motion. "I've heard the name before."

"You have?"

"Yeah. His cousin who always called was named O'Sullivan."

"Do you remember the cousin's first name?"

"Kate."

I pulled out the tiny tablet I'd stuck in my back pocket before I walked out of ALFA and started to jot down notes. This was one time I wanted to actually write shit down. I needed to go back to the office with a full report. Plus, I'd figured Fran would distract me and I'd probably forget half the shit she'd told me by the time I walked out the door.

"Do you know where she lives?"

"Somewhere in New York."

"Anything else about Kate?" She couldn't have had any more of a plain name. It would be like finding a needle in a haystack in the entire state of New York.

"She's a hairdresser or some shit in the Bronx."

That narrowed it down a lot. Couldn't be too many Kate O'Sullivans doing hair in the Bronx. "I'll start checking her out as soon as possible."

"Now that I think of it…" She placed her face in her hands. "Oh God," she wailed softly. "I'm a fool."

I reached out and pulled her hands away from her face. "Don't feel like a fool, babe. Just tell me."

She sighed before dragging her dark brown eyes to mine. "He always said I love you to her before they got off the phone. I didn't think anything of it. But he claimed they were cousins. How many cousins do you know who say that every time they talk?"

"I don't know." I shrugged.

"I bet she's his wife or some shit. That's just how my luck is."

"Don't jump to conclusions. Maybe it was his cousin."

She gave me a "don't be an idiot" look. "Let's be real here, Bear. He used me to get comfortable and stay under the radar at work."

"Now you listen to me, Ms. DeLuca, manipulators know just what to say and how to act to get their way. There's nothing you could've done to change things. He knew exactly what he was doing."

"Maybe." She shook her head. "Or I'm just a fool."

"Didn't he work at the track for years?"

"He owned it, and Race bought it from him."

I knew that, but it had slipped my mind. Something wasn't adding up. Why would a man sell a track and then steal from the very person he'd already had a windfall from… It didn't make sense.

"It's highly unlikely that she's his wife, Fran. Maybe she's his sister. If he lived down here for years, running a business, someone would've known about Kate. A man can only hide a wife for so long."

"True," she said in a soft voice and twisted her fingers together on top of the table. "She knew we were a couple. I actually spoke to her on the phone a few times."

I placed my hands over hers. "If that was you on the other end, would you want to talk to the woman sleeping with your husband?"

"I'd track that bitch down and kick her ass."

"Exactly." I laughed loudly. "So she's probably not his wife, but she's definitely a lead. Did Johnny act any differently lately?"

"He seemed more paranoid than normal." She stirred her drink, staring at the liquid swirling around the ice cubes. "He'd look out the windows a few times, double-check locks, and shit like that, but I thought he was just being cautious."

"Did Johnny gamble?"

She shook her head, and her hair skimmed across her shoulder, glistening in the light. "Not that I knew of."

"Who else do you remember him talking to? We're trying to get an accurate picture of who he is and who his associates were."

"Hmm." She paused and chewed on the inside of her lip. "He'd get texts all the time from someone named Trout, but I don't know if it's a nickname or a last name. I heard him reminisce about an old friend named Sawyer too. I'm sorry," she said and rubbed her forehead with her delicate fingers. "I guess I didn't know as much about him as I thought."

"Some people are just guarded, Fran. Usually, it's just out of habit, but sometimes, like with Johnny, there are other reasons why someone doesn't open up about who they really are." I took a large swig of gin, but I kept my eyes trained on her.

"You're kind of like him, Bear. You're very private. I don't even know your real name."

My hand stilled with the glass still pressed against my lips. I never hid my name, but I also never told people openly. My closest friends knew it, and my family, but years ago I stopped answering to it. I set down the gin and licked my lips, taking a moment to debate telling her. When I looked across the table at her sad smile, I couldn't stop myself from answering. "It's Murray."

Her smile widened, like I'd let her in on a very private secret. "I like that name. It suits you." Even though I cringed, she whispered, "Murray."

Usually, hearing my name would bring back too many memories, but coming from her mouth, it sounded as sweet as the most beautiful song. "That's me." I played it off like an idiot.

She placed her hand on my forearm and stroked my skin, sending chills skidding up my arm. "Do you mind if I call you that? Bear is cute, but Murray is more…manly."

"Cook for me again, and you can call me whatever you want." I smiled at her, relishing the feel of her skin against mine.

"Shit. I forgot about your beautiful dessert. Let me grab it." When she removed her hand and stood, I instantly missed the connection.

She disappeared into the kitchen, leaving me alone in the dining room. "What the fuck am I doing?" I whispered and glanced toward the ceiling. Closing my eyes for a moment, I took a deep breath and told myself, Fran is off-limits, asshole.

"You okay?" she asked, catching me off guard.

I peered over at her as she stood in the doorway, holding a tray of freshly made cannoli. "I couldn't be better. Good food and great company, but I wish I were here under different circumstances."

She placed two powdered-sugar-covered, chocolate-dipped cannoli on my plate. "Well, let's talk about other things besides Johnny. Ever have any kids?"

I tried to hold back my cringe. My life was something I didn't discuss with many. "I have two," I told her, which was surprisingly easy.

She sat down and placed one cannoli on her dish before setting the napkin in her lap. "How old?"

"Ret's around thirty now, and Janice is just a year older."

"Do they live around here?"

"Last I heard, he lived somewhere in Texas." I took the

largest bite of the cannoli, hoping my mouth would be too full to answer any more questions. "And she lives nearby."

"Jesus, I couldn't imagine my kid living so far away. He's my only baby and has been my life since my marriage ended."

"How long ago was that?" I asked with a mouth full of ricotta filling sticking to the roof of my mouth like wallpaper paste.

"He left right around the time Morgan graduated from high school, but the marriage was over long before that." She mindlessly traced the chocolate on the tip of the cannoli tube, and my mind went into overdrive.

It was like something out of a wet dream. Fran's tongue moved slowly across the dried chocolate, the pink beautifully contrasting with the darkness of the treat. Her eyes closed, savoring the taste, and for a brief moment, I pictured my cock in her hand with her making the same motion. When she let out a tiny moan, I almost fell off my chair.

"Anyway," she said before biting off the end and ending my fantasy. "Ray was a piece of shit. He's never had any contact with Morgan since that day. He served me with papers, and I haven't seen him since."

"I'm sorry."

"Eh." She waved her hand. "It was years ago and the best thing that ever could've happened. He was an asshole, straight up. Murray, what about your wife?"

"My wife, Jackie," I said and felt a pang of sadness. I rarely said her name anymore because it was still an open wound that hadn't fully healed. "She died during childbirth."

Her hand flew to her mouth, and her eyes widened. "I'm so sorry." When she dropped her arm, her hand found the same spot on my forearm, stroking me gently. "I can't imagine how hard that must've been."

"Even though it's been almost three decades, the pain is still like yesterday."

"It's different when someone is taken from you. I can't imagine what you went through with a newborn baby and dealing with the loss of your wife."

"I didn't deal well. I was a shitty father, Fran."

She gripped my arm tighter, the bite of her fingernails grounding me. "Men aren't meant to raise babies alone."

"Maybe," I whispered, pushing the cannoli around my dish. "I could've been a better father. Instead, I got involved with the wrong crowd, drank too much, and left Ret in the care of my sisters. I couldn't look at his cute little face every day. He was a constant reminder of what I'd lost."

"You can't correct the past, but you can try to make amends for the future." She patted my arm softly. "Do you talk to him now?"

"We talk, but I wish he were closer." I shrugged.

She smiled sweetly at me with the softest brown eyes. "Well, why don't you convince him to come here? Who doesn't love Florida?"

"I don't know," I mumbled before shoving the rest of the half-eaten cannoli in my mouth.

"Time is something you can never get back. At our age, it's the most precious thing we have, Murray."

"Fran." Pieces of the cannoli fell from my lips, and I scooped them into my hand and dropped them on the plate. "I love when you say my name, but when we're not alone, can you call me Bear?"

She winked playfully. “Sure. I know you have an image to maintain.”

I couldn’t hide my smile. “Something like that.”

“So…” She dragged her drink in front of her and settled back into her chair. “That makes you about how old? Fifty?”

“Somewhere around there.” I winked. “How about you?”

“About the same.”

I dabbed at the powdered sugar that I was sure had fallen into my beard with each bite. “I didn’t think I’d ever live to see the big five-oh.”

Fran licked her finger and scooted forward. “Let me get that.” She raised her hand, and I nodded.

My body froze the closer she came with her arm outstretched, running her fingers through my beard. Each hair that moved sent tiny prickles through my system. “There,” she said and stroked my face before pulling her hand away.

“Thanks.” No one had cleaned my face since Jackie. The small gesture made my heart ache with sadness. “It’s getting late. Let’s finish up about Johnny so you can get some rest.”

“Oh, okay,” she said, and I could tell my response wasn’t what she expected.

I didn’t veer off course for the rest of my visit. We only talked about Johnny and the track. After an hour of jotting down notes, I thanked her for the dinner and made my way to the door.

“Are you sure you don’t want to stay a little longer?”

I let out a fake yawn. “I need to get to bed. Thank you for a lovely meal and even better company, Fran.” I leaned forward and kissed her soft, round cheek. “I had a good time tonight.”

She placed her palm flat against my chest, and I could feel her warmth through my T-shirt. “It was nice to cook for someone who actually likes to eat what I make."

"Whenever you need company, just call." The words just came out of my mouth without a filter. If Morgan were here, he'd punch me right in the back of the head for coming on to his mom.

"I may just take you up on that offer." She smiled and backed away through the door. "Have a safe trip home, Murray."

I had started to jog down the driveway, but I stopped when I heard my name. I turned, smiled at her, and waved. "Sweet dreams, Franny."

I couldn't wipe the stupid grin off my face as I pushed my bike down her driveway to avoid pissing off her neighbors. I kept my eyes on her in the side mirror, watching her watch me from the doorway.

Don't look back.

I was in so much trouble at this point, I'd let Morgan get in a free shot or two without even defending myself. I broke the guy code. He was my buddy and coworker, but Fran… She was a real woman who made me feel something for the first time in as long as I could remember.

FRAN

The phone rang before the sun even shone through my sheers. "Hello," I said in a groggy voice, still half asleep even though the call had startled me.

"Late night?" Maria, my sister-in-law, asked with a small giggle.

I rolled onto my side and squinted to see the numbers on the alarm clock. "What the hell are you doing awake at this ungodly hour?"

"It's almost eight, sleepyhead. We have tennis this morning, but it's raining."

"Ugh," I groaned because I fucking hated tennis, but I played it with Maria weekly to make her happy. The only bright side was that my body had never looked better since I started chasing that stupid neon ball around the court.

"Let's meet for coffee and breakfast instead."

Resting the phone against my shoulder, I rubbed the sleep from my eyes. "Fine. That sounds better than tennis any day. I'm too tired today to actually do much else."

"I heard Bear came over last night."

"From whom?"

"I talked to Tommy last night."

I grabbed the pillow from the other side of the bed and placed it over my face, muffling my voice. "You're already gossiping about me?"

"No."

"Hmph," I mumbled. "Sounds like you were."

"Stop being a baby. Get your ass up and meet me at the diner in an hour."

"Fine," I told her before kicking off the covers. "Bye."

"Don't keep me wait—"

I hung up the phone before she could keep talking. I hadn't even had a cup of coffee, and the last thing I wanted to deal with was Maria and her questions.

After I rolled out of bed and made my way to the kitchen, I dialed Morgan while I waited for the coffee to brew. "Hey, baby," I said when he answered.

"Morning, Ma. How are you today?"

"It's too early to form an opinion. I'm just waiting for the coffee and thought I'd call to check in with you."

"How did it go?"

"Fine," I said, keeping my answer short.

"That's all you have to say?"

I heard the annoyance in his tone. "We had a little dinner, talked, and then he left."

"You made him dinner?" His voice cracked on the last word.

"It helped keep my mind occupied."

"But, Ma," he replied with a deeper tone.

"No buts, Morgan. It was a nice evening."

"It was work."

"I know, son. Trust me, Bear was a complete gentleman."

"Doubtful," Morgan mumbled into the phone.

"He even complimented my cooking."

Morgan was silent for a moment. "Now I really don't trust him."

"You trusted Johnny and so did I, and where did that get us? Bear is a good man. He was kind to me last night."

"I'm sure he was," he grumbled.

"Stop with the shitty attitude, mister."

"Just be careful."

I laughed as I grabbed the half-filled pot and poured myself a cup. "You have nothing to worry about. I just hope I gave him enough information about Johnny to help."

"I'm sure you did, Ma."

"I feel responsible, Morgan. I mean, Johnny and I didn't go steady, but I spent enough time with him that I should've seen the signs. I should've known he wasn't a good guy." I took a sip, savoring the warmth and caffeine.

"Don't be ridiculous. He manipulated everyone. But that's what I'm saying about Bear. You never really know someone until it's too late. Don't think he's a good guy, Ma. He's not."

"Morgan DeLuca, I raised you to think better about people. He's your friend and a friend of the Gallos. Don't confuse your feelings for Johnny with Bear."

"I'm just putting it out there."

"Well, you've said it now. I'm a big girl and can make my own decisions." I placed the mug on the counter and glanced at the clock. "I have to run. Maria is waiting for me to have breakfast. Have a good day, honey."

"We're not done talking about—"

I hung up on him. It was becoming a normal thing for me. When I didn't like what someone was saying, I'd hang up the phone before they could finish. Although I loved Morgan dearly, I was a grown woman, and I didn't have to justify my life to him. I'd made it this far without his "wise words" and worry.

By the time I walked into the diner, Maria was already seated and sipping on a cup of coffee. "Nice of you to finally make it," she said with a lopsided smile. "Bear wear you out last night?"

I slid into the booth and set my purse at my side. "Don't be ridiculous."

She giggled like a teenage girl. "I see the way you look at him, and he's always watching you."

I waved my hand across the table in front of her. "You're imagining things, Mar."

"Am I?"

"Coffee, Fran?" Martha asked, holding an empty cup in her hand.

I smiled at her because I couldn't have timed the interruption any better. "Yes, please."

Maria and I stared at each other while Martha poured a full cup, but we didn't speak. When the waitress was out of earshot, Maria started right where she left off.

"So did you at least kiss him?"

My sister-in-law was a nosy thing. She and Morgan could form their own little club. "No." I rolled my eyes as I brought the mug to my lips.

She pursed her lips and raised her eyebrows. "Did you want to?"

"Maybe," I said, drawing out my answer.

"He's a bit rough around the edges, but he's one of the nicest, most loyal men I've ever met."

"Morgan says he's trouble."

"If Morgan had his way, you'd enter a convent and be celibate the rest of your life."

"You got that right."

Martha came back, pulling the pencil from behind her ear. "You ladies want the usual?"

"Yeah," we answered together before Martha walked away.

"We're really getting predictable, aren't we?" I asked Maria.

"You can think you're old, but I feel like I have a new lease on life. I plan to live with no apologies and no regrets." I smiled and glanced out the window just as I heard the sound of a motorcycle. For a moment, I hoped it would be Bear barreling down the street, just to catch a glimpse of him. But it was a girl in short-shorts and flip-flops, with her long blond hair waving in the wind. "I figure I have twenty good years left in me. I don't plan on spending them crocheting and watching soap operas."

Maria rubbed her face with her fingertips, making tiny circles near her temples. "You just depressed the hell out of me."

"Why?"

"Twenty years? I want to turn back the clock and go back to my youth. Time moves so fast now, it'll pass in the blink of an eye."

"I know, girl, I know. That's why I don't plan on spending it at home—what a waste that would be."

She cupped the dingy cream mug in her hand and leaned back in the booth. "Do you have a plan?"

"No, but I know just where I'm going to start." I rubbed my hands together with the biggest smile on my face.

"I feel there's going to be a rocky road ahead."

"Morgan forgets who the parent is in this situation. He's not the boss of me. He'll just have to deal."

"Oh, this is going to be fun." Maria laughed. "You know…" Her voice trailed off.

"What?"

"We should really get you a new wardrobe if you plan to whore it up."

I glanced down at my favorite pink tracksuit and pulled at the collar. "Why?"

Maria's eyes traveled around my top before connecting with my eyes. "You look like you live in an assisted-living community and are about to play bridge. You certainly don't scream 'fuck me' in that ratty old thing."

"But it's comfortable."

"So is an old shoe, but there's a time when you need to replace it."

“Fine,” I muttered. “When do you want to go shopping?”

“I’m not doing anything today,” she replied quickly with a partial grin.

“Let’s do this, then.” I shrugged. “I’m ready for a change.” I lied right through my teeth. Some change, I could deal with, but the way I dressed was more of a security blanket to stop the advances of men.

“Fuck, this is going to be epic!”

“When did you start using the word epic, Mar?”

“Izzy seems to like it, so I figured I’d try it out.”

I giggled, and Maria quickly followed. As soon as Martha delivered our breakfast, we ate quickly before heading to the mall.

Maria had my head spinning the way she shopped. She twirled around the department store, plucking pieces off the racks and holding them against me.

“What size are you?” she asked, with a top that looked more like a scrap of material pressed up against my chest.

“Medium, maybe.” I cringed because I hadn’t bought anything new in so long, I wasn’t quite sure.

“And your pants?”

“Medium too.”

Her eyebrows drew together as her eyes flicked to mine. “Real pants don’t come in medium. What’s your actual size?”

I glanced down at my track pants and pulled at the elastic. “Last time I checked, these were real pants.”

She laughed softly at first, but every time she looked at my face, her laughter grew louder. “I can’t.” She tried to catch her breath but couldn't. "Those aren't—"

"Can I help you?" a saleswoman asked after hearing Maria laughing like a hyena.

"We're good," I told her, already embarrassed enough by my sister-in-law. "Thank you, though."

"Can I start a dressing room for you?"

With all the ugly tops piled high on my one arm, I couldn't say no. "Yes, please. I don't think she's done yet."

Maria cleared her throat to try to get rid of her giggles. "No, we're far from done," she said in a strangled voice.

I rolled my eyes and handed over the pile of "real" clothing, as Maria would've called it, before the saleswoman scurried away.

"Are you done laughing at me?"

She shook her head, walking away from me quickly, but I could still hear her laughter as I followed behind. She grabbed some pants in various sizes from the rack to cover the bases before we headed to the dressing room to try on the first round of items.

She stood outside the door, tapping her foot against the cold, white tile. "How does it look?" she asked.

My arms didn't want to go into the tiny opening in the long-sleeved top she'd picked out. I kept sticking my hand through the cutout near the shoulder. "Great."

"Let me see."

When I finally got it on and looked in the mirror, it wasn't as bad as I'd imagined. "Gimme a minute. I have to put on some pants." I grabbed the size eight, figuring it was my best bet, and pulled them on easily. "Wrong size."

"Which one?"

"Eight."

"Too small?"

"Too big," I admitted, feeling slightly ashamed that I didn't know my right size. Track pants were easy. They always fit. Even if I gained a few pounds or lost a few, the elastic always made them right. I threw the eights to the floor and grabbed the size six from the hook. "What the hell are skinny jeans?"

"Just put them on," she said in an annoyed tone.

"I'm doing this for you, so you better drop the attitude, Mar."

"Shut up, Franny. This is for you and that poor, lonely vagina of yours. Put the jeans on, and get your tiny little ass out here."

My vagina wasn't lonely. The thieving bastard Johnny had taken care of it for some time. I just wasn't a talker like Maria. I didn't have to share my sexual experiences to validate that they actually happened.

Once I had the jeans on, I turned around and looked at my ass in the mirror. My bottom never looked so nice. The soft denim had a bit of stretch, making it easy to breathe, and it was comfortable. They looked more like leggings from the way they clung to my body. The outfit was pretty, but I looked younger—too young, in fact.

"I look stupid," I whined, but secretly I liked the outfit. I didn't look like a grandma anymore, but like a woman.

"I'm coming in if you don't come out."

Damn her. She was so damn pushy. Years of being with my brother had turned her into a bossy little thing. "Don't!" I yelled before finally turning the handle and walking out for her inspection.

She clapped the moment she saw me. "You look hot," she said with the widest smile. "Turn around." She twirled her fingers in a circle. Instead of fighting her, I followed her command.

She whistled loudly when my ass faced her full on. "You can bounce a quarter off that thing."

"Please," I groaned in horror. "It's aged too much for that shit."

"You're getting that outfit."

"I don't know. The top really isn't me."

She smacked my ass, causing me to jump. "That's the point. We're retiring the tracksuit. It's too you, and that shit ain't working."

I turned, glaring at her for a second. "Fine." I wanted the outfit, but I'd never admit it to her.

"Go try on the next one."

I closed the door and turned around in front of the mirror, smiling as I did. I really did like the way the outfit hugged my body and showed my curves.

"We have to get you a new bra."

"Why?" I called out when I started to pry the shirt from my body in the most ungraceful way.

"Your boobs shouldn't be near your elbows."

As I tossed the top to the floor with the size-eight jeans, I stared in the mirror and turned to the side. She was right. They were hanging low. The bra I had on was the same style I'd worn for years.

"They're fine."

"No, they're not. Does it even have underwire?"

I grimaced at the thought of wearing something so constrictive. "Underwire?"

"You need a push-up bra to get those girls back toward your chin."

"For the love of God," I muttered, pushing up my tits to the spot they'd sat twenty years ago.

"Let's find more clothes, and then we're on to raising those babies a few inches. You need to show off that cleavage."

In my head, I kept hearing Morgan. He was going to flip his lid the moment he saw me. The entire thing might be worth it just to freak him out.

But then I thought of Bear. What would he say when he saw the new me?

5
BEAR

"I got a lead!" James yelled from the hallway around noon. "The bastard's in Raleigh."

"Conference room," Thomas said as he walked by my office.

I grabbed my laptop and followed him down the hallway along with the other guys so we could figure out what to do from here.

"Want me to head up?" I asked, sitting down at the table.

"Not yet," he replied.

Once everyone was inside, James asked. "Who do we know in Raleigh?"

"I have a buddy who used to be in the FBI there. I can call him," Sam said quickly.

"Do that. Get eyes on him and verify that it's Johnny. If it is, have them keep him under surveillance until we can get there," James told him, rubbing his chin with one finger before Sam pulled out his phone and sent a text.

"I'll head up," I said again. There was no point in waiting for confirmation. "Raleigh's only nine hours away."

Thomas shook his head. "I don't want to waste the manpower if it's not him."

I grumbled. "You're the boss," I bit out through gritted teeth. Sometimes working for someone else left a sour taste in my mouth. The guys at ALFA had their shit together though and made the right call.

Thomas leaned back in his chair and rocked back and forth. "If it's him, we'll be there within hours by plane. We won't let him slip from our sights. Do you agree, Morgan?"

Morgan rubbed his hands together and thought a moment. "Yeah. Get eyes on him first, and then we'll handle him. I don't want to chase after a ghost."

"It's him," Sam said when his phone started to ring. "I'll be back in a few."

Angel cleared her throat in the doorway as Sam brushed past. "Um," she mumbled and peered over her shoulder. "Mrs. Gallo and Ms. DeLuca are here."

Our entire table turned with the same perplexed looks on our faces. They'd come to visit separately, but never together. There must be something wrong.

Thomas's eyes narrowed on his wife. "Show them in, Angel."

She smiled and glanced behind her again. "I have to warn you—"

"What's wrong?" Morgan asked, wondering the same thing I had been thinking.

"Nothing. They just dropped by to say hi," Angel said and giggled as she walked back toward reception.

"This oughta be good," Frisco added after finally looking up from his laptop.

"Those two cause more trouble…" Thomas muttered.

Mrs. Gallo came into view first, smiling wildly. "Hey, guys. Just wanted to say hello."

Thomas walked over to his mother and kissed her on the cheek. "What are you two doing today?"

All I could see of Fran were her feet. From the angle I was sitting and with Maria in the doorway, I couldn't see any more. Maybe she regretted our dinner last night and didn't want to see me. The thought made my heart a little heavy, although I'd never admit it to anyone.

"Holy shit, Aunt Franny," Thomas said.

I sat a little straighter in my chair and tried to get a better glimpse without being obvious.

"Oh God, now what?" Morgan said from my side.

Maria held up her hand to stop the hysteria before it started. "We went shopping."

"I'll say," Thomas said and held out his hand to his mother to move her to the side. "Looking good, Auntie."

I craned my neck a little more and kept my ass glued to the chair because I didn't feel like getting into a brawl with her kid. He already didn't like that I had dinner with his mom. He'd made it very clear when I came into work today, but I told him what I always did—we're adults and nothing happened. It wasn't his business anyway. She may have birthed him, but she was a grown-ass adult.

When Fran stepped into view, my mouth dropped open. She had on the sexiest pair of dark blue skinny jeans and a white top that showed just the right amount of cleavage. My mouth watered at the sight. I'd only seen Fran in her tracksuits and thought she was still a stunner, but now… Now she was drop-dead gorgeous.

"Holy shit!" Morgan jumped up from his chair and almost covered her body with his. "What are you thinking, Ma?"

Maria slapped him in the back of the head, and he flinched. "Don't make a big deal out of this. She looks wonderful."

"Where did my mom go?" he asked while he rubbed the spot she'd just hit.

"I'm here, baby. Do I look bad?" She glanced down and swept her palm over the front of her shirt.

"Well," he mumbled and shook his head. "No. You look different."

"Different bad or good?" she asked, looking for validation.

"Good."

Her eyes wandered around the room and locked on mine. For once in my life, I was speechless. Fran DeLuca had it going on. Who knew underneath that frumpy shit she had a killer body?

I sure as fuck didn't.

I couldn't stop my mouth from hanging open as I checked her out, letting my eyes cascade over her body and imagining the dirtiest shit that I reserved for the naughtiest women.

Frisco elbowed me in the arm. "I'd stop looking at her like that if I were you."

I righted myself and snapped my mouth shut. Fran kept staring at me, ignoring everyone else in the room.

"Let's go to my office." Morgan tried to usher her from the room and probably my view.

"Don't be silly." Fran swatted his hands away. "We wanted to say hi to everyone and see how the investigation was going."

"Everything is good here. Nothing to see and no new information." Morgan couldn't be any more uncomfortable.

"We wanted to show off Fran's new look too. I figured, where else is better than in an office full of men?" Maria smiled directly at me, and I knew instantly that I was really the target of the fashion show.

"You look great," James said.

"Fantastic," Frisco added.

I was at a loss for words, and I was never out of shit to say. Usually, it was some sarcastic comment, but I had nothing.

"Now's the time to talk," Frisco whispered. "Dumbass."

"You look very nice," I said, even though I wanted to say so much more, and Fran's eyes sparkled at the compliment.

I glanced to her side and caught Morgan glaring at me. I must not have been as under the radar with my reaction as I'd thought. I squirmed in my chair—not from Morgan's look but from the sexiness oozing off Fran DeLuca.

My cock approved.

"Well, boys," Maria said and looked right at me, "Franny and I are off to get all sweaty playing tennis."

I realized in that moment that Maria Gallo was a wicked woman. My head filled with images of Fran bouncing up and down, her tits following suit, and covered in a thick veil of perspiration.

"Have fun," James said as he stood from his seat and went to give his mother-in-law a kiss on the cheek.

I couldn't speak because I was too lost in my fantasy.

"Don't overdo it," Morgan told his mother. "It's hot outside."

She placed her hand on his chest and leaned in to kiss him, but her eyes were on me. "Don't worry. I'm in great shape and can last for hours."

"Fucking hell," Morgan groaned and hugged his mother.

I swallowed my tongue and started to choke. Fran was just as rambunctious as Maria. If I was going to make it through the day, I needed to wipe all mental images of Fran running around the tennis court, grunting with each hit, and glistening in the sunlight.

Fran gave me a mischievous smile as she backed away from Morgan. "Don't work too hard today and keep me posted about Johnny."

"We will," Thomas assured the ladies before they walked out of the conference room.

All I could see was Fran's tight little ass swaying back and forth as they made their way down the hallway, following Morgan out.

It would be impossible to work today. Fran made sure of that by putting the images in my mind that would leave room for little else.

"You better get that shit under control," Frisco said.

I turned to face him and snarled. "Mind your own business."

"Morgan's going to have a fit."

"I didn't do anything."

"If I could read your mind, I'm pretty sure it would be X-rated, brother."

I scrubbed my hand down my face and tried to wipe the vivid images from my mind, but all I saw were her perky tits and jiggling ass.

Fuck.

I was in so much trouble.

FRAN

"Did you see the look on his face?" Maria said over the phone as I wiped the kitchen counter.

"Who?" I feigned ignorance.

"Bear. He almost swallowed his tongue." She chuckled.

"I know," I finally admitted. The poor guy—he did look like he was about to hyperventilate when he finally caught a glimpse of me.

It had been a long time since I'd seen a man look at me that way. Ray used to, but that was before he became an uncaring asshole. It felt like as soon as the wedding ring slipped on my finger, he lost his manners and stopped courting me.

But Bear made me feel sexy again. My belly did that weird thing where it flipped a few times, and my fingers tingled just from the way his eyes crawled across my skin. It wasn't lost on me, and based on Morgan's reaction, it wasn't lost on him either.

"You should invite him over for dinner again."

"Maria! I just had him over yesterday." I was protesting too much, but the thought had crossed my mind since I walked out of ALFA PI.

"So what? Live a little, Franny."

"What about Johnny?"

"Were you two even dating?"

"Not really. We'd go to dinner, and sometimes, we'd end up in the sack."

"There's your answer. It's not like you're rebounding or anything."

She was right, but I couldn't give in so easily. "But what about Morgan? Bear's his friend."

"Now you're just making excuses."

I was, too. Bear wasn't normally my type. I don't even know if I had a type anymore. "We'll see. Let me figure out what to do and do it in my own time."

"Fine. Be a pussy."

"The mouth on you."

She laughed loudly. "Your brother taught me well. Speaking of the devil, he just walked in. I got to run."

"Bye, Mar. Say hi to Sal for me."

"Will do. Bye."

With the dishrag still in my hand, I stared out the windows overlooking my backyard and thought about what to do next. Last night had been nice. Bear wasn't exactly the man I thought, and I wanted to know more about him. But was it the right time to go down that road?

Maybe I'd read the signals wrong. I'd never chased a man. Not even Ray. It wasn't my style, but my daughter-in-law Race told me it's what women do in the twenty-first century. My mind was still stuck back in the seventies where there were rules and proper etiquette.

My phone rang before I even had a chance to put it back on the charger. "Hello," I said after seeing it was Race calling.

"I heard you made quite a splash today."

"He already called you."

"He's worried, Ma."

"I'm an adult, Race."

"I know. I think it's cute."

"It's payback from that brat."

"Are you going to ask Bear out?"

"I don't know. I was just thinking about it."

"Do it. He's a great guy."

It seemed like the women in the family were conspiring against me. If Morgan knew Race was calling me, he'd be livid. "How would Morgan feel about that?"

"Who cares? You deserve to be happy too."

"Someone's at the door, Race. I gotta run." I lied because I wasn't ready for this conversation. Everyone was chirping in my ear, and I didn't need their opinions.

"Maybe it's Bear," she said through her laughter.

"Bye, busybody."

"Bye, Ma."

The sky was dark in the distance as the usual afternoon thunderstorms started to roll in. I walked to the mailbox, trying to beat the rain, when my neighbor Meredith caught me before I could sneak back inside.

"You're looking nice today," she said, her eyes raking over me, but not in a complimentary way.

"Thanks, Mer."

Her tiny mouth, one so small I wondered if she was ever able to suck a dick, pursed. "I saw a motorcycle in your driveway last night. Did you have a man over?"

Living in an older-resident community had its disadvantages, and this was a prime example. It was filled with a bunch of bored, nosy people who had no life but to spy on their neighbors.

I plastered a fake smile on my face. "Just a family friend." Thunder sounded in the distance, and I saw my out. "I better get inside before it storms. Take care." I started to walk away, waving over my shoulder at her.

"Bye," she grumbled from behind me, still standing near the driveway where I'd left her.

After I walked inside and flipped through the mail, I tossed it on the countertop and noticed I'd missed a phone call. My eyes widened when I saw the name. Bear. Maybe I hadn't interpreted his vibes wrong. After all these years, maybe I still had the ability to read a man.

I couldn't wipe the smile off my face as I waited for his voice mail to play. "Hey, Franny. It's Bear. I wanted to touch base with you and let you know that we may have a possible lead on Johnny. I know you're upset and would want to know what's going on. Call me back…ya know…if you want."

For a moment I was sad because I was hoping for something a little bit more…flirtatious. Even though it wasn't what I'd hoped to hear, I called him back anyway.

"Hey, Bear. It's Franny," I said as soon as he answered the phone.

"I know." He laughed softly.

"I wanted to say thank you for the update." I paced around my living room. "Morgan hasn't really been telling me much."

"He's just busy. Cut him a little slack."

"I know."

"Hold on one second."

The phone became muffled, and I could hear voices in the background.

"No go?" Bear asked and then a pause. "Fuck."

A few more things were said, but I couldn't make them out no matter how hard I pressed the phone to my ear.

"I'm back," he told me. "False alarm on the lead, but don't worry… We'll find him."

"I know you will. Was that Morgan?"

"Yeah."

I smiled because Bear hadn't told him that I was on the other end of the phone. "Well, I better let you go. I know you guys are busy."

"Hey, Franny?" he asked softly.

I stopped pacing, and butterflies filled my stomach. "Yeah?"

"Want to grab a beer tonight?"

I moved the receiver away from my mouth and took a few quick, deep breaths. "I'd love to." My feet started to move on their own, breaking out in a cross between a happy dance and the running man—but more of a senior version.

"Great. I'll pick you up at seven."

"I'll be ready."

"Later."

"Bye," I said, and when the call disconnected, I stared at it like maybe I'd heard him wrong. But when I realized I hadn't, I broke out into a full-on celebratory dance in my living room.

Wait.

Was this a date?

Fuck. I didn't know how shit worked anymore. I'd spent my good years at home after Ray left me. I couldn't even look at another man for a long time. Then Morgan joined the military, and all I could do was think about him. I didn't have time to get involved in a relationship, and I figured, why bother since I was in my forties.

I thought Johnny and I were dating in the beginning, but he made it quite clear that he didn't want any type of relationship. I couldn't understand why, but now it's completely clear.

I guess, with Bear, I'd just have to wait and see. Maybe he was only being nice to me because was Morgan's mom, and I was feeling so much guilt for not seeing Johnny for the lying, cheating asshole he was.

I'm either going to have to grow a pair and ask what his intentions are or just wait it out and hope that he wants more than just a drink and a hot meal.

***

When I heard his bike pull into the driveway just before seven, I ran into the bedroom so it wouldn't seem as if I'd been waiting for him. I had been. I'd been ready for a half hour, and I'd been pacing back and forth in the living room, checking outside for any glimpse of him.

"This isn't a date," I told myself as I waited for him to knock. "It's just a drink."

My heart leapt when he knocked on the door, and I took one last look at myself in the mirror. I had on the same jeans from the office earlier today, but I had changed my top to something a little more revealing.

I leaned forward and checked my cleavage, heaving it up with my hand and giggling. The bra Maria picked out really did help them reach a height I hadn't seen since my twenties. Bear was probably used to women much younger, and if this padded, underwire-lined thing ever came off in front of him, he'd be shocked at where they swung.

I hummed the tune to "Swing Low, Sweet Chariot" as I walked toward the door. When I finally worked up the nerve to open it, I was pleasantly surprised by what I saw.

"Good evening, Franny." Bear held out a small bouquet of flowers as his eyes traveled down my body. "You're looking stunning."

I graciously took them and gave them a quick sniff. "Thank you. They're beautiful," I told him. "Would you like to come in while I put these in some water?" My voice wavered.

He nodded. "Sure."

I tried not to skip to the kitchen from excitement. Bear brought me flowers. I don't think anyone, not even Ray, had ever brought me a bouquet. "I'll be quick." I bent over and grabbed a vase from under the sink and caught a glimpse of Bear standing behind me. His eyes were glued to my ass, and I slowed down to give him a longer look.

He cleared his throat when I started to stand and turn around. "How was your day?" he asked as I started to arrange the flowers in the clear vase, and I noticed the redness in his face.

"Busy. Yours?"

He turned his body, adjusting himself and trying to be discreet but failing completely. "Busy too."

"So where are we headed?" I couldn't stop myself from chattering because I was so nervous. There was an awkwardness tonight I hadn't felt before.

"I thought we'd head down to the little place by the beach."

I smiled because the sun would be setting soon, and it'd been too long since I'd watched it descend below the horizon of the Gulf of Mexico. "That sounds lovely." Suddenly, I sounded more like June Cleaver than Fran DeLuca.

"Ready?" he asked, jostling back and forth on his feet, just as nervous as I was.

"Yeah. You?"

"Yep." His answer was short, and he was heading to the door before the vase was entirely filled with water.

I heard him mumbling to himself in the front room. He was giving himself a pep talk, and I could only make out a few words. I couldn't wipe the smile off my face as I set the flowers on the table near the window. A man like Bear never seemed to have a problem with self-esteem, and I found it endearing that he had to give himself a talk.

"Let's hit it," I said as I breezed into the living room to a pacing Bear.

When we went outside and I locked the door, he asked, "Are you good with being on a bike?"

"It's been a while, but yeah."

I hated bikes, but I didn't tell him that. I knew the man rode his faithfully, and who was I to stop him? Ray had one too, but after my third time on the bike, I never went on it again. I ended up punching him in the ribs when he took a turn a little too sharp for my liking. After that, he never asked me to go with him on another ride, and I was perfectly happy riding in my car instead.

After Bear got situated, he held out his hand like a perfect gentleman and helped me climb onto the back. I set my hands on his shoulders and waited.

"You have to wrap your arms around me," he said, glancing over his shoulder at me. "And hold on."

"Sorry." I smiled, and as soon as he turned around, I swallowed hard, looked up toward the sky, and said a silent prayer.

Wrapping my arms around Bear was like anchoring myself to a mountain. His chest was so wide that my fingers barely clasped in front of his chest. The muscles underneath my hands flexed when my arms tightened. The butterflies that had fluttered in my belly earlier started to move as if they were on hyperdrive. My body slid forward, pressing my chest against the warmth of his back. I wanted to lay my head against him and close my eyes, but I didn't want him to think I was a weirdo—even though I was.

"You good, babe?" he asked and patted my hands.

"I'm good," I whispered softly, shimmying my body so there wasn't a sliver of space between us.

He slid on his glasses that had been hanging near his handlebars and started the bike. The roar of the engine caused the entire machine to vibrate, sending tiny shock waves of pleasure through my system.

I wondered if that was part of the charm of a motorcycle and having a woman on the back—the closeness, the large vibrator in the form of a bike, and the wind through our hair. It was like an aphrodisiac that couldn't be replicated by anything else.

As we pulled out on to the street, I couldn't stop myself from resting my head against his back and closing my eyes. The mix of fear, adrenaline, and lust had me light-headed.

BEAR

The last woman who had wrapped her body so tightly around me on the back of the bike was Jackie. It felt like home the moment Fran put her head against my back, and I took off down the road.

The ladies from the bar that I'd sometimes take home on my bike were so comfortable they'd barely hold on, let alone plaster themselves to my body.

I forgot how nice it was too.

"Tell me more about your wife," Fran said after our first beer.

We'd spent the last half hour talking about our pasts, something I rarely did with anyone. "She had one of those smiles that could light up a room. When she laughed, no matter what was happening around me, I couldn't help but laugh too. Sometimes I try to remember the sound of it, but it's so faint that it just brings me sadness."

"I'm sorry. It sounds like she was a great girl."

"She was one of the best."

She moved the empty glass around on the table and avoided my eyes. "Why didn't you ever remarry?"

"I went to a dark place when I lost her." I picked at the label on my beer and stared out into the ocean, watching the waves roll in and crash against the shore. "I wouldn't have been good for anyone."

"It's been almost thirty years, Murray. I'm sure you're settled by now."

My eyes flickered to her. "I'm an old bastard now, Fran. Why didn't you get hitched after Ray?"

She frowned, dropping her gaze. "He was a mean fucker. When he left, I swore I'd never fall in love again. I've been really good at not getting close to anyone."

"Put all your effort into the kid?" I asked with a small smile.

She laughed softly and bit her lip. "Yeah. Poor Morgan. He was eighteen when Ray left, and I became what they now call a 'helicopter parent.'"

"Ain't nothing wrong with that," I told her and reached out to touch her hand. "I should've been that way with Ret and Janice. They deserved to have me in their life, but I was too self-absorbed and lost in my own sadness to be there for them."

"We all have regrets. But time isn't up yet. You can still make amends for the past." She curled her fingers around mine. "Just don't wait too long."

"Eh," I muttered, caressing the tender skin on the back of her hand with my thumb. "It'll probably cause more hurt after all this time. Sometimes it's better to leave things unsaid."

"Is this a date?" she blurted out with a nervous smile.

I froze for a second and began to laugh as the waitress arrived with our food. "I suppose it is."

Her lips curved up, almost kissing the corners of her eyes. "Good to know."

I was suddenly curious about the tracksuit-loving feisty woman I'd admired since the day I'd met her. "Go on a lot of dates?"

Her hair skimmed her shoulders as she shook her head. "Not really."

"Me either."

She laughed so hard she snorted. "Don't lie. I heard you're quite the ladies man."

I chuckled softly as my face heated. "I wouldn't say that."

"Well, I've heard the stories."

"Fran," I said, suddenly feeling guilty and whorish.

"You don't owe me an explanation, Bear. I'm just making a general statement."

I stabbed at my pasta, capturing a few flimsy noodles on my fork. "Oh."

"I bet you're pretty good in the sack," she said just as I put the fork in my mouth. I stared at her for a moment, chewing as fast as I could so I could respond, but she kept talking. "Probably a wild man." She made a small roaring noise in the back of her throat.

The fork fell from my hands and clattered against my plate. A noodle lodged in my throat, and tears formed in my eyes as I tried to cough it away.

"Are you okay?" she asked, starting to stand.

I grabbed her hand and kept her in the seat as I cleared my throat. "You have to stop doing that."

Her eyebrows rose, and she smiled innocently. "What?"

My grip tightened on her hand. "Talking about sex with me."

"Sex with you or sex with you?" She smirked.

I closed my eyes and muttered a few curse words under my breath. "Both."

"Isn't that what usually happens on dates?"

"How's everything?" the waitress asked, interrupting us at the worst moment.

"It's great," I told her without looking up. "Thank you." When she finally scurried away, I continued. "I'm trying real hard not to think about banging the fuck out of you, Fran. I've never tried so hard not to think about something."

She leaned forward, giving me a better view of her spectacular cleavage. "Why would you do that?"

I licked my lips, my mouth watering from the view more than from the food. "Because we should take things slower. Morgan would kill me if he knew I even said this was a date."

"He doesn't have to know." Her words came out quickly and quietly.

I laughed and rubbed the spot where my hand had held her down before releasing her. "I don't really like to keep secrets from him, but…"

"There are some things he should never know."

She piqued my curiosity. "Like what?"

Her smirk turned into a wicked grin. "I'll save all my secrets until another day. We'll see if you earn the right to know them."

"Fuck," I muttered softly before picking up my fork and

stabbing my food with a little more force. She had me on edge and needy.

We sat in silence, exchanging glances as we ate. I couldn't drag my eyes away from her mouth and the way her lips slid against the fork when she pulled it out. I kept thinking about my dick being in the same spot and the softness of her skin sliding against my shaft while the back of her teeth pressed against my head.

"Are you okay?" she asked after catching me adjusting myself in my seat for at least the tenth time since we sat down.

"I'm fine." I wiped my mouth, tossing the napkin on top of my plate, and watched her in absolute heaven.

"This is so good," she said and let out a loud moan.

Vixen. She knew exactly what she was doing when she made that sound.

"Hey, will you take me to the Neon Cowboy for a drink after this? I've heard so much about it, and I'd love to finally step foot inside."

I should've said no. Morgan and the guys were often there and taking his mom there was a huge risk, but I couldn't say no. She looked too excited, and I wasn't ready to take her home yet. "Sure."

I knew I'd regret it the moment the words left my mouth.

***

"Are you fucking crazy?" Tank asked when Fran excused herself and went to the ladies' room.

"Clearly, I am."

"What the hell are you doing with Fran DeLuca?"

"Just having a drink." I shrugged and feigned innocence.

Tank's hand connected with the back of my head, and my body lurched forward. "Don't be a dumbass."

I turned and glared at him, balling my hands into tight fists under the table. "You got a free shot—the next one I'm hitting back, fucker. We're adults. She wanted to have a drink so I brought her."

"What are you going to do when Morgan hears about it?"

"He won't, and if he does, I'll handle him."

Tank started to laugh so hard that he almost fell off his chair. "You're a dumber shit than I thought."

"I really like her, Tank," I admitted to him, feeling a weight lift off my chest from finally saying the words out loud.

"You're fucked, buddy. Totally fucked."

I glanced toward the ceiling and exhaled. "I know."

"Hey, guys. What did I miss?" Fran said as she sat down, brushing her hair back off of her shoulders and smiling.

"Not a thing," Tank replied before taking a slug of his beer and diverting his eyes.

"This place isn't really what I thought."

"What did you think it would be?" I asked.

"I thought it would be more like a hole-in-the-wall honky-tonk."

"Nah," I laughed and pulled my beer a little closer. "It's just a good ole-fashioned biker bar."

She looked around the bar, slowly taking in the crowd. "Do people dance?"

"Sometimes," I lied.

"Will you dance with me?"

"Um…"

"Come on, ya big baby. I'm sure you have some moves," she teased me while nudging me in the ribs.

"Okay," I said, unable to resist her even though I knew every set of eyes in the place would be on us.

"Dumb fucker," Tank muttered under his breath so only I could hear.

Rising to my feet, I glared at him before holding out my hand to Fran. She slid her hand in mine with the biggest grin on her face. Just as our feet touched the empty area of the bar that was typically the dance floor, Brantley Gilbert's "If You Want a Bad Boy" started to play.

"I love this song," she said as I wrapped my arms around her and pulled her closer, but I still left a little space between us. As if she knew what I was doing, her arm hooked around my neck and she closed the tiny gap.

It took me a minute to find my footing because I couldn't get Tank's words out of my head, and having Fran's tits pressed against me only made things worse.

We locked eyes, our feet moving with the beat, and everything else seemed to disappear. All I could see, feel, or hear was Fran. Her tiny laugh when I spun her around, and the feel of her body crashing into me when I pulled her back.

The only time my eyes left hers was to glance down at her cleavage. No girl wears a bra like that without wanting to be noticed. My hand slid lower down her back, just above her ass, when something caught my attention.

More like someone.

Standing near the doorway with his arms crossed and a very pissed off look on his face was Morgan, flanked by City.

"Fuck," I grumbled and closed my eyes, but I didn't let go of Fran.

"What's wrong?" she asked, rubbing my back gently with her palm because she hadn't caught sight of them.

Very slowly, I slid my hand up her back and spun around so she could see them too.

"Fuck," she groaned, finally catching a glimpse of them. "This is a shitshow."

My thoughts exactly.

I'd hoped to keep this evening to us so I didn't need to deal with Morgan, but now I had to face him and hope he didn't flip his shit. "Let's get this over with."

City leaned over, whispering in Morgan's ear as we approached. Morgan's face was unreadable, but his body language wasn't.

"Hey, baby." Fran spoke first, leaning forward to kiss his cheek.

"Mom." He glared at me as she kissed him.

"What are you guys doing here?" she asked as she backed away.

Morgan's eyes hadn't left mine. "The real question is what are you two doing here?"

Fran came back to stand next to me, but I didn't dare wrap my arm around her. Not that I was worried that Morgan could take me, but because I didn't want to get into a fight with him. He was Fran's baby. If I punched him in the face, it wouldn't be pretty and would be the end of us before we even started.

"I was talking to Franny about the case, and she wanted to come for a drink. Who am I to say no to her?" I shrugged, hoping that it would pacify him.

"A word?" City asked and motioned toward the bar with his head.

"Sure," I replied before glancing down at Fran.

She nodded her approval. "Morgan, buy me a drink and sit with me."

"I think we should leave."

She stepped into his space and smiled. "Baby, I'm an adult. I want a drink with my son. Now shut the fuck up and buy me one."

I bit my lip and tried to stifle my laughter. It wasn't the time or the place to laugh my ass off at the way Fran handled him. Morgan wasn't the type of guy many people fucked with, but as with any big man, they were brought down to size when their mother was around.

"One drink," Morgan replied as I walked away to meet an already waiting City.

"What the fuck is wrong with you?" he said before I had a chance to say anything.

My head jerked back in surprise. "What?"

"Why the fuck would you bring her here?"

City had been my friend for years. We'd walk through fire for each other, but his response shocked me. "Where am I supposed to bring her?"

"You knew word would get back to me."

"No one knows her."

"Sure as fuck do."

"How?"

"She's been to all my parties. The guys here know her, stupid fucker."

"So what? We're having a drink. It's not like I'm banging her on the table for everyone to see."

He dug his fingers into his eyes and shook his head. "I can't unsee that image."

He turned to the bartender. "Tequila."

"Make it two," I mumbled before he could walk away. "How pissed is he?"

"I'm lucky you're still alive." City chuckled softly and grabbed the two shot glasses as soon as the bartender set them in front of us. Handing me one, he said, "I may need more than one if I'm going to get through the rest of tonight."

"You know I can't fight back if he hits me."

"I know. After a few of these, you won't feel the pain when he punches your fucking lights out."

As I lifted the shot glass to my lips, I watched Fran and Morgan talking at the table. Her hands were moving wildly as she spoke, and I knew the conversation was heated but it looked like Fran had it under control.

"Were you really talking about business?" he asked, slamming his shot glass down on the table. "Because your hand on her ass made it seem…"

I cut him off with a wave of the hand. "She's a big girl, City."

"I know you'd never hurt Fran on purpose, Bear, but she's my aunt. You're my best friend in the world, but she's family."

"You think I'm going to bang her and treat her like shit."

"It's what you usually do," he said flatly.

How could I explain to him that this was different? Fran wasn't a club whore or a barfly. She was a good woman and reminded me of Jackie. For years, I'd found the trashiest girls, ones I knew I wouldn't feel anything for, and had a good time until they became too clingy and I'd kick them to the curb.

"It's different with her."

He raised an eyebrow, calling bullshit on that statement.

"It is!"

"Uh-huh."

"Fucker, listen to me. I can't explain it, but I really like Fran. She's like a breath of fresh air in my fucked-up life."

Thin arms wrapped around my waist. "Hey, baby."

City's eyes widened, matching my own as soon as I heard the voice. Fucking Molly. Peeling her hands from my body, I turned slowly and pushed her away gently.

"Molly."

"Wanna have some fun, big boy?" she said with a slur, hanging on to the word boy a little too long to be classified as sober.

"No. I told you I didn't want to see you again, and I meant every word of it." When she reached up to touch me, I grabbed her by the wrist and stopped her forward progress.

"Come on. I can make you feel good." Her eyes dipped to my cock, and she smirked. "I know just how you like it."

"Molly," I said quieter. "I'm not going to explain this again, so listen carefully. We're nothing. Nada. Zip. Zilch. So move along and find your next victim."

She pouted before a small smile spread across her face. "I love when you're like this. It's so hot. I know you want it rough, baby. Take out all that stress on me."

I glanced toward the ceiling and caught a glimpse of Morgan watching me. Quickly, I released Molly's wrist and put some space between us. "Lose my number and forget I exist," I told her because I didn't know what else to say. The woman clearly didn't understand the word no.

"City can join us if you want." She smiled brightly, running her eyes over his body.

City was over a decade my junior. His large body and chiseled good looks made it easy for him to bag the ladies—at least, before he found the love of his life, Suzy. His eyes darkened, and his body stiffened next to me. "I'm out. You clean up this mess and come over to the table," he said.

"Don't fucking leave me here," I told him and reached for his arm.

He took a few steps and turned to face me. "Get rid of her," he mouthed with a snarl.

As if this night couldn't get any worse—Molly had to show up, drunk off her ass, and wanting something I wasn't willing to give her again. With Morgan and Fran here, it added a whole new dimension of fucked up.

Could this night get any worse?

FRAN

"Girlfriend?" Morgan asked as Bear took a seat next to me and set a new pitcher of ice-cold beer on the table. I kicked him under the table because it was none of his fucking business.

"No," Bear replied, but it wasn't exactly convincing.

"Clusterfuck," Tank muttered so quietly I barely heard him. His dark caramel eyes shifted, giving Bear the side eye.

"What?" Morgan asked, turning his attention to someone else. My handsome son fit right in with this group. In his beauty and darkness, he was one of them.

Tank ran his hand across his jet black hair, which was cut in the most perfect military flat top I'd ever seen. "Nothing, man." His unusually wide shoulders hunched forward, making his neck disappear.

In the murky lighting of the seating area of the Neon Cowboy,

Bear looked rougher than the man who'd sat across from me at dinner earlier. There was a darkness in his eyes I hadn't seen before.

"You okay?" I asked, leaning over and speaking softly so only Bear could hear.

He glanced down at me, his steely gray eyes connecting with mine. He gave me a quick nod, grabbing my hand underneath the table and giving it a tight squeeze. I smiled up at him, but I wasn't convinced.

"Well, it's getting late. I better get you home, Ma," Morgan said, interrupting the little moment Bear and I were having.

"No." I didn't even look in his direction. It was time that I put this boy in his place. I may be his mother, but that didn't give him the right to dictate my life.

"It's too dangerous for you here."

I turned to face him and narrowed my eyes. "I'm surrounded by four strapping men. I highly doubt anyone will fuck with me, Morgan. So just zip it and have a beer—relax a little bit and enjoy your friends as much as I am." Bear's hand tightened around mine underneath the table.

The last statement didn't earn me a smile, but I hadn't expected it to either. The boy had some serious control issues. I never really realized it before tonight, but then again, I never hung out with his people.

He dragged the pitcher across the table and started to pour himself a glass. "Fine, but I'm driving you home."

My eyes didn't leave him, and I waited a moment to answer. "I'm going home with Bear."

He slammed the pitcher against the table, and some of the beer splashed out onto the table. "Like fuck you are!"

"Morgan, put your pencil dick back in your pants and calm the fuck down," Bear said, moving his arm from under the table and sliding it across the back of my chair. "Your mom is a grown woman, and we're just friends. Would you rather her be home watching reality television?"

Morgan's face turned the brightest shade of red. "Bear, you know I love you, man, but you better keep your paws off my ma. She's off-limits, and she doesn't need your kind of friendship."

Bear stood quickly, tipping his chair over, and Morgan did the same. I could see that the conversation was becoming heated and that I was the only person who could calm the situation.

"Boys!" I yelled, standing up and placing my face between theirs. "Both of you sit your asses down. Now!"

They didn't move initially, just stared each other down in the ultimate pissing contest. Morgan moved first, snarling at Bear as he sat down slowly. Bear growled in response, easing down into the chair with his eyes still locked on Morgan.

"You two are ridiculous," I scolded them like children. "Morgan." I paused, waiting for my lovely son to give me his full attention. When he did, I continued. "Bear has been kind and respectful to me. He's been nothing but a gentleman. I asked him to bring me here because I didn't want to sit at home alone tonight. Would you rather I use that Tender app I have on my phone?" I tapped my foot, still hovering above them.

Morgan's face scrunched up, and his head jerked back. "Do you mean Tinder?"

I shrugged and rolled my eyes. "Whatever it's called. Would you rather I use that to go out for a drink? I was told all I have to do is swipe, and voilà, I'd have a date."

He rested his elbow on the table and covered his face with his hand. "Tinder is not a dating app, Ma."

"Yeah, it is," I told him and put my hands on my hips.

"Fran, it's not," Bear said, giving me the sweetest smile.

"Well, what the hell is it, then?" Glancing around the table, I saw Morgan was horrified and the other guys at the table were almost in hysterics. I threw up my hands and finally sat my ass down with a huff.

"It's a hookup app." Bear smiled indulgently.

"A what?"

"Oh, God," Morgan groaned, dropping his hand to the table with a loud thump.

"It's how people find each other for one-night stands. It's not to find a long-term relationship."

"That can't be true."

"Sorry, Aunt Fran, it is," City said, clearing his throat to hide his amusement.

"Well, fuck. I'm glad I didn't 'hook up' with Fred last week," I said, using air quotes. "I thought he meant hooking up to have a drink. I didn't know he wanted to have sex with me."

"When the hell did you download Tinder?" Morgan asked with a suspicious look that made me want to spank him like he was a little boy.

"Newsflash, kid… I'm a woman, and I'm single. I can't sit at home alone for my entire life."

"But you had Johnny," Morgan replied quickly.

"Johnny was just a…" My voice trailed off.

"A what?" Morgan's eyes widened.

"We were never a couple."

"I can't." He waved his hands in surrender. "Let's just have our beer and talk about something else."

My mouth turned up into the biggest smile. I'd finally worn his ass down. Maybe now he'd learn to zip it. "I'd like to finish the dance you so rudely interrupted."

"Fine, Ma. I'll dance with you," he grumbled.

"I wasn't talking about with you. Bear," I said, turning to the hot guy sitting next to me.

"Anything you want, Franny." He held his hand out, and I slipped mine into his, loving the roughness of his callused skin against mine.

Morgan sat like a petulant child, gawking at us as we rose and made our way to the same spot we were in before he walked through the door.

"You know this isn't going to end well," Bear said as he wrapped his arms around me, but he didn't dare put his hand anywhere near my ass.

"I'll handle him."

"Babe, you're his mom and you have some sway, but there's a man's code I have to deal with."

"Murray, sweetie, he'll calm down. Just ignore him." Taking my own advice, I rested my head against his chest and followed his lead.

The beat of his heart matched the slow, steady rhythm of the music as we moved. I couldn't wipe the stupid grin off my face while we danced. He smelled too good, and he felt ever better pressed against me. Bear had that animal magnetism I'd always found sexy. There was nothing soft about him, except for the way he spoke to me.

I could see the man underneath and sometimes a hint of the man who had deeply loved and lost. In the years I'd known him, I'd never really taken the time to get to know him. I just knew that he worked with Morgan, and he was City's best friend. He was always in the middle of a shit storm, willing to put himself in harm's way for his friends.

I liked that about him. He wasn't a pussy and knew the meaning of loyalty.

When the song started to come to an end, I said, "This is nice."

His hand tightened around my waist, and he buried his face in the top of my hair. "I haven't felt this at peace in years, babe."

"Are they staring at us?" I asked into his T-shirt.

"No, not anymore."

I peered up at him and smiled. "I enjoyed myself tonight."

His eyes softened, and I fought not to reach up on my tiptoes and kiss him. "Me too. Want to do it again?"

"Yes, please."

"Wanna get out of here?" he asked, quirking an eyebrow at me with a mischievous smile.

"Thought you'd never ask."

When we made our way back to the table, I cleared my throat until City, Tank, and Morgan looked up at us. "We're going to go. I'm exhausted." I faked a yawn. "Bear's going to drop me off."

"I'll take you home, Ma," Morgan said again, even though I'd shut that conversation down before.

"No, Morgan. Bear's going to drive me home. You go home to your wife."

"Night, Aunt Fran," City said with a deep, low laugh.

"Night." Tank tipped his head and gave Bear a funny look.

"Ready?" Bear asked behind me but not close enough to feel his body heat.

"Yep."

As soon as we made it outside, a woman dressed more like a washed-up hooker approached with a wild look in her eyes—the same woman Bear had spoken to at the bar with City.

"You're taking this old bitch home?" she seethed as her eyes raked over my body. "What the fuck, Bear?"

Bear placed his body between us. "Shut the fuck up, Molly. Go back to the hole you crawled out of."

Her hand slid over his shoulder. "You know I can make you feel good. She's all dried up."

Bear wrapped his hand around her arm and pushed her away. "Watch your mouth. I'm in no mood for your shit tonight."

She peered around his body and glared at me. "I just fucked him. If you want sloppy seconds, he's all yours."

"I think the man asked you to leave." Somehow, I tried to be diplomatic, when the woman really needed a punch in the face.

"He'll come back… They always do."

Bear glanced at me over his shoulder and looked up toward the sky. "Molly, if I have to tell you again that we're not a couple, you're going to regret it."

"Whatcha gonna do, Bear, spank me?" She laughed loudly and licked her cracked lips, trying to be sexy.

Bear reached behind him and took my hand. "Get a fucking life and leave us alone," he told her as he guided me toward his bike.

"You're going to regret not being with me, Bear!" Her frizzy hair flopped around as she stomped away from us, talking to herself like a crazy person.

"I can't believe you stuck your dick in that."

He turned and grimaced. "Would it make it any better if I blamed it on alcohol?"

"It's the only way I'd ever believe you'd do it."

"It was only once." He pressed his body against me, and using his fingertips, pulled my eyes to his. "I promise."

I searched his eyes and knew he spoke the truth. "She sure seems to be head over heels for you."

"She's a crazy bitch, Fran. Ignore her."

Placing my hand on his arm, I swept my thumb against his skin. "She's forgotten."

He smiled down at me as his fingertips brushed against my cheek. All I could think was, kiss me, kiss me, kiss me, but it didn't happen.

As I climbed onto his bike and wrapped my arms around him, I felt a pang of jealousy. Skanky Molly had a piece of Bear that I never did.

I wasn't sure I ever would either.

BEAR

As soon as I shut the engine off, Fran asked, “Want to come in for a nightcap?”

This was where I should’ve declined and been on my way, but that had never been my style.

“Sure.” I knew it was a dumb-ass move, but I didn’t give a fuck.

I liked Fran.

More than I should, actually.

I never mixed business, friendship, and sex together. That combination could be nothing more than a recipe for complete disaster. But I’d hit a point in my life where I didn’t give a fuck what anyone thought.

I trailed behind her up the walkway, watching her cute little ass swaying back and forth and her sleek black hair matching the rhythm as it swished through the air. She glanced over her shoulder and smiled as she placed the key in the door lock.

For a woman of her age, she had very few wrinkles, and her skin almost glowed, even with her caramel Italian complexion. She had just a few lines near the corners of her eyes that made them seem more mysterious, giving her more character and intriguing me even more.

"What's your poison?"

"Anything you got." I didn't care if she brought me a glass of water. All I knew was that I wasn't ready to go home to my empty place and say good night to her.

I watched her, while I sat in her living room as she moved around the bottles in her cabinet, bent over with her ass in the air, and all I could think about was seeing her in the same position without the jeans.

"Gin?" she asked without looking in my direction.

"Sure," I replied, unable to drag my eyes away.

She straightened and finally glanced over her shoulder. "Ice?"

I nodded without speaking because I was at a loss for words, and to be quite frank, I was still lost in the fantasy of bending Fran over in the same position.

"Sex?" she said quietly as she carried two glasses in my direction.

My eyes cut to hers in complete shock. "What?"

"You're looking at me like you want to eat me, Bear." She laughed softly and blushed.

I rubbed my neck, trying to ease the tension, but it wasn't the right part of my body that needed relief. "To be honest, Fran, the shit I want to do with you is illegal in about forty-five states."

She handed me the drink and sat down next to me, smoothing back her hair. “Only forty-five?” she teased.

“Fran.” I set the drink down on the coffee table and turned to face her. “I’m trying to be a good guy here, when everything in me wants to be bad. You’re not making it any easier, sauntering into the office in clothes that scream sex and a dirty-ass mouth to boot. I’m hanging on by a thread, babe.”

She swallowed hard, placing the cold glass against her neck. “Why do you have to be good?”

Rubbing my hands together, I exhaled loudly. “There are a dozen reasons I shouldn’t be here right now.”

“Don’t you dare name my kid.”

“He’s the first reason.” My palms started to sweat, and I knew that the further we got into this conversation, the harder it was going to be to come up with excuses.

“Would you let your kid tell you who to fuck?” she shot back with a smug look because she knew she had me.

“Hell no.”

“Well, I’m not going to let mine either.”

“I’m not good for you,” I admitted. But it was the truth. My police record read more like an issue of Reader’s Digest, filled with stupid-ass antics that I knew were bad ideas, but I did them anyway.

“There’s that word for again. I’ve spent the last twenty years being ‘good.’ I’m over it.” The Fran sitting next to me didn’t look like she had an ounce of angel in her. She was a sex kitten with the mouth of a truck driver. The black eyeliner around her chocolate eyes made her seem even more naughty. Gone was the tracksuit, replaced by a wardrobe that said she was on the prowl.

Had she done it for me?

I wondered if I was the cause. I had one dinner with the woman, and the next day, she made a grand entrance at the office, sporting an outfit that would have most men's tongues wagging like a dog in heat.

She didn't give me a chance to respond before she crawled into my lap and straddled me with her legs squeezing my thighs. "Bear," she whispered while she stared down at me with a look that could only be described as lustful. "Kiss me."

I thought about it for a grand total of two seconds before I reached up and cupped her face in my palm. The heat from her pussy had my cock hard a few seconds later. I could no longer deny myself what I wanted—and what she wanted too. I dragged the rough pad of my thumb against her soft, plump lip. "Are you sure, Franny?" My voice was deep, yet gentle.

She nodded with a tiny smile on her lips. I took a deep breath, already light-headed at the thought of tasting her. Instead of leaning forward to kiss her, I wrapped my fingers wrapped around the back of her neck and pulled her down to me. Without hesitation, my lips connected with hers. A soft moan escaped her throat, vibrating into my mouth as her body relaxed and her pussy ground against my already aching dick.

Tasting her was like sinking my teeth into the sweetest fruit for the first time. Describing the feeling of her against my body was impossible. Her soft to my hard had my head spinning and my body in overdrive.

She rocked against my body as she opened to me when I tried to deepen the kiss. I couldn't do gentle with her. The need to touch her was more than I had prepared myself to deal with, but I stilled her body by holding her hip and stopping the through-the-clothes fucking she was giving me.

My fingers tangled in her hair, and her mouth opened more. Our tongues danced together in a perfect harmony, our moans the chorus to the most beautiful kiss I'd had in a long, long time. It wasn't soft. It wasn't hurried. There was nothing but need and lust between us, and I couldn't slow down the momentum even if I wanted to.

Tugging on her hair, I tried to pull her backward, but it only poured fuel on the fire. "Don't stop," she moaned against my lips before her tongue plunged back into my waiting, greedy mouth.

My hand slid from her hip to the middle of her back as I pushed her body against mine, leaving no space between us. She smelled like a mix of beer and flowers, but when my mouth finally blazed a trail to her neck, I caught a whiff of her perfume. The sweet, musky smell made my cock twitch, the familiar scent one I'd smelled somewhere before but couldn't remember where.

When I sank my teeth into her neck, hard enough to make her shiver but not enough to break the skin, she tipped her head back, following the pull of my fingers, and exposed her neck to my mouth more. The position made her core press harder into my cock, making my breath catch.

Her silky fingertips slid underneath my shirt, slowly raking over my sides before tangling in my chest hair. When her fingertips bit into my back, I grunted in approval and wanted more.

Like horny teenagers, we quickly dispensed with of our shirts before my mouth found a way back to her bare flesh and her fingers dug into my sides. When our lips found each other's again, our hands started to roam, caressing the other's skin frantically.

My hand cupped her breast, kneading the lushness through her bra. Everything about Fran was soft—except her mouth. Her mouth was harsh and brash and drove me fucking wild.

Scratching her skin with my beard, I kissed my way to her chest, lingering where her tits met and losing myself in the plumpness. The velvet of her skin met my lips, softer than any silk I'd ever touched, and I groaned softly.

Her eyes were closed when I peered up at her before pulling the top of her bra down and exposing the most perfectly erect nipple I'd ever seen.

I lowered my head and closed my lips around her nipple, stroking the stiff peak with my tongue and moaning. She shivered in my arms and melted against me, lowering her even farther and bringing her chest to an easy to reach level. I took my time, not wanting to rush having my face pressed against her chest, buried in her cleavage, and praying I'd die just like that.

When her hands started to tug at the button of my jeans, I pulled back. "Fran, I didn't bring protection."

Her eyebrows shot up, shocked at my admission. "You didn't?"

"No. I wasn't planning on fucking you tonight."

"Oh." She chewed on her bottom lip and cleared her throat. "I'm clean. Are you?"

"I am. I get tested regularly and haven't been with anyone without protection since…"

She frowned, probably knowing I was going to say since Jackie. I had always been prepared, but tonight I didn't even think about it. I planned on dinner and a kiss—because Fran was different.

God, I sounded like a pussy. I sure as fuck thought like one. Fran did that to me.

"Well, lucky for you, big boy, that I can't get knocked up." She giggled softly as her hands roamed my bare chest, toying with my nipples on each pass.

"You can't?"

"Nope." She shook her head with a smirk. "Menopause. It has its advantages."

"Oh, fuck. I didn't even think about that." Fran seemed too young to be in menopause. I don't know why it didn't even dawn on me before that moment. Most of the women I'd been with were younger, and it wasn't a conversation we had. Typically, I'd take what I wanted, wear protection, and be done with it.

"I trust you," she whispered, pressing her chest against mine. Her lips lingered just above mine as she stared into my eyes. "Do you trust me?"

I wouldn't have said I was a trustworthy guy when it came to pussy. I was unapologetic and greedy, but with Fran, I felt that I'd do anything in my power never to hurt her, including never lying to her about anything.

"I trust you," I whispered back before crushing my lips against hers.

It was like someone opened up the floodgates with those words. I lifted her off me, depositing her on the floor and rising to stand in front of her. Although I wanted to undress her fully, there wasn't enough time or patience to make that a reality.

Watching each other, we unbuttoned our pants and threw them to the floor. The entire time, we were appraising each other, drinking in the other for the first time. I took in her entire beauty, while Fran stared at my stiff cock, bobbing and weaving like it was in a boxing match.

The ravages of time and having a child hadn't affected Fran's body much. I couldn't see more than a few scars left as remnants of the baby she'd once carried. Her naturally tan skin shimmered in the dim lighting of her living room.

My hands itched to touch her, my dick ached to be inside her, but my mind kept reminding me that I was about to open up a can of worms that I could never put back.

But I didn't listen.

I never did.

It was how I got myself into half the shit in my life. It was how I ended up in jail and let my life spiral out of control.

Fran was just another notch in that belt.

"Come here," I told her and motioned for her with my hand.

She took tiny steps, tiptoeing her way to me. "Yes, sir," she said with a smug smile and laughter. My cock waved, loving her response.

God, she was beautiful. The way her eyes sparkled when she laughed and the tiny lines near the corners deepened.

I could get lost in them.

The little devil on my shoulder stabbed me with his spear. "Pussy," he whispered in my ear, but I silently told him to fuck off and decided to show him exactly what kind of man I was.

When she stood before me, shifting nervously on her feet and naked as the day she was born, I wrapped a hand behind her neck and pulled her to me. Before she could speak or I could chicken out, I slammed my lips against hers and devoured her as if my very life depended on it.

Reaching down between us, I slid my fingers through her slickness with ease… Fran was ready for me and just as greedy as me. She wanted it. I knew it. The kissing and touching on the couch made it clear, but there was no denying the need that dripped from my fingertips.

I tore my lips away, gasping for air. "I can't go slow."

"Take me," she proclaimed and waggled her eyebrows.

If my balls hadn't been about to turn blue, I'd have laughed.

Normally, I'd toy with the girl, driving her mindless with lust so she'd be willing to let me do anything I wanted just to get off. But Fran was different. I didn't feel like playing games, and I had a feeling she was just as big of a freak as me—if not, I'd bring it out in her.

I turned her around to face the back of the cushy chair and pushed her down, folding her over it. Starting at her neck, I traced a path to her ass and cupped it roughly.

I leaned forward and rested my lips against her ear. "Ever been taken here?" I asked as I ran my finger over her asshole.

She gasped and turned her face ever so slightly to look me in the eyes. "No," she said, clenching her ass and looking away. "I haven't."

"Good," I murmured. "Don't worry, sweetheart. That's not for tonight. I have to earn that."

Parting her cheeks with one hand and holding my cock with the other, I nipped at her shoulders until she waggled her ass against my tip. "Careful now, girl."

I wanted to put it in her ass so fucking bad I wanted to jump out of my skin, but this was our first time and hopefully not our last. Before I even had the tip inside her pussy, she slammed back against me, impaling herself. I chuckled briefly, but when she started to move before I could, all laughter fell away.

Fran and I moved in synchronized rhythm like the perfect waves in the most ferocious storm, our bodies ebbing toward each other and flowing away.

As our bodies slapped together, I tried to hold it together. I didn't want to be a two-pump chump. But the way her body responded to mine and clamped down against me, I didn't know how long I'd last.

Reaching up, I placed my hand on her shoulder to take the reins and control the pace. “You have a greedy little pussy, don’t you?” I grunted.

She answered with a shake of her ass as she tried to take control again. My grip tightened on her shoulder to remind her who was really in charge. “Bend over more.”

She peered over her shoulder with a pout. “But I’ll be on my tiptoes.”

“Exactly.” I smirked.

She started to bend forward, and I pushed down on her shoulder to help her, while my cock was still buried inside of her. I moved too, making sure not to lose the connection.

When she was barely able to stand, I slammed into her as hard as I could, causing her feet to dangle. She grunted her dissatisfaction at the position, and I responded with a growl before pounding into her without remorse.

Fran screamed out a moan, calling my name and dropping a few curse words in there too. My hand wandered to her waist, holding her in place as I repeatedly crashed into her.

And there it was. Her asshole. Taunting me. Teasing me. Beggin’ to be taken. I couldn’t take it anymore. The torment was too much. She gasped when I pulled my cock out of her, but I filled her with my fingers before she had a chance to whine. I plunged them into her, wetting them with her need and rubbing her G-spot with each pass.

“Oh, God…” she moaned, dragging out the word as if it were a song.

Instead of pulling out, I kept going. Diving deeper, feeling every inch of her insides and keeping the pressure on her G-spot as she writhed against the chair. When she gasped for air and bore down against my fingers, trying to push me out—I knew I had her right where I wanted her.

She stiffened, and her legs strained as my fingers assaulted her in the most pleasurable way. Fran DeLuca came for me for the very first time, and it was the most magnificent thing in the world. The way her body tensed and her mouth fell open, breathless and lost.

When her body started to calm, I withdrew my fingers and replaced them with my lonely, needy, and still hard-as-fuck dick. She melted against the chair, pliable and ready, just how I wanted her.

My fingers rubbed the remnants of her orgasm against her asshole, and she moaned softly with her head buried in the back of the chair. Slowly, I stuck the tip of my finger inside, and she moaned louder, clamping down on my finger like a vise.

Fran's pussy fastened itself around me, just as needy as her ass, and I took it as a sign that she wanted more—fuck, I knew I did. Slowly, I added a second finger to the mix, and I could no longer keep my eyes open. Fucking heaven. The feel of her ass wrapped around my fingers and her sweet cunt around my cock, I couldn't imagine anything better.

Working out of sync, I finger-fucked her ass and pummeled her pussy until her body grew slicker with sweat and I couldn't hold out any longer. My balls ached, retracting toward my body as if they knew they were home. The release washed over me, sucking the air from my lungs and leaving my legs shaking. She followed me over the cliff, pushing my fingers out of her with her orgasm.

"Fuck," I groaned and collapsed against her.

Our bodies stuck together as we both tried to fill our lungs with air. My cock was still buried inside of her but making a slow retreat—being forced out by the aftershocks that racked her body.

"Damn," she whispered with her face still buried in the green fabric of the chair.

"You okay?" I asked, even though I knew the answer.

"Yeah," she muttered and tried to right herself, but she couldn't.

Pulling her by the waist, I helped her find her footing and instantly missed the heat of her skin and the heaven that was her pussy.

"I just didn't…" Her voice trailed off as she began to sway, but she caught herself and held on to the back of the chair. "I didn't know it could be that good." She turned around with a flushed face and sweat dotting her brow.

I cocked an eyebrow and smirked. "Just good?"

"Okay," she laughed. "I just didn't want you to get too cocky."

"Sweetheart, it's only cocky if you can't back that shit up." I turned her body to face me. "The way you came on my fingers and pushed against my cock, I know I did it right."

"Fine. It was fucking amazing."

My smirk grew bigger. "Best sex you ever had?"

She pursed her lips and tipped her head to one side, studying me. "I see you have a self-confidence issue."

"Want to see if I can do a repeat performance? Maybe I just got lucky." I shrugged, but I knew I was good. I'd spent too many years with way too many women to suck at it. Plus, I watched thousands of hours of porn in the name of education.

"I couldn't. I'm too old to do it twice."

"Franny." I wrapped my hand around her neck and rubbed

her cheek with the pad of my thumb. "What's the longest any man's ever eaten your pussy?"

Her eyes widened. "I don't know."

"I'm not leaving this house until you pass out from exhaustion, completely spent by too many orgasms and a lack of oxygen."

"Fuck me," she whispered and gawked at me.

"I plan to. A lot. Lie down, spread those legs, and let me feast on that greedy pussy," I told her.

By the time the sun rose, Fran was passed out, with one arm hanging over the bed and the other draped across my chest.

I banged her brains out and mine too. Hopefully, I had just enough energy left to deal with Morgan because he wasn't going to be happy about the way I'd defiled his mother when he found out.

And he would find out.

I knew nothing stayed secret in that family for long.

FRAN

“I want all the details,” Maria demanded over the phone before I even had a chance to get out of bed.

“There’s nothing to tell.” I lied for good reason. Morgan would freak the fuck out, and I didn’t feel like dealing with my son’s shit first thing in the morning.

“I can keep a secret.”

I burst into laughter because nobody in my family could hold on to anything for too long. “Don’t lie to me. I’ve been your sister-in-law for far too long.”

She made a hmph sound. “Did you fuck him?”

“Yes.”

“Did you suck his cock?”

“A time or two.”

She gasped. “Two?”

"I wasn't counting how many times his dick was in my mouth." I stretched and felt the effects of one too many orgasms on my muscles. The last few I had to strain for, but I couldn't let them slip away.

"Did you have an orgasm at least?"

"A few," I said coyly and smiled into the pillow I'd placed over my face.

"My girl," she said before she whistled.

"I lost count, but I sure as hell feel it. My muscles ache like I ran a marathon."

"When has your ass ever run a marathon?"

"Never." I laughed. "But I'm sure I'd feel something like this."

"Tell me more."

"Want me to draw you a picture, Mar? We sucked and fucked until I literally passed out."

"My God," she said softly. "Bear's a beast."

"Yep. The nickname fits."

"You passed out, passed out?"

"Yeah," I replied and thought about all the naughtiness of last night that almost felt like a dream.

"I did that once. Best night of my life."

"I don't want to know." Sometimes I wished Maria was married to someone else. I wanted to talk with her about sex and relationships, but Sal was my brother, and the thought of him having sex made me ill.

"Why?"

"He's my brother, and I'll vomit."

"Fine. Are you still in bed?"

"Yes."

I felt like I was on an episode of Family Feud in the bonus round with the way she was rapidly firing questions off at me.

"Get dressed and meet me for lunch. I think we need to go shopping again."

"Why?" I grumbled and struggled to sit upright. "I don't think I can walk around the mall."

"Get your slutty ass up and get dressed. You need more lingerie and clothes. It's time to throw out the tracksuits and keep that man coming back for more."

I kicked off the covers and stood on wobbly legs. "I don't think he cares about my clothes, Mar."

"He's Bear. He's a badass biker. He doesn't want Sophia standing next to him, with her glasses hanging by a chain."

"Fuck off," I told her as I spotted a note on the floor.

"You know I'm right. One o'clock by Macy's," she told me before she hung up.

I rubbed the sleep from my eyes and tried to focus on the blurry words.

Franny,

I didn't want to wake you. I'll call later. Rest up, sweetheart, I'm not done with you yet.

Bear

When I woke, my heart had been the only part of me that didn't feel battered. But after reading his words and thinking of all the possibilities, it started to beat wildly. I collapsed backward onto the bed and clutched his note to my chest. The scent of him, musky and strong, clung to the paper.

Fuckin' Maria. She was right. I needed to break out of my shell a bit further. I needed to shed my skin, ala my favorite tracksuits, and join the dating world again. To trap a man like Bear, I had to dress like a woman and not a grandma.

***

Walking through the parking lot, I had to stop more than a few times to rub out the aches in my calves. Each one a reminder of the delicious night I'd spent with Bear.

"Jesus," Mar complained before I even had a chance to step onto the sidewalk. "I'm melting out here."

"No one told you to wait outside." I walked past her and opened the door, loving the feel of the air conditioning as it washed over me.

"I need something cold to drink before we start shopping."

It was her code for getting my ass in a seat and prying all the details of last night out of me. "I'm not giving you the details."

"You're a cruel woman, Fran. Cruel," she complained, following close behind me as her heels clicked against the linoleum flooring of the department store.

I stopped walking and spun around, narrowing my gaze. "How did you even know I was with him last night?"

"Joe told me."

"Aha." I pointed at her. "That's my point. Nothing is secret."

"What?" She shrugged before smiling. "He called to tell me that it's all my fault. He knows I took you shopping, and he blames me for setting you two up."

I walked away from her and headed toward the mall entrance nearest the food court. "Tell him to mind his own business."

She caught up, standing at my side. "I did."

I rubbed my neck and tried to ease the stress of the entire situation out of my muscles. "Fucking kids. They're so goddamn nosy."

"Don't I know it."

"I swear they're trying to get us back for being good, caring mothers."

As we were peering up at the coffee shop menu, she said, "You were a little over the top."

"Shut up, Mar. I had one kid to look after. I got carried away. I can't help that you pushed out a small army."

"I hover. I know I butt into their lives, but sometimes they seem to forget that I'm the parent."

"I'll take a trip caf half non-fat mocha," I told the pimply faced teenager behind the register.

She turned around and stared up at the menu. "I'm not sure what that is, ma'am."

I looked at Maria and rolled my eyes. "Order me something sweet, please. I don't know why coffee has to be so fucking complicated."

Maria motioned toward the bustling food court. "Go find us a seat, and I'll get the coffee."

"Fine," I grumbled under my breath as I walked away and found a seat nearby.

I glanced around the food court and felt like I fit in for the first time in a long time. No more elastic-trimmed pants and front-zip jackets. Those were gone and replaced by skinny jeans and form-fitting shirts. I couldn't forget the latest high-tech bra from the store that reeked of too much perfume, just down the way from where I sat.

"Here," Maria said, startling me as she placed some cold,

blended beverage in a clear cup in front of me.

"What is it?" I stared at it like it had two heads.

"Some fracka something. I don't know." She pushed the drink closer to me. "It's good. Just drink it."

I wrapped my lips around the green straw and took a sip. To my surprise, it tasted amazing and hit the spot on such a hot, sticky day in Florida. "Thanks," I said after licking the remnants of the concoction off my lips.

"So let's talk trash." She rubbed her hands together and smiled. "Tell me every dirty detail."

I fidgeted with the cup, wiping away the moisture that started to dot the outside. "What do you want to know?"

"Is he big?"

"Um, his nickname is Bear."

"I know, dumbass. I'm talking about his cock."

"It's pretty." I giggled and felt my cheeks flush. "And larger than I expected."

"Really?" She tapped her finger against her coffee. "Tell me more. If you leave anything out, I'll tell Morgan."

My eyes widened in shock. "You wouldn't."

"Try me. I've been known to blackmail a person or two. I have leverage, and I'm not afraid to use it."

I sighed and knew it was futile to fight with her and keep quiet. She'd eventually get it out of me. And I was actually excited also—I needed to share what happened with someone, and Maria was the only option who could possibly keep my secret without judgment.

By the time I finished telling her every detail, down to the way he tasted, she was sweating and holding her drained yet still perspiring cup against her neck. "Well, fuck. That's hot."

"Yeah," I said and drained the last bit of fracka-whatever from my glass, but I still felt parched.

"Are you going to see him again?"

"Yep. He wants to see me again, and I can't say no. Especially after last night."

She straightened in her chair and leaned forward, becoming serious. "How are you going to explain this to Morgan?"

"Um," I mumbled and mimicked her by leaning forward too. "What is there to explain? I'm an adult, he's an adult, and it's none of his fucking business."

She laughed and bit down on her lip. "It's about to get really interesting around here."

I crossed my arms on the table and lowered my voice. "He doesn't need to find out."

"Keep living in your dreamland."

"Just keep your trap shut."

She pretended to zip her lips. "My lips are sealed."

At least I knew I had a little time until the shit hit the fan. Morgan hadn't even entered my thoughts last night when I'd crawled into Bear's lap. He smelled too good and spoke to me too sweetly for my body not to respond. I hadn't expected it to be…so…so amazing. I hadn't planned on him being a gentleman with a raging sexual appetite more befitting a twenty-year-old. But the only thing I knew was that I wasn't willing to walk away from him just yet.

"Are we going to shop or sit here all day?" I asked when I felt stiffness start to seep into my leg muscles.

"Let's go get my girl some gear that screams 'fuck me.'"

"Great." I rolled my eyes and pushed back the chair, letting it scrape against the tile just to annoy her.

By the time we walked out of the mall, the sun had set in the sky and the cement let off heat in waves that looked like a mirage. "I'm exhausted," I said as I threw ten bags of clothing, underwear, shoes, and bras in the back of my tiny little SUV.

"Go home and nap. Recharge for round two," she snickered while she fished her keys out of her purse.

"I could use some sleep."

She leaned forward and kissed my cheek. "I have to get home and cook dinner. Sal will be home soon from the golf course."

"Make him take you out," I told her as I slammed the door closed on the back of my SUV.

"No way. I'm cooking, and he's eating." She waggled her eyebrows up and down, and I pretended to vomit.

"I've got to go."

"Bye," she said as she laughed and walked toward her car in the next row.

"Talk later," I called out and waved.

"Only if Sal unties me!"

I glanced toward the sky and sighed. She always had to leave me with the most disturbing mental images. I needed to scrub that one from my mind if I was ever to have sex again. "Fuckin' Maria," I muttered as I climbed into my car that felt more like an oven than an automobile.

Even after the air conditioning blasted me in the face the entire way home, looking like some old, haggard supermodel in an eighties' rock-band video, I was still hot. But the heat wasn't from the sun. It was from the memories of last night, playing in my head like a porn video.

When I walked through the front door with my hands full of packages, the phone was ringing off the hook. Before I could get to it, it switched over to my answering machine.

"Fran?" a man said, but the voice didn't sound familiar. There was urgency in his tone as he spoke. "It's Johnny. I need to talk to you."

I tossed the bags to the floor and went running to the phone. "Hello!" I sucked in a breath, trying to recover from the long run across my living room. "Hello," I repeated when I didn't hear anything. "Fuck!" I stared at the phone, knowing he'd already hung up.

I hurried up and dialed the one person I knew would want to know. "Bear," I said as soon as he picked up. I didn't even give him a chance to say hello. "Johnny just called."

"It's Morgan, Ma."

I pulled the phone away from my ear and glanced down at it, confused. Did I dial the wrong number? "Morgan?" I asked and placed the phone on my shoulder so I could pick up the clothes scattered across the carpeting.

"Yep. It's me. What did he say?"

"Nothing. Just that he needed to talk to me, and by the time I got to the phone, he hung up."

"I really wish you had caller ID sometimes, Ma. I'm going to call my buddy at the phone company and have the number traced. If he calls back, play along and try to get his location from him. Okay?"

"I will. Promise."

"And, Ma?"

"Yeah, honey?"

"We'll talk about why you called Bear instead of me later."

"Bye, Morgan," I groaned and disconnected the call before he could say anything more. I peered around the living room and tipped over onto my ass. "Fuck."

Just like Lucy, I had some 'splaining to do.

11

BEAR

I flipped through a file Sam had gathered about Johnny when I walked into my office and found Morgan talking on my phone. "Why are you behind my desk?"

He held up a finger, but he didn't look up. Sitting down across from him, I kicked my feet up on the desk and shuffled through the information.

"He just called her." He then rattled off Fran's phone number, and I glanced up at him and narrowed my eyes. "Trace it and get back to me with a location," he told the person on the other line before hanging up the phone.

"Who called your ma?"

He glared at me and leaned back in my chair. "You know her number by heart already?"

"I've called her about the case enough that I have it memorized." I fucking lied my ass off because I wasn't ready for the talk.

"We'll talk about it later. Johnny just called her."

I threw the folder on the edge of my desk and leaned forward. "What exactly did he say?"

Slippery fucker. I couldn't believe he had the balls to call her after running off with fifty thousand dollars of Race's money.

"Just that he needed to talk to her."

"What the fuck is there to talk about? He stole money, lied, and ran away." My hand started to shake and I fisted it, then I released it because I couldn't pound Johnny in the face.

"I don't know. It's funny how she called your phone and not mine."

"What?"

"I was in here dropping off a file when her number flashed across the caller ID."

I rubbed the back of my neck and tried to come up with some bullshit excuse. "I've talked to her more than anyone about the case, so it's only natural she called me first."

"Listen, Bear. You've been a great friend to me for years now, but what in the fuck were you thinking, taking my mom to the Neon Cowboy?"

I crossed my arms in front of my chest, cocking my head at the man and the question. "What's wrong with it there?"

He scrubbed his hand across his forehead and exhaled loudly. "It's dangerous. It's no place for a woman her age."

I held my hand out and stopped him from continuing. "Hold up. What kind of shitty statement is that?"

"Well, it's true. It's a biker bar. My mom isn't really the typical clientele."

"You go there."

"But I'm a man."

And here I'd thought the younger generation wasn't a bunch of sexist pigs—my mistake. "There's nothing wrong with that bar. Your mom wanted to go, and I had no problem taking her with me." I eyed him with suspicion. I assumed it had more to do with her being there with me than the actual type of bar it was. "Where should she be?"

"I dunno." He shrugged. "Church."

I couldn't hold my laughter in as I doubled over and slapped my leg. "You've got to be shitting me, man."

"Just don't bring her there again. And—" He cleared his throat, and I knew what was coming next. "I'd appreciate it if you kept your relationship strictly professional. I don't need my mom to become another notch in your belt. If you get my drift."

"Kid." I shook my head because I knew he had a set on him, but I wasn't going to cater to his dreams. I wasn't about to confess my love or tell him how many times I'd already fucked Fran either. "Your mom is a grown-ass woman. She can make decisions for herself. I've treated your mother with nothing but respect, and I'll continue to do so, but you don't get to decide what type of friendship your mother and I have."

Leaning forward, he pinched the bridge of his nose, and I was ready for him to leap across the desk. "I've seen you with enough women to know what you do, Bear. I'm trying to be nice and talk to you man-to-man, but I won't stay so cordial for long. Friendship only goes so far, my friend."

The phone rang, but just as I was about to answer, Morgan grabbed it first. "You got it?" he said to the caller and grabbed a pen that sat near the top of my desk calendar.

Fuck, don't look at what it says.

I spent the morning scribbling Fran's name around the edges

while I made various phone calls. He didn't give it a second look but jotted down a number on a blank space.

"Thanks, Tim." He tapped the pen against the calendar and stared straight at me as they continued to chat for a few more seconds. "Well," he said as he hung up the phone. "Looks like he's in a small town in Georgia."

"I can leave now," I told him because it was partly my case too.

"No, I'll go. You stay here in case he's already gone."

"Okay." I smiled. "I'll keep Fran busy." I knew that would piss him off and make him sing a different tune.

His face reddened. "Like hell, you will. Get your shit, and let's get out of here."

I got to my feet quickly and grabbed my cell phone off the desk, shoving it in my pocket. "I'm ready."

"Don't you want any clothes? We'll probably be gone at least a night."

"I have a bag just in case of emergencies."

"Of course you do," he grumbled and gave me a sideways glance as he stood.

Although I always loved a road trip, especially when it could lead to some trouble, I wasn't exactly thrilled about being trapped in the car with Morgan. "I'll run and get my car."

"No. I'll drive," he corrected me. "You're just coming so I can keep an eye on you."

"I'm not twelve."

"No, but you're making the moves on my mom, and I can't be worried about you instead of having my head in the game."

I wasn't about to tell him that I'd already made my moves.

He'd probably shoot my ass before I even had a chance to defend myself. "Anything you want." I smiled wryly.

***

We made it to the tiny town outside of Valdosta before sunset. Most of the drive I slept since Morgan decided he didn't much feel like talking to me.

"What a shithole," I said as we scouted the tiny bar where the phone call had originated from.

"I've been in worse."

"Excuse me." I waved the lady bartender over. "Hey," I said with a smile to the almost pretty woman behind the bar. "We're looking for someone and hope you can help."

She looked me up and down, her lifeless eyes drifting over to Morgan for a second. "You gonna order something?"

"Yeah, we'll take two Millers." I slid a twenty on the counter. "Keep the change, doll." I winked.

She smiled brightly before snatching the money away and shoving it in her front pocket with her bony arms. "Lots of people come in and out of here." She dug in the beer cooler under the bar, but she never took her eyes off us. "I don't know if I can help."

"He was just here." Morgan reached into his pocket to retrieve a photo that was taken of Johnny last year at the track. "He placed a call from your pay phone."

Her yellow-toothed smile vanished as she set the beers in front of us. "You two cops?"

"Honey, do I look like a cop?" I laughed.

She lifted her chin in Morgan's direction. "He does."

"He's not. Cops aren't usually my type of people anyway. He's looking for his dad is all, sugar."

She eyed us warily. "I may have seen him." She glanced toward the end of the bar to a group of rowdy guys and frowned. "I'll be right back."

"What the fuck?" Morgan gawked at me. "He's not my father, dipshit."

I shrugged. "He could be. Anyway, she'll help if she thinks he's family. This isn't the type of bar where people go to stand out, and it doesn't seem like the type of town where they welcome outsiders. Just shut the fuck up so we can get the information and head home."

"Sorry," she said, wiping her hands on the rag that was thrown over her shoulder. "So he's your daddy." She pointed to Johnny in the photo.

"Yeah."

She lifted it closer to her eyes and squinted before glancing at Morgan. "He doesn't look like you."

"I'm adopted," he said quickly. "He disappeared last week, and my mother is in a panic."

She slid it across the bar with a single finger. "Usually, people who vanish don't want to be found."

"How much do you want to make your conscience feel better?" I asked, knowing how the game was played.

She leaned forward, resting her elbows on the bar. "A hundred should do it."

I reached into my pocket and grabbed my money clip. "Is he staying around here?" I asked when I held a hundred-dollar bill between my two fingers.

She grabbed it quickly and stuffed it in her bra. "He's been staying at the inn next door for a few days. He'd wander in here for a drink each night, but I haven't seen him in a few hours."

"Thanks for the information."

"Sure. Anything else you want to know?" she asked. "Maybe I could interest you two in something else. Seems like you have more money to burn." Her eyes drifted to my money clip still in my hand.

"No, that's it. Thanks," Morgan said and yanked on my T-shirt after he stood up.

"I get off at two," she yelled out as I followed Morgan through the crowd.

"Do women just throw themselves at you?" he barked before we made it to the door.

"I think she was talking to both of us, kid."

"Yeah, 'cause that's gonna happen."

I laughed behind his back because he was wound so fucking tight I thought that if the right string were pulled, his head would start to spin around like a top. He grumbled, talking to himself as we made our way to the motel next door. The woman called it an inn, but in no way did it resemble anything other than a by-the-hour, dirty-ass motel that I'd spent my fair share of time in throughout the country.

"Hello," Morgan called out after the bell on the door finished ringing.

A man with a wild comb-over that looked more like a gnarly bird's nest sitting on his head walked out of the office. "How can I help you?" he asked, seeing Morgan first and then sneering when he saw me. "Sorry, guys, I can't rent a room to two men. It's not biblical."

He could not be serious. This wasn't the Ritz, and in no way was this anything other than a place to hit it and quit it. "I highly doubt anything that happens in this place is biblical."

He smoothed down his hair, but it didn't help. It still looked a mess. "Then what can I help you with?" he asked as he hitched up his brown polyester pants.

"We're looking for someone who's staying here," Morgan replied and pulled the photo from his back pocket and set it on the counter in front of the man.

He didn't look at the photo as he sat down. "I don't make it my business to remember faces."

Morgan fisted a handful of bills in his hand. "How much to make it your business?"

The man glanced down and took stock of the wad of bills. "Two hundred."

"Here," he said, plucking two bills off the top. "What do you know about him?"

Once the balding man had the money in his hand, he said, "He checked out three hours ago."

Morgan glanced at me over his shoulder, and I shrugged and shook my head. That type of information wasn't really worth the amount he'd paid. "Did he pay cash?" I asked, trying to get as much as we could out of him.

"Cash."

"What name did he use?"

"I don't ask for names," he said quickly. "Sorry I couldn't be more help."

"I'm sure you are," Morgan sneered, but I rested my hand on his shoulder to stop him from saying anything more.

"Thanks for your time," I told the guy and started to back up, hoping Morgan would follow.

"What a cocksucker," he said when we were outside in the sticky night air.

“I didn’t expect to get much out of him. Should we head back?”

“Got a hot date?” he asked and quirked an eyebrow. “Wait, don’t tell me. I don’t wanna know.”

“Nah, man. I’m just tired.” I waved him off and tried to play it cool as we walked through the parking lot.

“Right answer.”

“What the fuck!” Morgan ran toward his car and bent down near the tire.

“What’s wrong?”

“It’s flat.”

“Shit,” I groaned because that meant we were going to be in this shithole town longer. “Let’s put on the spare and get the hell out of here.”

He pointed at the tire and growled. “This is the spare.”

“Dude, you didn’t replace it?”

He shook his head.

“I can push it to the nearest station.” Because at that point, I’d carry the car just to get home.

“I don’t even remember where one is. I saw one about five miles back.”

I closed my eyes and cursed. “I’ll call for a tow.”

Pacing the parking lot, I listened to the worst elevator music I’d ever heard as I waited on hold for roadside assistance to answer. When they finally did, their response was that someone would be out as soon as possible, but the expected wait time was close to eight hours.

“They coming?” he asked when I hung up and almost crushed the phone in my hand.

"They'll be here in the morning."

"Seriously?"

"I wouldn't lie about something as sad as this."

He scrubbed his hand down his face and grunted. "Might as well get a beer. It's going to be a long-ass night."

"Aren't you happy I'm here to keep you company?"

"Yeah, couldn't be any fucking happier about anything in my life," he grumbled, walking ahead of me toward the honky-tonk.

Even though it was late, I sent Fran a text because I wanted her to know I wouldn't be back in the morning and that I was with Morgan. She'd already texted me earlier, worried about my safety, being alone with him. I assured her that I could handle him and that he seemed clueless about anything that happened the night before.

"Two Millers," he said as we sat down at the bar next to each other.

The woman from earlier fished out two beers, but she kept her eyes pinned on us. "Find what you were looking for?"

I shook my head.

"Didn't feel like leaving tonight?" she asked and smiled, sliding our beers across the counter.

"Just grabbing a drink before we're on our way."

"Don't leave so soon." She placed her hand on top of Morgan's and toyed with his wedding ring. "Might as well have some fun while you're away."

Morgan pulled his hand back like her hand had burned him. "We're fine. Just wanted a drink."

"Come on. It's not often we get new blood in here."

"Ma'am, we're not looking for anything other than a drink.

We're both taken and have no plans to cheat, so why don't you move it along?" I shooed her away.

She pursed her lips. "You don't know what you're missing out on, handsome," she drawled, sauntering away from us and swinging her hips wildly.

"She's just…" Morgan started to say but didn't bother to finish before taking a gulp of his beer.

"Yeah," I mumbled, knowing exactly where he was going.

"Well, what do we have here," a man said from behind us in the twangiest Southern accent. "Chase, I think we have a couple of city slickers."

I closed my eyes because I knew where this was going. A couple of macho country shitheads felt the need to mark their territory and give us shit.

"Move along," I said without turning around.

"Big shot here wants us to move along." He repeated my words like a moron. "Should we do that, Chase?"

"Nah, man. They look like some uppity fuckers that don't know this isn't their bar."

God, I thought I dealt with some dumb motherfuckers at the Neon Cowboy, but these backwoods, inbred shitheads took the cake.

"They're not worth the time," Morgan said next to me.

I lifted the bottle to my lips and pretended they weren't behind me. The last thing we needed was to get into a fight in the middle of Bumfuck, Georgia late at night. We were interlopers in their world, and it wouldn't turn out well.

"I'm talking to you, boy," the guy, not Chase, said and hit my shoulder.

Was he fucking serious? I'm fifty fucking years old and

hardly a boy, but I knew he meant it as a derogatory statement, trying to get my blood boiling. He accomplished his goal.

I spun around on my stool to come face-to-face with a redneck. Not just any country bumpkin, but a real-life, moonshine-making, shit-shoveling, cousin-fucking country boy.

"What's your fucking problem?" I barked, already curling my hand into a tight fist and ready to swing at any moment.

He yanked on his red ball cap, adorned with a Confederate flag and covered in dirt. "You are. You don't belong here." He shoved his stubby little finger in my chest.

I glanced down and laughed. "I don't see your name on the bar. It's a free country last time I checked." I tried to play it cool, but I didn't feel like sitting in jail tonight. Even the fleabag motel next door was preferable to a metal bench in a cell.

"This is my town," he announced and spread his arms out and raised his chin like he was king of the world.

I didn't have to look around to know that everyone in the bar was staring at us. He was talking loud enough that everyone heard him, and the music had been turned down for those too far away to hear over it.

I crossed an arm in front of my chest and stroked my beard. He couldn't be more than 5'10", barely taller than me while I was seated. Probably at some time he had muscles, but his flabby arms stuck out from his sleeveless plaid dress shirt. "I'm just having a beer, guy. Why don't you bother someone more your…" I looked him up and down "…size."

Morgan laughed next to me before finally turning to face them. "Chase, why don't you take your buddy and get out of here before you get your ass kicked by an old man and a city boy."

"Who the fuck you calling old, kid? I can kick your ass with one hand behind my back," I replied to him but kept my eyes trained on Chase and Shithead.

"Come on, Travis, let's leave them alone." Chase told Travis, the inbred motherfucker, and averted his eyes. "They're not bothering anyone."

"Listen to your friend," I told him and cracked my neck, slowly turning it side to side.

"I think you're done drinking here, city slicker. This is my bar, and you're not welcome." Travis snarled and cracked his knuckles.

Here we go.

There was a point in every hostile conversation when you knew what was going to happen. No matter what I said or did, he was going to swing at me. It wasn't that I was in his bar, but he wanted a fight and figured he'd pick on the stranger.

I don't know why I looked like a good mark. I'm well over half a foot taller than him, my muscles were still thick and strong, and I wasn't friendly looking. My graying beard and dark, weathered eyes didn't convey softness. Maybe he thought my gray was a sign of weakness, but I knew different. I'd taken on bigger men than him and won. It wasn't all about power, but brains too. Travis clearly didn't have much of either.

"Let's get this over with," I said and stepped down off the stool and towered over him.

"Finally, something smart came out of your mouth," he replied and nudged Chase with his elbow.

"I'm still waiting for you to say something smart. Where's your mama? Or is she your cousin?" I teased him because I was done pussyfooting around. I wanted him to swing on me. It had been forever since I'd knocked some country bumpkin on his ass, and Travis was an easy mark.

His face reddened, and a vein in the side of his neck bulged. "No one talks about my mama."

I waited, standing tall and straight, and watched his hand closely. He swung on me moments later, and I jerked my upper body backward to make him miss. He looked like a child trying to hit a piñata that was way too high for him to reach.

He grunted, but it didn't deter him from trying again. This time, I let him connect with my face, just for shits and giggles. My head snapped to the side, all for show, of course, because I had to fuck with him and let him think he got one in. "Best you got, Travis?" I smirked.

He swung again, but this time, I grabbed his hand and crushed it in my grip. "Hit me like a man or don't even bother, pussy," I goaded him before releasing his fist.

He shook it out and looked around the bar. He wasn't looking like such a tough guy in front of his "friends" at this point. An old-ass city guy was showing him up.

"Want any help?" Morgan asked before he took another sip of his beer.

"I got this," I told him and waved him off before I turned my full attention to a fuming Travis. "I'm going to give you five shots to knock my ass out before I put you down."

He swiped his thumb down the side of his nose and started dancing around, using fancy footwork like in the boxer movies. I couldn't hold back and started to laugh. "You've got to be fuckin' jokin'. Is this kid for real, Morgan?"

"Seems like he's going to give you everything he's got, Bear. If he beats you badly, I'll step in and put him out of his misery."

"Shut up," Travis the douchebag said to Morgan and continued to move around like he was Rocky.

"I'll make it easier for you. I'll put my hands behind my

back, give you five shots, and if I'm still breathing, I'm going to take you outside by the feet and beat you bloody. Sound like a deal?"

Again he swept his thumb down his nose, and I wondered if he was high on coke or just trying to act tough. I placed my hands behind my back and stuck out my chin to make it easier. Every set of eyes in the place was on us, and a crowd had gathered around.

He swung once, but my head barely moved. I'd had kids hit me harder than that. "One." I counted each blow, if I could even call them that, taunting him.

"This is ridiculous," Morgan said after I called out four.

"I'm a man of my word." Just one more attempted takedown, and I was going to wipe the floor with Travis and teach him a lesson about southern charm and hospitality.

"You're next," Travis said to Morgan through his heavy breathing.

I laughed but kept still, waiting for number five and my chance to knock his ass out. He hit me twice in the face, once in the ribs, and once in the stomach, but it didn't matter—I didn't feel a thing.

The fifth and final blow landed against my chin. I grunted and gave him an uppercut right in the corner of his jaw. I didn't want to knock him out, not yet. I had a promise to keep and a lesson to teach. Travis stumbled backward and lost his footing, falling to the floor with a loud thud.

As promised, I grabbed his leg and started to drag him toward the door. The crowd parted, giving me room to pull a screaming, cursing Travis toward the parking lot. "It's time you learn some manners, country boy."

An older gentleman tipped his hat and held open the door for me with a smile. Travis's head bounced against the threshold as I pulled him on the sidewalk and finally let go. "Get on your feet and take it like a man," I told him and let him climb to his feet before I tried to punch him again.

His body swayed back and forth, and he tried to put his hands in front of his face to block the blow he knew was coming. Leaving his ribs exposed, I gave him a quick jab, forcing his hands downward and his body sideways.

"Fuck," he howled and grabbed his ribs. The crowd hooted with excitement.

Using his position to my advantage, my fist connected with his jaw—harder than inside the bar. He teetered on his heels, the cowboy boots unforgiving and stiff. Before he could fall backward, I grabbed him by the arm and righted him again because I wanted five blows before I left him on the cement.

He shook his head, probably seeing stars, and tried to grab on to me for support. "You need to learn manners, son." I brushed him off and made him stand on his own two pathetic feet before I hit him again.

But I made an error and hit him harder than I'd planned. He hit the ground with a loud thunk and didn't move.

"Maybe you killed him," Morgan said from behind me.

"Would serve his ass right."

"Well, what do we have here?" a voice said toward the back of the crowd. They parted like the Red Sea, and just when I thought we were going to get out of here without any trouble, a local sheriff dressed in a perfectly pressed brown uniform stepped forward.

"I received a call about a fight, but this seems more like an assault," he said before whistling. "I need you to turn around and put your hands behind your back, sir." His hand was already positioned on his gun, and I knew that nothing good would come from this.

"Fucker," I muttered to Morgan as I turned slowly and placed my palms flat on the back of my neck so the Andy Griffith wannabe could reach.

"I'll get you out," Morgan said to me before the sheriff cuffed me and hauled my ass to jail.

***

"You have a rap sheet a mile long," Andy said, sitting at his desk only feet from my cell. Of course, it was my made-up name for the guy, but I didn't feel like learning his real name.

"Yep," I replied, stretching out on the cold metal bench in my lonely cell. The joint looked like something from out of an old Western. Wooden walls, three cells, and a desk were all that made up the police station. I guess Podunk, Georgia didn't get much action.

"B&E, Grand Theft, Assault." He rattled off my charges and convictions while I sat there, staring at the ceiling and wondering where the fuck Morgan was—it had been three hours. I could barely keep my eyes open as he went on and on. "I don't think the judge is going to give you bail. You're a menace, Mr. North."

I wanted to argue with him, because I wasn't the same dumbass I was ten years ago, but I didn't bother. It didn't matter what I said, he wasn't going to let me go.

"Served hard time back in the eighties, even. Folks around here don't take kindly to people like you coming here and starting trouble."

I sighed loudly and thumped the back of my head against the bars. "I didn't start anything. Travis hit me six times before I even laid my hands on him."

"You weren't the one on the ground, North. I don't even see

a mark on you."

"I can't help it if the guy can't fight for shit." I was grouchy, tired, and not in the mood for any more of his bullshit. Just as I opened my mouth, about to spout off, Morgan breezed through the door.

"Can I help you?" Andy asked him without even standing to greet him.

Morgan gave me a quick chin lift before greeting the sheriff. "I'm here for Mr. North."

"Sorry, sir. He's stuck here until the judge comes in."

"There's a phone call coming for you about Mr. North."

Andy glanced back at me with the most unimpressed look. "Rules are rules, son. He's going to be here for a—" He was cut off when the phone rang. Morgan's eyes slid to mine when Andy answered the phone. "Hello, Lowndes County Sheriff's Department." He leaned back in his chair, rocking back and forth but not speaking.

Morgan walked up to my cell and sighed. "Sorry it took so long, man. It isn't easy getting in touch with everyone at this hour."

I motioned toward the douchebag. "Who's on the phone?"

"I called Thomas, and he got in touch with an old buddy at the DEA. He called in a favor and is getting you released."

I smirked. "Andy isn't going to like that."

"Andy? You guys buds now?"

"Fuck no. I'll explain later."

"Yes, sir," Andy said and swiveled around in his seat, glaring at us.

"Guess he heard the news." I chuckled.

"Fuck him. That asshole deserved to be laid out."

"So I didn't fuck up for once?"

Morgan sighed and shook his head. "I can't say that you did."

"Looks like you're off the hook," Andy said as he hung up the phone. "It pains me to let you out, but when the US government calls and says to release you, I don't have much to argue about." He stalked toward the cell and fished his keys from his belt buckle.

"Thanks," I told Morgan, but Andy thought I was talking to him.

"Don't thank me." He motioned toward Morgan before finally opening my cage. "Thank your buddy over there."

I climbed to my feet and stretched before stepping outside the last jail cell I ever planned to inhabit. If I never came back to this shit town, it would be too soon.

"If I were you, I wouldn't stick around town," Andy warned.

I gave a curt nod. "I didn't plan on staying."

"We're on our way out," Morgan said.

"Good idea." Andy took a seat at the desk and pulled out a manila envelope with my personal belongings.

I grabbed them without a thank you and followed Morgan into the parking lot. "Elvira ready to roll?"

"Yep. I made friends with someone at the bar after you left. He fixed it, but it cost me three times the normal amount. I didn't give a fuck. I just want out of this shithole."

"Perfect. Get us the fuck out of this place. Don't stop until we hit Florida."

"On it," he said, unlocking the doors to Elvira, his sleek black Challenger.

She purred like a kitten when he started her engine, and he peeled out of the parking lot, the back tires fishtailing all over the road.

"Yeah, that won't have Andy coming after us."

"He can't catch us. Don't worry. I've done this before." His smile was visible in the dull blue lighting of the dashboard.

"That makes me feel all warm and fuzzy."

"Just close your eyes and shut up. We'll be home before you know it."

"Bossy motherfucker. I'd argue with you, kid, but sleep sounds too good right now," I said as I closed my eyes and thought about Fran until I drifted off to sleep.

FRAN

The doorbell rang just after noon, and I ran to the door, excited to finally see Bear. But when I opened it, it wasn't him filling my doorway but Morgan instead.

"We gotta talk," he barked and pushed past me, walking into the hallway and kicking off his shoes.

I slammed the front door and turned to face him with my hands on my hips. "Nice to see you too."

He didn't seem amused today. "Drop it, Ma." He stalked off into the kitchen, and I followed close behind him.

"What's the problem?"

"Bear." His voice was flat, and I couldn't read him.

"What about him?" I asked, toying with the cross around my neck.

He pulled a coffee cup out of the cabinet and helped himself to the fresh pot I'd brewed for Bear. "I want you to stay away from him."

I glanced toward the door, hoping Bear wasn't about to knock. I'm sure once he saw Morgan's car in the driveway, he'd wait until the coast was clear. "Why?"

"'Cause he's trouble." He carried the cup to the table and made himself at home.

Sitting down across from him, I rested my chin in my palm. "I'm an adult, Morgan."

He leaned back in the chair and stared out the window. "I can't have my mom messing around with a fellow employee. I have to look him in the face every day, and I shouldn't want to punch his lights out. It's not fair to either of us."

"You know I love you, right?" I tried to be diplomatic, but in no way was my son going to run my life.

"Yeah." He dragged his eyes to mine and narrowed his gaze. "What's that have to do with anything?"

"You need to mind your own business."

"This is my business. I work with Bear. I can't have you gallivanting all over town with him like some love-sick kid."

My head jerked back. "Gallivanting? Is that what I'm doing?"

"What do you call hanging out at the Neon Cowboy with him, Ma? Seriously, you need to act your age."

I placed my hands flat on the table and moved them back and forth across the cool wood to stop myself from slapping his pretty little face. "Should I just move into the nursing home now?" I asked sarcastically.

"No, but don't go to bars and dance with men. At least, the ones I know, please."

Oh, no, he didn't. "So you'd rather me go on Tender and hook up."

His head cocked to the side like he hadn't heard me, when I knew he did. "Tinder?"

"Yeah. Want me to just go on there and find a man? I mean, there are millions of them on there that would love to get a piece of this." I motioned toward my body and giggled.

Poor Morgan looked like he was about to pass out. "Ma, you gotta stop with this shit. You can't go on Tinder. It's too dangerous."

"Bear's dangerous. Tender is dangerous." I mispronounced it just to aggravate him and waved my hands around like a lunatic. "Should I just sit home and crochet until I die?"

He turned the coffee cup in his hand and grimaced. "Fuck! You're so hardheaded."

"Listen, kid. I stopped trying to run your life a long time ago. I know you're worried, but you need to stop your shit. I'm an adult. Bear's an adult. I'm barely fifty. I'm not ready to become an old lady just yet."

He stared at me as he lifted the mug to his lips. "I want my mom back," he grumbled into his coffee.

"I'm still here, kiddo. For the first time in a long time, I actually enjoy spending time with someone, and you want to shit all over my parade."

"You were spending time with Johnny," he said with a cocky smirk.

"And he was a thief and a liar. Bear isn't any of that. You didn't have a problem when I was with Johnny, so you're just going to have to swallow your pride and move the fuck on, baby." I added the little term of endearment to ease the blow of my curse words.

"Fine, Ma."

"And I had you when I was barely legal and got hitched right away to your piece of shit father. I'm ready to actually have some fun before it's too late."

"Okay, okay." He threw his hands up in surrender. "I get it. Just be careful and tell Bear to keep his hands off you for now. I couldn't handle seeing him paw you."

I stood and took two steps to stand over him. "Sure, sweetie," I lied, placing my lips in his silky black hair. "I wouldn't want to make you uncomfortable."

"Thanks." He smiled up at me when I gave him a pat on the back.

"Shouldn't you be getting back to work?" I glanced toward the door again.

He looked down at his watch and yawned. "Yeah, it was a long night, but I should at least make an appearance."

"Okay, baby," I said, already walking toward the door so he'd be gone before Bear arrived.

Morgan leaned over and gave me a kiss as I opened the door for him. "I'll call later and check on you."

I smacked him on the chest playfully. "I'm fine. Spend some time with your wife and stop worrying about me. I'm playing bridge with the ladies later anyway. I won't be home."

"Have fun." He jogged down the front steps toward his car.

"Yeah, it's going to be a wild night." I laughed nervously and looked down the street for any sign of Bear, but nothing.

When Morgan's engine roared to life, he gave me another wave before backing out of my driveway like a maniac. The boy never did learn to drive slowly. It probably wasn't the best choice for him to get a car with over 400 horsepower either.

I waited for him to pull away before closing the door. Hurrying into the kitchen, I put his coffee cup in the dishwasher and checked my makeup before Bear arrived.

Just as I picked up my phone to call him, there was a knock at the door. "Coming!" I skipped to the door like a kid—at least, feeling like one with butterflies fluttering around my stomach on warp speed.

I yanked the door open and immediately became shadowed from the sunlight. The man was so large that his entire body filled the space, letting no light inside. I smiled gleefully and squinted up at him. "Hey, handsome."

His gray eyes were hooded as they raked over my body. "Hey, sweetheart. Aren't you a sight for sore eyes?"

I could get lost in him. The years had been fair to him. His eyes weren't large, but narrowed and focused from his life on the road. The tiny lines in his cheeks and near his eyes gave him even more character but were marred by his beard.

"Wanna come in?" I asked like an idiot, but I was too nervous even though this wasn't our first time together.

He leaned in and lowered his voice. "I'd bang you out here, but I don't think the neighbors would appreciate it." My body began to sway with his words, but he wrapped his large hands around my arms and steadied me. "You okay?"

I laughed and my cheeks burned, but luckily he kept his hands on me. "You just get me so…" My voice trailed off.

He leaned forward and kissed my cheek, sending a shiver throughout my body. His lips grazed my ear and he whispered, "Horny, Fran?"

My toes curled from the vibration of his voice. "I can barely walk, Bear."

"It's a good thing you don't need to stand for what I have

planned."

"Bear," I said and cleared my throat, trying to get myself out of my lusty haze. "We better go inside before—" I glanced around to see if any of the busybody neighbors were watching.

"Want me to put my bike in the garage?"

"Great idea. I don't need Morgan coming by again and seeing your bike in the drive."

"You go inside and get naked, and I'll stow it."

"Wait," I said with one foot inside the doorway. "You expect me to get undressed now?"

"Fran, sweetheart, don't question me. I only say what I mean, and what I want is your fine self naked and waiting. Hurry or I'll have to spank that pretty little ass of yours for not following commands."

"Well," I said and pulled the cross still dangling from my neck from side to side. If I weren't already going to hell, Bear would make sure to get me a one-way ticket.

I ran to the kitchen to open the garage for him before making a beeline to the bedroom. My clothes couldn't come off fast enough as I contorted to work my way out of the super clingy pieces Maria claimed I had to have. Dear God. If Bear had to remove them, it would be a nightmare.

I stood in front of my bed and wondered if I was supposed to lie down or stand here. I fidgeted and shifted on my feet, glancing over my shoulder. When the garage door started to close, I hopped on the bed and tried to look sexy by stretching out on my side with my head propped up in my hand. The girls in Playboy always made it seem like a sexy position.

"For the love of God," I muttered when I glanced down and caught sight of my belly flowing into the mattress like a mound of half-melted ice cream.

When he walked into the hallway just outside my bedroom, I flopped onto my back to help hide my fluffy stomach. I sucked in a breath as the door swung open, and I waited.

"I love a woman who can follow orders." He kicked off his boots, and I stared down the length of my body to watch him undress with so much excitement that it was hard to be still.

My chest heaved, and my breathing grew more ragged. The anticipation of what was going to come next was killing me. My heart pounded against my insides so hard I wondered if my old ticker would just give out. God, I hoped he'd at least dress me before calling the coroner to remove my body. My greatest fear has always been to be found like this, sprawled out and naked as the day I was born.

The other night, I didn't really have a chance to take in the beauty of Bear. We were too busy undressing and getting down to business to really appreciate each other. Even though his face was hairy, he only had a smattering across his chest. There had always been something about a man with chest hair that just screamed manly to me. I wanted to run my fingers through it.

I was so lost in the moment, taking in all of him, including his "pretty dick," as I'd told Maria, that I hadn't noticed him stalking toward me. He grabbed my ankles and pulled me down the bed so quick I didn't even have time to squeal my surprise.

My feet were in the air and over his shoulder moments later. When his mouth came down against my pussy, I twisted against the sheets and lost my breath.

"I missed this beautiful pussy," he mumbled against my skin before clamping down hard over my clit.

I fisted the comforter, writhing back and forth because of the way he ate me like a starved man. Two nights ago, he'd spent so much time licking me that my head spun. I'd had some good oral sex in my time, men who took their time and treated my vagina more like a sacred flower that they didn't want to break. But Bear… Bear chowed down like it was the best thing he'd ever had in his mouth. It wasn't that he rushed it. Fuck, he spent over an hour licking and sucking every inch between my legs.

"So fucking good," I moaned and dug my heels into his back to trap him against my body.

"Greedy," he murmured with a tiny chuckle that vibrated against my clit, causing me to spasm uncontrollably.

I ground myself against him and dug my fingers into his hair. I'd always been meek and mild in the bedroom, but there was something about Bear that brought out a different side of me. One that didn't give a fuck what he was thinking, even though I knew Bear wouldn't judge me. For once in my life, I was out for me. Greedy, he called me. And I was. Unapologetically, take-what-I-want greedy.

He watched me, our eyes locking on each other as he worshiped me with his mouth. I'd always been the turn the lights off before we get down to business type of gal, but with Bear, I wanted to see him the way he saw me.

It was written all over his face. His attraction. His need. The want he felt for me was almost electric. Why hadn't I seen it before?

"I'm so close," I said, pushing his face deeper and holding his mouth hostage against my flesh.

The man had a tongue that worked magic. Swiping to the left, then to the right before making a complete circle that could only be described as magnificent. My feet moved back and forth, my muscles strained as I felt the orgasm building inside me.

His mouth was that good. So good that I wanted him to do it all day, but I also wanted the feeling of euphoria I hadn't ever experienced, except for the few times I'd experimented with drugs.

When two fingers dipped inside me, stroking that spot that made me lose my breath, I couldn't hold it back any longer. Everything inside me seized up, including my ability to see straight.

I stared down at him through blurry eyes as he hummed his satisfaction against me, drawing out my climax and my inability to breathe. As each wave crashed over me, his fingers still stroking my insides, I let oblivion take me.

"Franny…" Bear's voice was soft at first, almost distant.

Mmm. This is so nice. Heavenly.

"Franny." There was more urgency in his voice this time.

He's just the best.

"Franny!" he yelled as my body began to shake back and forth.

"What?" I asked, finally opening my eyes and snapping back to reality.

"Fuck," he hissed above me, his eyes serious. "I thought you were dying."

I laughed and cradled his face in my hands, even though my arms felt like they weighed a thousand pounds. "It's the perfect way to go."

"Don't do that shit to me, woman. I thought I was going to have to explain this to Morgan. I kinda like livin'."

My laughter grew louder, and I dug my fingers into his salt-and-pepper beard. "I was in that perfect spot until you pulled me back."

His eyebrow drew down, and his jaw clenched. "What spot?"

Pulling my head up, I kissed his lips softly and tasted myself. "The darkness and warmth where you're alive, but on the edge of nothingness."

"You're crazy, Fran. Simply crazy." He slammed his mouth down against mine, pushing the back of my head into the pillow.

My arms snaked around his neck as I opened to him, letting our tongues tangle together in the most beautiful dance. I felt his passion and need in the way his lips covered mine and in his ragged breaths that fed me.

When he collapsed onto his back and took me with him, I was shocked when he said, "Just lie here for a few and close your eyes. The day is young."

My fingers slid through his chest hair, settling against the space between his pecs. "Don't you want me to take care of you?" I asked softly with my lips against his skin and my hand covering his massive erection.

He kissed my forehead and let his lips linger against my skin. "I had a long night last night. Just lie with me."

Snuggle?

Bear wanted to snuggle me?

Never took him for a man who wanted to cuddle a woman. Hell, I'd never been much for it either. But the pull of the nothingness I'd felt before started to grow heavier behind my eyelids, and the last thing I thought was—I liked being greedy.

BEAR

City stood over me and laughed. "You look like shit."

"Thanks," I grumbled, pulling at the label on my beer.

I'd been sitting there for an hour, nursing it and thinking about Fran. We'd spent the last two weeks holed up at her place or mine to keep from being seen by her kid, and I was done with it.

I no longer wanted to hide.

For the first time in my life, I actually liked someone and wanted the rest of the world to know it.

"Still seeing my aunt?"

His words caught me off guard. I turned, pondering what to say and stroking my beard. "Yep," I finally answered because, fuck it, I wanted him to know.

"Thought so. She the one making you look like you got one

foot in the grave?"

"You really wanna know?"

He blanched but righted himself quickly. "I suppose I don't, but you're my friend, so I'll pretend we're talking about someone I don't share blood with."

"She's in my bed or I'm in hers every night. But that's not the most tiring part. Hiding is."

"I imagine it is. It's like having an affair, but your wife is your friend, and you're bangin' his mom."

"Nice," I muttered with a tiny smile.

"So what are you going to do? Have you felt Morgan out about it?"

"Dude." I leaned back in my chair, kicking my feet out underneath the table. "He made it quite clear that he wanted me to stay away from his mother."

"I don't blame him for standing his ground. You have to remember, Fran hasn't really been with anyone since his father left. No matter who she's with, it won't be easy for him." He motioned toward the waitress, asking for two more.

"That's stupid."

"Eh, men aren't always rational, especially when it comes to our women—even when they're our mothers." He studied me for a moment. "So you really like Fran?"

Once our beers were on the table, I dragged mine toward me and pushed the old one away. "I do." I sighed and scratched at my beard, catching a whiff of her perfume that had been left from when I kissed her neck earlier. "She invited Janice over for dinner tomorrow."

He spat the beer he was just about to swallow all over the table. "What? Did you just say—"

"Yep." I nodded and downed half my beer in one giant gulp.

He wiped his mouth with the back of his hand. "How do you feel about that?"

"I don't know. Janice has never approved of my lifestyle, but maybe, if she met Fran, she may soften a bit."

When I left her with my sisters, she cried. Her wails still rang in my ears, and I'd never forget the look on her face when I kissed her good-bye.

Time hadn't healed the wound either. We were cordial, but by no means did she love me like she had. When she was a baby, she'd sleep on my chest for hours. There wasn't anywhere I'd go without her attached to me in some form.

Being her first heartbreak is something I'd never forgive myself for, and I suppose, neither would she.

"She's a tough cookie," City said and sipped his beer, staring off into the distance. "Maybe you should invite Morgan to dinner too."

My head jerked back at his stupidity. "Are you fucking crazy? He'll just add flames to the fire. She doesn't need any more reason to hate me."

"True."

Like the four horsemen of the Apocalypse, James, Morgan, Thomas, and Frisco came bursting through the front door of the Neon Cowboy. Maybe they caught wind of my tryst with Fran and were all here to kick my ass.

Frisco stopped off at the bar, but the others marched directly to our table and sat down. Thomas spoke first, "We found him."

James continued, "We have eyes on him until we can get there."

"Where the hell is he?" I asked just as Frisco pulled over a chair, twirled it around, and sat.

"Back in Lowndes County. Same spot we went to." Morgan shook his head. "Guess after we left, he popped back up. Probably figured we wouldn't look for him there again."

"When do we leave?" I asked, ready to leave now if needed.

They glanced around the table, avoiding my eyes as the waitress dropped off a bucket of beer. "You're not going," Morgan said and glanced at City.

My fist clenched so tightly around my beer bottle I thought it would burst in my hand. "My ass is going."

"No, buddy, you're going to stay here and man the phones," Thomas told me with a straight face.

"Isn't that what Angel's for?" I just kept shaking my head in disbelief.

"She'll be there too, but you have to keep in contact with the clients. You and Sam will stay behind while we head to Georgia and take care of Johnny."

"But—" I started to say, ready to argue my point, when Morgan cut me off.

"The Lowndes County Sheriff would be happy to have you back in town. I'm sure he'd haul your ass back to jail just for looking at someone funny. We don't have time to deal with the hick cops there. Just stay here, watch the business, keep an eye on the ladies, and let us handle Johnny."

"Fine," I grumbled. "I'll stay here with Sam."

"Good." Thomas eased back into the chair. "We're out of here first thing in the morning. I'll let the service know to forward all the messages to you or Sam. If we aren't back tomorrow night, you need to make sure your ass is in the office first thing in the morning."

I smiled, even though I was anything but happy. "Sure thing, boss." The sarcasm in my voice wasn't missed by anyone.

"Would you rather sit in jail with Andy?" Morgan remembered my nickname for the asshole.

"Not really, although he was entertaining." I smiled.

"You're lucky I got you out. It wasn't easy with your record." Thomas tried to hold back his laughter. "People don't seem to understand how I hired a convicted criminal to work for me, but I know you're an upstanding dude."

"Wish everyone felt that way," I muttered under my breath.

Morgan glared at me from across the table. "You talking about me?"

I shook my head and glared right back. "Never."

"What's the problem?" Frisco asked because he wasn't in the know about anything between Fran and me. It had stayed "within the family."

"Bear and Fran," James said casually, like it wasn't a big fucking deal.

Frisco spat his beer out. "Come again?"

"Yep, you heard me right. Bear and Fran have a 'thing.'" James used air quotes, driving the point home for effect.

Morgan still held my eyes, giving me the look of death. "We had a drink together." I shrugged off the lie.

Thomas cocked an eyebrow and smirked. "Is that all?"

"Yes." My answer was short, but I was being thrown under the bus right in front of the very person I was trying to hide from.

With a scowl on his face, Morgan peered around the table. "Is there something I don't know?"

"Nah, man. We're just fucking with Bear and you." City

tried to stop whatever train wreck was coming, but it's hard to stop one once it's set in motion.

Morgan's eyes bounced back and forth between City and me. "You've been with my ma?"

Before I could answer, City stuck up for me. "What's so wrong with Bear seeing Aunt Fran?" He crossed his arms and stared down Morgan. "He's the best friend a guy could ask for. He sticks to his word and has a level head."

"You want him fuckin' your ma?" Morgan snarled and kept his eyes on me. "I sure as fuck don't. Good friend or not, he's not the right man for her."

"When did you become such a shit in the pants?" James laughed, trying to break the tension but failing.

Morgan turned his scowl on him. "Fuck off."

"I wasn't exactly happy about my best buddy being with my sister," Thomas said, giving James the stink eye. "But at some point, you gotta let go."

"We'll see about that," Morgan replied before taking a long, slow slug of his beer.

"She's your mom. You can't boss her ass around," City, the usual voice of reason, chimed in.

"Fran isn't to be messed with," Thomas said through his laughter. "She's vicious. You should know better than anyone else."

"If you're worried Bear's going to step out of line, I'm sure Fran will put him in his place, just like she has you," City stated, and his words were true.

Fran wasn't a shrinking violet. She had a wicked tongue and an attitude to match. Maybe that's why I liked her so much. She didn't put up with my shit or anyone else's for that matter—

including Morgan.

Morgan eyed me warily. "She's been off my back for weeks. It's been…" His voice trailed off.

"Nice?" City nudged him in the arm.

"Yeah," Morgan laughed.

"When her attention is elsewhere, she'll stay off your ass," Frisco said, knowing firsthand what it was like to have a parent who hovered.

"But I don't like that it's him." Morgan pointed his skinny little finger in my direction.

"When did I become the bad guy? It's nice you're all talking about me like I'm not even here too. Fuckers."

Morgan leaned back and swung his arms out wide. "Look around the room. Which girl hasn't Bear fucked here?"

He had a point, but there were a few I hadn't been with. Fuck, I'd been single for thirty years, and I'm not a priest. Women offered, I accepted—end of discussion.

"Point?" I asked in defense of myself.

"You're a manwhore, Bear," Morgan said matter-of-factly.

"I've been single almost longer than you've been alive, kid."

"He has a point," City said with a nod.

"I never lied to any woman I've slept with either. I never promise anything more than what it is."

Sometimes they were delusional and thought after a single taste of their pussy that I'd get down on one knee and proclaim them as mine, but that's my fault. I should never get involved with the nutty bitches. They aren't worth the headache.

Morgan leaned forward, his face still serious as a heart attack. "And what are you promising my mother?"

Shit. That was something Fran should be answering, not me. But I had to break the news because I couldn't have this shitty-ass tension between us.

"We're dating," I answered simply.

Morgan's entire body stiffened as his eyes widened. "Dating?"

"Yep, dating."

"When was the last time you dated anyone?" Morgan asked, not realizing the seriousness of my words.

"Once since 1985."

Morgan looked at me funny. "Once?"

"Yeah, dumbass. I don't date unless I'm seriously into someone."

His body rocked backward like someone punched him in the face. "You're seriously into my ma?" he asked with the biggest eyes I'd ever seen.

I shrugged it off like it was the most nonchalant statement to make. "Yeah."

Morgan rubbed his face, digging his fingers into his eyes and mumbling under his breath. I couldn't make out what he was saying, but I didn't care either. Nothing was going to change the fact that I did like Fran and I wanted to date her.

"We're happy for you, Bear." Thomas smiled and gave me a quick, curt nod.

Morgan hopped from his chair and glared at Thomas. "Like fuck we are!"

James grabbed his arm and stopped him from leaping over the table at me. "Sit your ass down and stop making a scene."

"Dude," Morgan seethed, keeping his eyes pinned to me as

he sat again. "It's my mom we're talking about."

"And it's Bear. He's not going to fuck over your mom." James glanced in my direction. "He knows that we'll all kick his ass if he does."

"I do." I didn't dare smile. It wasn't the time or place. This was serious talk about an important person. "I'd expect nothing less."

Morgan clenched his fists on top of the table, his entire body tense. "If I even think you're doing my ma wrong, I'll fucking end you."

All I could do was nod. It didn't matter what I said. I'd have to prove it through my actions and over time. Lots of time—maybe longer than I had left to live. Morgan saw me in a different light, and I wasn't sure I'd ever be able to change it.

14

FRAN

Bear didn't spend the night last night and I actually missed him, but I had too much to do this morning to dwell on it. Janice was coming for an early dinner, a fact that Bear wasn't so excited about, but I didn't give a shit about his lack of enthusiasm.

He explained to me that they were cordial, but he'd never been able to work his way into her good graces. He fucked up when she was a kid, and for that, he had to pay penance and make amends.

We all make mistakes as parents. Most aren't as big as his, but it's our responsibility to set things right. When I called Janice to ask her over, I thought she'd decline, but she jumped at the chance.

Maybe she was ready to forgive him. Maybe she wanted to tell him off. It didn't really matter. My only goal was to get them in the same room and let them sort their shit out.

"Janice," I said as I opened the door to the most beautiful pregnant woman I'd ever seen.

She smiled brightly with her hands resting on her belly. "Fran."

"Come on in, sweetheart." I stepped to the side, giving her enough room for her belly. "Aren't you a beautiful creature?"

"Thanks." She peered around the living room and frowned. "Is he not coming?"

"He'll be here. He's really excited about today." I lied as I closed the door, but I didn't want her to think otherwise.

Her eyes grew wide. "He is?"

I nodded as I walked up to her. "He's missed you. Does he know you're pregnant?"

She shook her head and glanced toward the floor. "No, I haven't told him yet."

"He's going to be a grandpa." I couldn't contain my excitement at the thought of little ones running around the house.

"Yeah, I guess he is, technically."

Ouch. One thing I knew was that Bear loved his kids, even when he couldn't take care of them.

"I guess so," I said softly. "Would you like to sit down, and I'll get you something to drink?"

"That would be great. My feet are killing me," she said as I wandered into the kitchen to grab a bottle of water.

When I walked back into the room, she sat on the couch, clutching her stomach again. "How far along are you?"

"Eight and a half months, but I feel as big as a whale."

I handed her the glass and sat next to her. "I remember when I was pregnant. I was miserable for the entire nine months." I laughed softly. “It probably had more to do with my husband than my son.”

The timer on the oven beeped just as there was a knock at the door. “Come in!” I yelled, knowing it was Bear, but I headed toward the kitchen.

I couldn’t fuck up this meal. Everyone knew I was a shitty cook. Maria gave me some homemade sauce to make lasagna. It was the one thing I could cook without fail, but usually, I used some jarred shit from the store. She’d insisted that only the family recipe would do for such a special occasion.

After I took out the lasagna and set it on the stove to cool, I tiptoed toward the living room and watched Bear and Janice from a distance as they stood in the center of the room.

She smiled up at him, a hint of a little girl mesmerized by her dad showing through. He placed his hand on her belly, his eyes bouncing between her face and the point at where their bodies were connected.

“Janice,” he said with a sad, soft voice. “I’m so, so…”

“I know, Dad.”

“No, baby, you don’t.” His hand moved away from her stomach to her face. He cupped her cheek in his palm, rubbing his thumb against her cheek.

Her eyebrows drew together, but she did nothing to move away from his touch. I didn’t dare move or intrude on their moment. They needed this time. Their relationship had been severed, and words needed to be spoken without me in their presence.

“Let’s sit.” He guided her toward the couch, his hand gripping her elbow in case she tripped. “We need to talk about something that I’ve put off for too many years.”

I looked back at the lasagna and shrugged. It could wait—

that was the best thing about this type of meal. It was pretty hard to fuck up and only got better with time. So thankfully, it would still be edible.

Even though I knew it wasn't right to eavesdrop, I did anyway. I couldn't drag my eyes away from them. She looked like him with eyes that were the color of gray clouds on a rainy day. Her dark hair shimmered in the sunlight, streaming through the window behind her. He still had a smattering of the identical shade in his, but the white had started to overtake the darkness. Even the roundness of their cheeks matched. Somehow, even though they had so many similarities, she was feminine and petite while Bear was big, burly, and hard-looking.

She sat down, smoothing her dress down with her palms. "What's wrong, Dad?"

"Nothing, Jan. We've never had a talk about what happened, and I need to talk to you now before it's too late."

Her hand flew to her mouth, and her eyes widened in horror. "Are you dying or something?"

He shook his head with a faint smile visible beneath his beard. "Not today, but I'm getting older." His large hand pulled hers down from her face. "I don't even know where to start."

"You don't have to say anything."

"No. This needs to be said." He pulled in a shaky breath and then began to speak. "Your mother and I had you when we were young, probably too young to really be parents, but we made the best of it. We loved you so much and never let you leave our side. God." He took another deep breath. "I loved Jackie so much. I couldn't imagine my life with anyone else. We were crazy for each other. So much so that Ret came less than a year after you were born."

Janice placed her hands over his. "I heard that from Aunt

Caroline. She said you two couldn't keep your hands to yourself. She called it undignified."

"She would say that," he grumbled just loud enough for me to hear. "We loved you so much we couldn't wait for another baby. My world revolved around my family. I can't describe how much I loved your mother, because I've never felt that way about any woman in my life."

My eyes suddenly filled with tears. I shouldn't be jealous of Jackie and the way Bear loved her, but a tiny, greedy piece of me was and probably always would be. It was hard to compete with the memory of someone taken too soon, even if it was almost thirty years ago.

"Your mom and me had big plans. We wanted to have at least four kids. The more, the merrier because you were such a great baby. We wanted an entire house full. We wanted to build a house in the country and just have our own piece of heaven with no one else but us."

"That sounds…" Her voice trailed off.

"Yeah," he said in the sweetest voice, and I could almost feel his longing and heartache. "When she went into labor, it never even crossed my mind that she could die." His voice cracked.

Seeing him like that, choked up and in pain, wasn't the Bear I'd always seen. He was so full of life and jokes that no one saw the pain hidden beneath the surface. Only in fleeting moments when we were lying in bed would he confide to me all the regret and sorrow he had about his past. He missed Jackie and loved her to this day, but his biggest regret was his children—Ret and Janice. He never got the chance to be a father, to teach them how to do things, and to be there for many of their biggest life firsts.

He clutched her hands tighter, and his shoulders slumped forward. "When it happened, I was in shock. I refused to believe she was really gone. I barely remember the following days. They passed in a blur because my mind couldn't comprehend that she was actually gone."

"I wish I could remember Mom," Janice said to him, her face softer than when they had first started talking.

"I saved a box for you."

"You did?" Tears welled in her eyes and quickly trickled down her cheeks.

"I did, babygirl. I had to save some of your mom's stuff so that someday you'd have a piece of her with you."

"Dad," Janice whispered and placed her hands over his.

"I was a shit father. I know it. I'm not making an excuse for how I acted, but I want you to understand the depths of my despair. Seeing you now, with that baby in your belly… It should be a happy time for me. But it's not. I'm scared for you. Frightened that you'll be like your mother, and I'll lose you too."

She smiled softly before wiping away a tear before it fell from her jaw. "I'm fine. The doctor said everything is good, so don't worry."

"Aunt Caroline watched you right after it happened. She knew I couldn't look after you two because I could barely take care of myself. I thought I'd heal and be able to move on, but I couldn't do it. I wasn't strong enough," he admitted. "I was mad at the world. I hated God and couldn't fathom why he took Jackie from me…from us."

"Things happen. We can't control them." Her hands twisted in her lap as she stared down at them. "But why didn't you come back for us?" She dragged her eyes to his, and the pain in them was heart-wrenching.

He grimaced. "I wish I had a reason that sounded right, but I don't. Nothing can justify what I did. I went off the deep end when the dust settled. You kids were being taken care of, and I got mixed up in some bad shit. I had a death wish after losing your mom. I wanted to be with her so bad that I didn't care if I had to die to do it."

"Dad," she gasped. "That's horrible."

"But you kids would've been fine. Or at least, that's what I told myself. Not long after, I ended up in jail for a bit, and when I got out, I didn't see a point in coming back into your lives. Caroline told me how well you both were doing, and we both decided it was best I stayed away. I couldn't argue with her either."

The tears in my eyes dropped down my cheeks as I plastered my back to the wall. I couldn't imagine walking away from Morgan, but I also couldn't imagine the pain Bear went through losing the love of his life.

"It's my biggest regret in life—not being there for you kids. I should've been a stronger man. I should've been a better man. But your mom made me better. I don't know how to make it up to you and Ret for being a shit father."

I peered around the corner, unable to stop myself.

She scooted closer and placed her hand on his arm. "You can be here for us now, Dad. We're always going to be your kids. Just because we're grown doesn't mean we don't need you."

"Babygirl, what do you need me for?"

"Everything. Jeff left me. I'm all alone with the baby on the way. I'm so lost with no one to lean on. Aunt Caroline is great, but you know how she is."

"I'll kick his ass," Bear barked, his body growing rigid.

"Don't bother. He's not worth the jail time. I need you more than I want his ass knocked out."

"Whatever you want, Janice. I'll do anything you want or need as long as you give me a shot at making up all our lost years."

I smiled, still hidden behind the wall as they embraced. When I invited her over, I'd hoped they'd make up, but I never thought it would be this great. I busied myself in the kitchen, tinkering with the table settings until they were done. Luckily, the lasagna was still warm, safely covered by aluminum foil and ready to be devoured.

When they entered the kitchen with their arms locked, I melted a little bit inside. This big, hunky tough guy had transformed into someone else—someone better.

"Ready to eat?" I asked, transfixed by the image of them together.

"I'm starving, Fran. Thanks for having me today." Janice glanced up at Bear and rested her head on his chest, leaning against him. "I finally feel like I have my dad back."

"Awww, honey. He loves you."

Her smile widened. "I know."

"Sit down, and I'll serve everyone," I said, grabbing the spatula.

Bear helped Janice sit and then came to my side. "Thanks, sweetheart. I'll have to thank you later." He waggled his eyebrows, and I giggled.

"Not in front of the kid," I whispered and glanced at her out of the corner of my eye.

"How do you think she got that way?" he smirked and grabbed my ass.

I swatted his stomach with the hard plastic utensil. "Behave, big boy."

"I will for now, but when the kid goes, all bets are off."

"Salad?" I asked with a strangled voice, unable to hide my excitement.

"No, I'm craving meat," Janice replied.

"Me too," I mumbled, catching Bear's eye.

He smiled easier, and his entire being felt different…lighter. Usually, my meddling brought headaches, but for the first time in a long time, I did fuckin' good.

15

BEAR

“Talk to your brother lately?” I asked after we’d finished dinner. Janice had forgiven me, but Ret wouldn’t be so easy.

He was too much like me for that to happen.

“I talked to him yesterday. I told him I was coming here for dinner.”

I hadn’t been able to take my eyes off Janice. She looked so much like Jackie that my heart ached. It was bittersweet. At least a piece of my wife lived on in our girl. “What did he say?”

“He wished me luck.” She laughed softly and wiped her lips.

“Funny guy,” I whispered and shifted in my chair. “Where’s he at?”

“Near Miami, but he’s ready to make a move as soon as he finds the job of his dreams.”

“What’s he doing now?” What kind of shitty father am I? I didn’t even know what the hell my kid did for a living. After he got out of the military, we lost touch.

"He's a bounty hunter."

My entire body rocked back in the chair. "No shit?"

"Yep. He's been doing it for a few years. He gets restless though and moves around a lot."

My kid, the bounty hunter. "Is he married?"

"Well," she said with a grimace. "He lives an…" Her voice trailed off, and she looked at Fran. "Alternative lifestyle."

"He's gay?" My mouth fell open.

Janice snorted. "No, he has a girl."

"A girlfriend?" Fran asked, saving me the awkwardness.

Janice scrubbed a hand across her face, but she couldn't stop her laughter. "Yeah, I guess you can call her that."

I looked at Fran, and she shrugged. "Well, what is she?"

"They met at a club."

I held up my hands. "Stop." I couldn't discuss this with my kid, no matter how old she was.

"Like Izzy and James?" Fran asked me.

I nodded. "Just tell me he's the boss, at least."

"Yes." Janice snorted again with the rosiest colored cheeks. "She calls him sir. It's kind of sickening."

"I like the sound of that." My fingers tangled in my beard as I stared at Fran.

"Never going to happen, big boy," Fran replied quickly and swatted my arm.

"A guy can wish." I smirked.

Janice placed her hands on her belly and stared at us. "It's nice to see you're at peace, Dad."

"I am," I said with a smile and placed my hand over Fran's on top of the table. "For the first time since your mother died, I am." Fran sucked in a breath and made a weird, throaty noise. "She's a good woman." I clutched her fingers tighter.

"You're an amazing cook, Fran. Thanks for a wonderful meal."

"Isn't she, though?"

"Oh, stop. All I did was make lasagna. It's not a big deal." Fran blushed before leaning over to kiss me.

Warmth flooded me. Having Fran and Janice with me felt better than I could ever dream. I finally felt at peace with my daughter. So much of her life I'd been gone, but I wasn't going to let that happen again. I had a lot to make up for, and I planned to be around to be the father I never had been to her.

"When are you due?" Fran asked as she started to clear the table.

"Three weeks, but I'm hoping it happens sooner. The Florida heat is killing me."

"Three weeks?" I felt sick. I knew it was irrational to worry that she'd meet the same fate as her mother, but I couldn't stop myself from worrying.

"I'll be fine, Dad. Calm down."

"I can't be calm. In three weeks, I'll be a grandpa. Jesus, fuck." Suddenly I felt dizzy. "Oh, God."

Fran turned around from the sink and rolled her eyes. "You're such a baby."

"That's easy for you to say." I held my stomach, trying to wrap my head around that little nugget of truth. Grandpa. I was going to be a motherfucking grandpa.

I wasn't ready for it.

When I looked in the mirror, I saw an older version of myself, but not a grandfather. Those men were hunched over, half-crippled shells of their former selves. I wasn't that. I still had life. I still had strength. Fuck, my dick still stayed hard without the help of that little blue pill.

"Bear, snap out of it." Fran waved her hand in front of my face as I sat there like a zombie. "For shit's sake," she muttered before touching my cheek with her hand. "You're still you, babe. You're still my Bear."

"Grandpa Bear," I whispered, my eyes bouncing between Janice's belly and Fran's tits. "Grand. Pa."

"Maybe we'll get the baby to call ya Pops," Janice said.

"Pops. Fuck." I hung my head and thought about it. It wasn't as bad as Grandpa and hell, maybe people would think the kid was mine. I sighed heavily. "It's fine. As long as its healthy and you're okay, I'll be just fine."

Janice stayed for a few more hours and left just before dark. I insisted on her leaving because I didn't want her on the road and driving in the sticks. It wasn't safe, and she had precious cargo on board.

As soon as Fran closed the door, I slammed her against the wall, using my body as the ram. "I want you," I said against her neck, running my lips up the side.

"What got into you?" She wrapped her arms around me, tipping her head back to give me better access. "Have something to prove, old man?" She laughed softly before moaning when I sank my teeth into the corner of her neck where it met her shoulder.

I pulled back, staring into her dark brown eyes. "This old man can still fuck until you pass out."

"I was just tired—"

I pressed my lips to her, devouring her words and her bullshit. I knew I still had it. Her lips opened, giving me her sweet softness as I kneaded her breasts in my palm. When she moaned, I knew I had her.

When our lips disconnected, she stood against the wall and panted. Backing away, I narrowed my eyes and took in her beauty. "Strip, Franny. I need to be in you."

"Right here?" she asked, using the wall as an anchor.

I pointed to her and motioned to her clothing. "Right here. Get naked."

She swallowed hard and nodded. Slowly she pulled her shirt over her head, exposing her red lace bra and beautiful tits, and tossed it to the floor.

I drew in a shaky breath, but I kept my eyes pinned to her. "Pants too."

Without hesitation, she yanked off her skintight pants, letting them pool near her feet before kicking them away.

I turned my fingers in a circle. "Face the wall," I told her, taking in all of her beauty and softness as she moved.

"You sure you don't want to go in the bedroom?"

"I'm sure, sweetheart. Stop talking and put your hands against the wall."

I took off my clothes at warp speed, giddier than a kid at Christmas and needing to prove my virility—still not over the fact that I was about to become a grandfather.

Pressing my front to her back, I placed my mouth close to her ear. "Who's your daddy?"

"Tom," Fran said with a bit of chuckle.

But her laughter died when I tangled my fingers through her raven hair and pulled her head back. "A smartass and greedy, but

I know how to shut you up."

My lips crashed against hers, stealing her breath and her words. My hand drifted down her body, cupping her ass gently in my rough palms before sliding between her cheeks and checking her readiness for me.

She moaned softly in my mouth and pushed her body against my hand. My fingers moved to her front, coated in her need, and slowly rubbed her clit in a circular motion.

Breaking our kiss, I growled. "Do you want me?"

"Yes," she said in an airy, wanton tone.

"Bend over and touch your toes."

Her eyebrows drew together. "Do you know how old I am? Fuck me, Bear. I haven't been able to touch my toes for twenty years."

"Fran," I said, trying to hold in my laughter. I hadn't even thought about her age as a factor in the scene I had playing out in my mind. "Bend over and hold the door handle."

"That, I can do." Gripping the door handle tightly, she bent at the waist, pushing her ass against my body.

Wrapping my hands around her hips, I pulled them out, bending her farther to give me better access. Before she had a chance to say anything else, I pushed my cock inside and shivered in ecstasy.

"I love your greedy pussy. So fucking good," I growled, pushing myself deeper until there was nowhere else to go but pull out and ram back into her.

"Fuck me," she moaned and met my thrust with enough force that she caused me to rock backward on my heels.

My hands tightened, stilling her movement as I controlled her motions and mine. I thrust into her with such force that her head tapped the wooden door, making a light knocking sound.

Neither of us cared.

We were too lost in the moment to laugh about it and too close to the precipice to stop. My fingertips dug into her flesh the closer to the edge I came. She hunched over, standing on her tiptoes and arching her back higher in the air to make me dive deeper and stroke her in just the right spot.

When Fran reached between her legs and touched herself—I lost it. My eyes blurred before fuzzy fireworks filled my vision, my body trembling through the orgasm that stole the air from my lungs. She followed me, moaning, and pushed against me, making my dick slide deeper inside.

"Jesus," I said, holding on to her for fear of falling.

"You did good, Grandpa," Fran said, yanking my proverbial chain and laughing.

I backed away, my cock coming with me, and slapped her ass. "Not yet."

She jumped, her hand coming around to touch the very spot my hand just landed. "Doesn't matter," she said. "You still fuck like a champ."

"Fran." I started to laugh too and stroked my semihard dick. "I may be old, but I can fuck you into oblivion."

She turned around with the naughtiest grin I'd ever seen. "Want to find out?"

I took a step forward and twisted my hand in her hair. "You and your greedy pussy are going to be the death of me, woman."

"You'd only be so lucky to go that way."

She was right too. I'd tempted fate half my life, and with my record in the good and evil columns, I was sure I wouldn't be lucky enough to go out inside a woman. With my luck, I'd be hit by a semi or some crazy-ass shit—something agonizing as payback for being a pain in the ass my entire life.

FRAN

I was absolutely buzzing by the time Bear left my house. The feeling stayed with me until the next morning when the phone rang. "Hello."

"Ma?" Morgan sounded weird. It was a mother thing. I could be hundreds of miles away from him and just know when something was off.

I stopped walking. "What's wrong?"

"We found Johnny," he said an octave lower.

"Good. That bastard," I whispered into the phone.

"He's dead."

"What?" I screeched, thinking I heard him wrong.

"He's gone, Ma."

Nervousness filled me, and I grabbed the sponge from the

sink and started cleaning in a manic state. "What happened?"

"Looks like suicide. Shot himself."

The guilt I felt after calling him a bastard started to eat at me immediately. "I can't believe it."

"He left a note. It looks like he wasn't working alone in the theft of Race's money."

My hand stopped scrubbing the black granite counter. "What did it say?" Sometimes getting information out of Morgan was more like pulling teeth than an actual conversation.

"I'll send it to you via text. The cops are taking it into evidence."

"Okay," I said, trying to hold back my tears.

"We'll be home later today. I'll stop by when I get a chance."

"Go home to your wife, baby. I'm fine," I lied.

"I need to talk to you, though, about Johnny and his circle of friends."

"I already told Bear everything I knew."

"I still want to talk with you. I gotta run, Ma. We're about to leave and head out. I'll call you later."

"Drive safely, Morgan. I love you."

"Love you too," he said before he disconnected.

Johnny killed himself. I couldn't believe it. Standing in my kitchen, I stared out the window and clutched my phone.

When it beeped, I glanced down, still in a trance.

I read the note five times, trying to figure out who "he" was and why Johnny felt it was his only way out. The information was too sparse and cryptic for me to really make any type of guess on what the hell was going on.

I couldn't sit here all day and replay everything in my head. There was only one place I could go to figure shit out—only one person who would talk to me like a person.

I grabbed my purse and headed straight for ALFA PI. By the time I walked through the front door, my stomach had filled with knots, and my shoulders felt like iron bricks.

"Hey," I said to Angel as she stood from the reception desk and came to greet me. Her auburn hair bounced with each step like a luscious red velvet blanket.

Her dark eyes didn't meet mine when she spoke. "Hey, yourself." She backed away and studied my face. "You don't look so good."

I waved her comment away. "Have you talked to Morgan?"

"He just called to say he's on his way back."

"Is that all he said?" Even though I was standing still, my foot tapped on the floor because pacing wasn't an option.

"No." She frowned and stared down at the floor. "No, he told me about Johnny."

I looked around her shoulder, down the hallway that led to the offices. "Bear around?"

She nodded and stepped to the side. "He's in his office."

"Thanks, doll." I gave her a quick peck on the cheek before marching straight to the man I knew could help me work through the shit in my head.

I knocked softly. "Bear."

No response.

"Bear," I spoke a little louder this time.

The door behind me opened, and a smiling Sam stood in the

doorway. “Hi, Ms. D. How are you today?”

“I’m well, Sam. Yourself?” I took him in—all his beauty and muscles. If I were twenty years younger, I would’ve taken a run at him. I could’ve climbed that tall drink of water and swung off his vine like a champion.

“I’m well.” His white teeth glistened against his tanned face. His white T-shirt clung to his muscles like it couldn’t get close enough. “He’s inside.” He motioned with his scruff-covered chin.

“I don’t want to just walk inside,” I told him, still eyeing him like a flesh-colored lollipop.

“Just go in. He’s probably asleep. We had a long night.”

If he only knew.

“Thanks, sweetie,” I said and stood on my tiptoes to place a kiss on his cheek. When I planted my lips against his skin, I inhaled his scent like a creeper.

When I came to ALFA, most of the men were my relatives. I was only left with Bear and Sam as eye candy, but they were more than enough to keep my imagination occupied.

“Anytime, Ms. D.”

As I backed away, I debated my next statement in my head a few times before finally blurting it out. “Don’t tell Morgan I was here, please.”

His smile vanished. “Why?”

“I just don’t want him to worry. I need to talk to Bear about the case, and I don’t want to hear Morgan’s shit. Got me?”

He nodded slowly. “Got ya. Whatever you say.”

“Good boy.” I waved and touched the door handle, waiting for Sam to go back inside. Once he finally closed his door, I opened Bear’s to find him on the phone with his back to me.

"I'm working on it. Just get your ass back here and calm the fuck down," he growled, swiveling around in his chair. His eyes raked up my body before a slow, lazy smile appeared. "I'll keep her safe. I have to go. Someone is here to see me." He disconnected the call and leaned back, staring at me.

I shifted on my feet. "Am I bothering you?"

"Come here," he said, motioning for me with his hand.

I walked around the desk and came to a stop in front of him. "I can go."

His big hands slid around my waist, and he pulled me into his lap. "You all right, sweetheart?"

"I'm okay," I told him as I nuzzled against his chest. "Better now that I'm here." My hand tangled in his white T-shirt, the tips of my fingers digging into his hard pecs.

His hand swept up and down my back, soothing me. "How much did you hear?"

I peered up into his silver eyes. "Not much. I assume you were referring to me in that phone call."

He grimaced. "Yeah. I'm supposed to keep an eye on you, and Sam's going to head to the track to be with Race until Morgan gets back."

I would've argued needing to be watched, but I wasn't in the mood, and it was Bear that would do the watching. "Did you see the note?"

"Yeah." His hand came to the back of my neck and gripped me gently. "You know it's not your fault, right?"

My eyes drifted away from his. "Yeah," I whispered.

"Franny, look at me." My chest tightened as I directed my eyes to his, and his hold on me increased. "Whatever Johnny got involved in had nothing to do with you. Do not feel guilty for his choices."

"But," I started to say, but I lost my train of thought.

"Don't worry," he said in the most soothing voice and pulled my head against his chest, cupping my face. "This isn't your fault."

"Bear, if I would've answered the phone, maybe…" I sealed my eyes shut as my chin began to quiver.

"It wouldn't've changed a thing. He was in too deep. He would've just dragged you into whatever mess he was involved in." His fingers swept my hair away from my face and tucked a few strays behind my ear. "It's bad enough that you're this involved. I couldn't imagine if something happened to you too."

I listened to the steady thumping of his heart and let his words sink in. I probably couldn't have changed anything, but knowing I didn't answer the phone would eat at me for some time.

We sat in silence for a few minutes while I gathered my thoughts. I finally straightened in his lap, staring into his steely eyes. "Well, he's gone now. There's nothing I can do to change it."

"You're stuck with me for the rest of the day."

"That's not a hardship." I smiled, and the tears that had collected in my eyes spilled down my cheeks.

Using his thumb, he brushed them away. "Want to go see Race? We could spend the day out at the track, and I can talk to some of the workers."

"Sure. I never mind spending time with my daughter-in-law."

"Sam!" Bear yelled over my head. His eyes dropped to mine. "Sorry. Didn't mean to yell in your ear."

"It's okay." I laughed.

"Yo," Sam said as he opened the door, filling the entire frame.

"We're heading to the track. Stay here if you want. I'll keep an eye on both of the ladies."

Sam chewed on his lip and thought about it before finally replying, "Sure."

"We're out." Bear lifted me off his lap and deposited my feet on the floor. "Ready?"

"Let's take my car and leave your bike here."

Bear's eyebrows drew together. "Although that sounds nice, I'd be more comfortable with you on the back of my bike."

"That makes one of us," I mumbled.

"I'll get your car back to your place, Ms. D," Sam offered.

"Thanks," Bear replied before I could protest.

"Call me if you need anything," Sam said before walking back to his office, leaving us alone again.

"I don't understand why we can't take my car."

"I have nothing against your sedan, baby." Bear stood and grabbed my chin, forcing me to look up at him. "But I'd rather have you on the back of my bike with your sweet thighs squeezing me like a vise and your hungry pussy pressed against my back."

"Okay," I whispered because I liked it too.

***

"Fran!" Race ran toward me with her arms outstretched.

"Hey, sweetie," I said to her as we hugged.

With her arms still wrapped around me, she said, "Bear. It's good to see you. I've heard a lot about you lately." She snickered.

I backed away and held her shoulders. "Don't believe a word

of what Morgan says. You hear me?"

Her deep green eyes sparkled. "Sure, Mom. Whatever you say."

"It's probably worse than you've heard," Bear said, which earned him a stern look.

"I know you're a dirty dog." Race slapped Bear's chest. "What brings you two by?" She blocked the sun from her eyes with her hand.

"Just wanted to go through Johnny's office once more, and I thought I'd take you two to lunch."

"Hmm." She turned around and glanced down at the track behind us. "I'm sure I can get away for a little bit. We're shorthanded without Johnny, but we can make do."

"You're always working. We barely spend time together anymore." I felt whiny, but I did miss her. She had been consumed by the track and making it a success, and with Johnny gone, it hadn't made her job any easier.

"Good. I'll go with Race, and you check out the office," I told Bear when I looped my arm with Race's and started to walk away.

"Meet back here in an hour, and we'll head out."

"You got it!" I yelled out before glancing at my daughter-in-law. "When are you going to give me a grandchild?" I asked because it'd been on my mind ever since Janice came to my house with her giant belly. Really, it'd been on my mind since the day they were married, but I'd been waiting patiently.

"We're working on it, Mom. I promise," Race said, and I believed her.

I'd learned over the last few years that Race never lied to me. Even when Morgan would complain, she still told me like it was—never sparing my feelings in the name of truth.

We walked toward the maintenance building with our arms still locked. "As long as you're trying, then I'm happy."

She looked at me with a quirked eyebrow. "What about you and Bear?"

I smiled so big that my cheeks hurt. "Oh, girl. It's a long story."

"It's a good thing we have an hour, then."

We gabbed the entire time, mostly about Bear, but also about Morgan. Race told me that he'd complained all week about us growing closer. He worried that Bear wasn't going to treat me with the respect I deserved.

I'm sure some of the feelings had more to do with his father and the way he treated me and left us, but I knew Bear was nothing like him. Ray was out for one person—himself.

Bear would do anything to shield his friends and family from any pain, even if it meant he'd take a hit to do it. He was that kind of guy.

17

BEAR

By the time we finished eating, my ears were ringing. Race and Fran never stopped talking. I was too used to the guys at the office and our limited conversation usually containing some grunts instead of actual words.

But these two—they talked and talked, jumping between topics so quickly that my head spun. The only other time I experienced something like that was being at a Gallo family function.

Race and Fran couldn't look more opposite. The color of Race's hair reminded me of sunshine and spring days with its yellow, pin-straight strands. Fran's sat on her shoulders, a stream of black silk that glistened in the light. Their builds were similar—tiny, not frail. Together they were a matched set of beautiful perfection with foul mouths to rival any biker.

But their talkativeness allowed me time to think about what I found while sweeping Johnny's office for clues. We did it when he first disappeared, but this time, we had solid proof that he wasn't working alone.

I found some Post-its that had been tossed to the side with phone numbers scribbled on them but no names. Any of them could be his accomplice. There were a handful of them underneath the desk that had been crumpled into tiny balls. All over his calendar, like mine, were notes I snapped photos of to follow up on later.

But there was one clue that had me worried. The name Ray was written in black ink and traced over numerous times. No phone number, no other information, just the name. I immediately thought of Fran's ex-husband. My mind reeled at the possibility that the slimy bastard was involved in some way.

Morgan had to know about this sooner rather than later. I slid my phone across the table and discreetly sent him a text.

Me: Gotta talk. Found something interesting.

"Whatcha doing?" Fran asked right after I hit send.

"Just seeing how the guys are." I turned off my screen, shielding the words from her prying eyes. She should be employed at ALFA, because she could sniff out bullshit like a bloodhound.

"Everything okay?" Her perfectly shaped eyebrow arched when she spoke.

"Great." I smiled and hoped she bought the bullshit. I placed my hand across the screen as I waited for his reply.

She narrowed her eyes quickly at the gesture. "We'll talk later."

Race started laughing, softly at first but grew loud in a hurry. "You two are so damn cute. I can't get over it. It's like a match made in heaven. Morgan has to get over his shit 'cause I need you two together."

"Don't be silly," Fran said to her and wrinkled her nose.

"No. No." Race shook her head, still laughing. "It's like Beauty and the Beast. I've never seen this side of Bear. Usually, he's stalking around, grunting and broody, but with you, Mom, he's like a sweet man with a heart of gold and scared as hell of you too."

"I'm not," I said quickly.

"He is kind of a beast, isn't he?" Fran's eyes moved between Race and me before she smiled. "You should see what's underneath those clothes."

"Get out." Race smacked Fran's arm. "Is he beastly everywhere?"

Fuckin' women.

I moved my hand to the side and read Morgan's message, trying not to listen to what they were about to say next.

Morgan: Meet at the Cowboy at 7.

Me: I'll be there. What about the women?

Morgan: Fuck. Don't leave them alone. Sam can stay outside my house, and bring Mom with you to the Cowboy.

I sat there in complete shock. He bitched me out for bringing her there before, and now he wants me to take her with me?

"What did he say?" Fran asked after she finished telling Race that I was pure man with a huge sword.

"He said we should meet him at the Cowboy at seven."

"Oh, I love it there," Race said quickly.

"He wants you at home." I couldn't look her in the eye.

She slammed her hand down on the table. "Like fuck. That's not gonna happen." She plucked her phone from her purse and started to type like a madwoman.

"I'm just following orders." I cringed when she paused long enough to glare at me.

"I'll be going. Morgan will just have to get over his macho shit."

"That's my girl. We have to stick together," Fran said as Race hit send.

"What time should I be ready?" Race asked, jamming her phone back into her purse.

"Six thirty," I told her and looked over at Fran. "And I'll pick you up at five."

Fran glanced down at her watch. "It's almost three now. Why don't you just come over for a bit? I'll give you something to eat." Her smile sparkled, and the wickedness in her eyes was evident.

"I'm sure you will." I winked at her.

"Well, all righty, then. Since we just had lunch, I know you two aren't talking about food." Race nudged Fran. "Lucky woman."

"You do have a husband," Fran told her.

"I'm too pissed at him. It's going to be a long time until he gets a piece of this." Race motioned up and down her body.

"Oh, Lord." I peered up at the ceiling and exhaled.

They were so filthy. I didn't want to think about Race and Morgan, and I sure as fuck didn't want Race thinking about Fran and me, but the two of them had no problem with it.

"Well, I have to get back to work, and you two have to…" Race's voice trailed off before she winked at Fran.

I didn't respond. What could I say to that? I didn't want to be the creepy old dude. Fran and Race had a relationship more like friends than mother-in-law and daughter-in-law. It was sweet and kind, and way too much information was shared between them. More than I ever wanted to know.

Fran scooted from the booth, letting Race out and coming to stand next to me. She put her arm around my shoulder and stroked my neck with her fingers. "We'll see you in a few hours."

Race smiled down at me before kissing Fran on the cheek. "Have fun," she whispered but not soft enough that I couldn't hear.

"We will." Fran grinned and glanced down in my direction. "Right, tiger?"

"Yep," I said, shifting in my seat and throwing the money for the check on the table.

After Race was far enough away, I pulled Fran into my lap, and she squealed. "You're trying to get me killed, right?"

"Come on," she said gleefully and slapped my chest. "Don't be crazy."

I nuzzled my face against her neck, kissing a path to her jaw. "Talking about my dick and our sex life with Race is a recipe for my execution at the hands of your son, sweetheart."

Fran tipped her head back and closed her eyes. "Race won't say anything."

"Uh-huh," I muttered against her skin. "If I die, know that I had fun."

"Just fun?" she breathed.

"Fuck," I hissed when my cock swelled in my pants. "Let's get out of here, or I'm going to have to fuck you in the bathroom."

"Ooh," she cooed and moved around just enough to send a jolt through my system. "I've never done it in a bathroom."

Note to self. “Not here.” I stood, taking her with me in my arms and stalked toward the door.

“Bear!” she yelled in protest, but she snaked her arm around my shoulders.

“Let’s go feed that greedy pussy of yours before we’re in public. I need you sated tonight.”

Her eyes grew wide. “You do?”

“Yeah. Remember… I like to live. I don’t need you rubbing all over me with Morgan there. I want no chance of anything going wrong.”

“I’m going to rock your world, baby,” she whispered into my ear.

My eyes rolled back, and my dick threatened to break through the material of my pants. I didn’t even give a fuck who was around, seeing the massive wood I was sporting. “Fuck, woman. I can’t drive like this.”

“I’m sure you’ve been in harder situations.” She giggled.

“I don’t know what I’m going to do with you.” I placed her on the back of the bike before adjusting my cock so it wasn’t so…noticeable.

She plucked at her bottom lip while she pouted. “I’ve been a bad girl. Maybe you should spank me.”

Turning my face up to the clouds, I whispered, “What did I ever do to you?”

“Come on, handsome. Take me home so you can go for a real ride.”

“Seriously,” I said again to the sky and growled loudly. I climbed on my bike with my cock screaming for relief and started the engine.

Fran slid forward, pressing her sweet little pussy against me and squeezing her thighs around me. "I need your cock, Bear. I need all of your cock," she said into my ear.

The woman didn't have to tell me twice. When we got back, I was going to fuck her until she could barely walk. She needed to be so sated that she wouldn't give any lip tonight or cause any problems. I'd fuck her into oblivion and then pull her out just enough to function.

***

Morgan rushed toward Fran as soon as we stepped foot inside the Neon Cowboy. "What's wrong, Ma?"

Fran grabbed his arms and stopped him before he hugged her. "I'm fine, baby." She didn't want him too close because the smell of sex oozed right off her.

Morgan looked at me before staring back at her and narrowing his eyes. "You look…different."

Race snorted. "She's fine. Just been a hard day for her."

I gritted my teeth, almost grimacing. "I need a drink. Anyone else?" I asked, trying to find a reason to make an exit from this situation before it got sticky.

"I'll take a strawberry daiquiri. I'm parched." Fran smiled lazily at me.

"I'll take a Dirty Martini," Race told me and brushed the hair off her shoulders.

"Coming right up." I walked away, moving straight to the bar where I saw City standing.

"What's up, man?" I asked and slapped him on the back as he leaned over the bar and sipped on his beer.

"Bear. I see you brought my aunt." He tipped his head backward toward the table where they all now sat.

"Yeah. Problem?"

"Nope."

Sandy, the longtime bartender and a one-time fling, approached. "What'll it be?" she asked, pretending not to know me. I accepted the fact that she hated my guts after I kicked her out of bed. As long as she didn't spit in my drinks, I didn't care what the fuck she did.

"Dirty Martini, strawberry daiquiri, and a tequila with a Miller chaser."

She snarled, but she stalked away without any bullshit.

City laughed. "Sandy still hates your fucking guts."

"Such is life." I shrugged and blew it off.

"Things good with Fran?"

"Couldn't be better."

"Good for you," he said, catching me off guard.

"Twenty bucks," Sandy said, all the while giving me the stink eye as she set the three drinks down on the bar.

"Twenty?"

"Yeah, you get the douchebag rate."

I growled, and City laughed at my side. "Just pay the woman."

"Fine," I said, slamming a twenty plus three more bucks on the bar.

"Only three?"

I couldn't believe she had the balls to ask me this after giving me the "douchebag" rate. "It's the bitch rate from a douchebag," I shot back quickly.

City laughed harder when she flipped me the bird and stalked to the other side of the bar without another word. "You're smooth."

"Fuck her, man." I grabbed the three drinks, balancing them in between my hands. "She doesn't deserve more. I shouldn't have given her the three. She already pocketed five of the twenty. Her pussy wasn't even worth the hassle."

"You sure you want to be with Fran?" He followed behind me, still laughing. "'Cause when you fuck that up, you're going to have bigger problems than the 'douchebag rate.'"

"I know. I know," I mumbled, but I cleared my throat when we came within feet of the table. "Ladies." I set the drinks down and slid Fran's and Race's across the table.

Morgan and Race were deep in conversation, talking too low for anyone to hear, but it seemed heated.

"Kids," Fran whispered and rolled her eyes.

"Yeah." Under the table, I entwined our fingers before slamming back my shot of tequila. The warmth of the liquid slid down my throat before working its way into my system.

If all the shit with Johnny hadn't been going on, I'd have said this has been the best damn week I'd had in decades. But the shadow of the theft and Johnny's death had sucked a bit of the happy out of everything.

"Bear," Morgan said, breaking my train of thought. "Can I talk to you at the bar?" He stood and leaned over to kiss Race on the cheek, but she ducked out of the way.

"Sure." I gave Fran's hand a quick squeeze before standing. Our relationship was already a bit heated, but with him and Race fighting, this couldn't end well.

As I walked toward the bar, I kept telling myself to stay calm. For Fran's sake—stay calm. "What's up?"

He leaned against the bar with his hand hanging over the edge, looking completely relaxed. "What did you find in Johnny's office?"

Reaching into my pocket, I pulled out the tiny scrap of paper and tossed it on the bar in front of him.

Morgan glanced down, and his eyes immediately shot to mine. "You think it's my Ray?"

"I couldn't say, kid. It's too coincidental to be anything else, in my opinion."

"It can't be. We haven't heard from my father in over a decade."

"Maybe he's been keeping tabs on you."

He shook his head. "I can't believe that. It can't be true."

"Stranger shit has happened, Morgan. Want me to follow up on it?"

"Nah, I'll do it. He's my dad."

"You got it." I patted him on the shoulder. "Maybe I'm wrong. It's a common name."

"Yeah." He sighed. "How did it go with the ladies today?"

"Piece of cake," I replied, but I didn't elaborate.

He eyed me suspiciously. "And things with my mother?"

"Good there too."

"Bear, baby," Fran said, coming up behind me and wrapping her arms around my waist. "Dance with me."

Morgan's eyes narrowed, and my stomach tightened. "Anything you want, sweetheart."

"Go," Morgan said with a pained look.

"Thanks," I told him, but I was going to do it even if I didn't have his permission.

Fran grabbed my hand, intertwining our fingers as we walked toward the dance floor. "You looked like you needed saving."

I wrapped my arm around her and pulled her close. "Actually, Fran, that was the most civil he's been in a long time."

"Huh." She smiled up at me. "Maybe he's finally realizing he can't control everything in my life."

I didn't have the heart to tell her that he had bigger things on his mind. Shit that had to do with her alcoholic ex-husband possibly being involved in the theft and Johnny's death.

It wasn't my place to tell her, and there was no point in scaring her yet. She had enough shit on her mind for me to clutter it with more bullshit.

"Yeah, I'm sure that's it, sweetheart." I kissed the top of her head, tucking her closer against me as we spun around the dance floor.

I knew shit was about to get stickier and more complicated before we got to the bottom of everything. Lord help us all if my hunch was right.

18

FRAN

I woke with my body tangled with Murray's and coated in sweat. The man was covered in fur, and when he slept, he threw off heat like a small campfire.

He'd stayed over for the past week, stating that he didn't want to be away from me, but I knew something was up. Morgan had been acting strange since Johnny's death, and Bear had become overprotective to the point of suffocation.

"Morning, sweetheart." Bear tightened his hold on me.

I kicked off the blankets, trying to find some cool air, but there was none to be had. "Morning, babe. Want some coffee?"

"I'm good just like this," he said as he buried his face in my neck.

Even though I felt like I was roasting in the sun, goose bumps broke out across my skin as he kissed me. "We can't stay in bed all day." I wiggled to try to break free, but I failed.

His cock stirred. "Why not?"

I shimmied away from his hardness. "Oh, no. Not now, mister. I'm going to the hairdresser and then to meet Maria for lunch."

"I'll come," he said, and I knew immediately that there was something no one had told me.

"What aren't you telling me?"

"I don't know what you're talking about. Stay here. I want to have a little Fran for breakfast."

I grabbed his balls and gave them a playful squeeze. "Why don't you roll on your back, and I'll give you a proper good morning?" The men in this family, including Bear, must have thought I was an idiot.

His eyes grew wide, and he quickly flipped onto his back, putting his hands behind his head. "This is the best fucking way to wake up."

I crawled between his legs and settled on my heels as I wrapped my hand around his stiff cock. "You like this, baby."

"God, yes." He let out a little moan when my hand moved.

"Do you want it rough or soft?" I asked in a breathy, sexy voice.

"Any way you want to do it." He licked his lips and closed his eyes. "I'm up for anything you've got."

He shivered when I dragged my tongue around the head. Placing the tip in my mouth, I grazed him with my teeth, and his hips shot off the bed.

"Gentle, baby," he told me, glancing down his body at me.

Pulling his cock out, I waved it in front of my lips. "You

want gentle?"

"I don't want teeth."

My hold tightened on his shaft. "You better start telling me what the fuck is going on, and do it quick before you get a blow job you'll never forget, Murray."

His eyes snapped to mine. "What are you talking about?"

"You've been up my ass, and Morgan's acting weird. You better tell me what's going on, or this is going to be the last time your dick is in my hands."

"Fran, let's be civil about this."

Civil? I was being civil. I hadn't punched him in the gut or kicked him out of my house. I was giving him a chance to explain and make shit right.

I stroked his cock slowly, and his hips moved. "You better start explaining, and do it now."

"Fran," he said my name as a plea.

"Talk." My fingers tightened, and my thumb grazed the tip. When he didn't speak, I leaned forward and placed my lips around the head, sucking lightly.

"Fuck, yes," he moaned.

I wasn't going to back down on answers. The men in my life needed to understand that I didn't need shielding from information. It was only fair that I knew what was going on since it had to do with Johnny, me, and a boatload of cash.

I sucked a little more and brought him close to the edge before backing away.

His hips followed my mouth. "I'm not allowed to say anything, Fran."

I shook my head and licked my lips. "Talk, or you get

nothing."

He mumbled something I couldn't make out before throwing his arm over his face. "Fine. I'll tell you anything you want to know."

I smiled and didn't feel one bit guilty. "What's going on with the case?"

His hands tangled in my hair. "He wasn't alone."

I swiped my tongue across the underneath of his head and pulled back. "Tell me something I don't know."

He closed his eyes, and his jaw ticked. "We haven't found anything solid yet."

"Talk, or you're going home with blue balls."

I felt proud of myself. Powerful, even. Women often forgot their ability to control a man with their sexuality. Give men a hard-on, and they're putty in our hands.

"All we found is a note with a name," he said through clenched teeth.

I quirked an eyebrow and glared at him. "Whose name?"

"It said Ray," he said quickly when I squeezed his dick like a vise.

My body went rigid, and my hand opened before his cock fell backward and waved. "My Ray?"

"We don't know," he said in a strangled voice. "Morgan is tracking him down."

I covered my mouth, my eyes wider than if I'd seen a ghost. "He can't track him down."

"Why not?" Bear asked as he sat up and scooted closer.

"He's a bad person, Murray. Whether or not he's involved, he's not someone I want back in either of our lives."

"Fran." He slid his legs around me. "We have to follow up on it. Whoever is involved is bad news. Johnny wouldn't kill himself unless it was too bad to break free of, sweetheart."

"I don't want Morgan finding him. Can't you handle it?"

"It's his case, but I can tell Thomas and James, and maybe they'll handle the search for Ray."

"Please," I begged and clutched his shoulders.

Ray DeLuca was one of the biggest pieces of shit I'd ever had the displeasure of being with. I stayed too long with him too. But times were different then. Once I became pregnant, there was no going back. Being raised a Catholic, divorce was a sin, one that my parents would never allow. I didn't have any way to support Morgan and myself, so I stayed.

Bear placed his soft lips against my forehead, tickling my nose with his beard. "I'll talk to them."

Ray had never hit me. He wouldn't be alive if that were the case, but he'd used his words as weapons instead of fists. Every time he drank too much, another side of him would come out. His sharp tongue would lash my soul with hurtful slurs about my body, my face, and my personality. There wasn't one thing he liked about me. He felt tied to me because of the baby and never liked Morgan from the day he was born.

He stayed, though. Just long enough to see Morgan reach adulthood, and then he took off, leaving me to fend for myself. I never really realized the full extent of the piece of shit that was Ray DeLuca until people started showing up at my door. They were looking for him because he had outstanding loans, mainly with local bookies, and he was a wanted man. We never saw him again, and that was just fine by me.

I often shielded Morgan from Ray's nastiness. Morgan didn't remember all the hate his father spewed, and I wanted to keep it that way. No child should feel unwanted, but if he found his father, he'd realize exactly the type of man he came from.

But it was more than Morgan finding out that his father didn't want him. I didn't want my son to think less of me for staying with such a person for as long as I did. I prided myself on my independence and strength, and I worried that Morgan would question my very sanity once he met the real Ray DeLuca. If Ray was involved in this, in Johnny's death and the theft, it would only cement the level of asshole he truly was and probably still is to this day.

"I need coffee," I said as I scurried toward the edge of the bed.

"But what about me?" He glanced down at his boner.

I giggled. "You do what I ask, and I'll make it worth your while."

A giant smile spread across his face. "Is this me earning the one thing you've never given any man?"

I turned around and shook my ass. "You want this?" I bent over and wiggled it. "Do what I ask, and it's yours." It was the only card I had left to play.

He hopped out of the bed like a kid and grabbed his jeans off the floor, jamming his legs inside.

"Where you going?"

"No time to waste," he said as he pulled up the zipper and buttoned them.

I laughed and watched him get dressed faster than I ever thought possible. "You have time for a cup of coffee, Murray. My ass will be here."

"Fran." He smoothed out his wrinkled T-shirt and shook his head. "Some things are more important than coffee. I'm wide awake anyway." He stalked toward me.

I peered up at him and slid my hand against his cheek. "But it's only 6:30. No one's at the office yet."

He smirked and kissed my thumb when it grazed his lip. "Early bird gets the worm, sweetheart. Or in my case, the ass." Leaning forward, his lips pressed against mine, and I melted into him.

I grabbed his denim-covered cock and stroked it roughly. "Sure I can't interest you in staying?"

He backed away and pulled my hand off of him, lifting it to his mouth and kissing the back. "I'm a patient man, Franny. I'm not fucking this one up."

Before I could reply, he was already marching toward the front door and grabbing his boots. With one on and the other in his hand, he opened the door and jogged down the walkway.

"Call me later!" I yelled as he climbed on his bike and slid his foot into the other boot.

"I'll call as soon as I know anything."

I waved, and he waved back before he started the bike and took off.

"A little ass and a man could move mountains without being asked twice," I said to myself as he disappeared in the distance.

I always thought blow jobs were the keys to the kingdom, but in Bear's world…a little ass made everything possible.

19

BEAR

"What are you doing here so early?" Thomas glanced down at the watch on his wrist and back at me.

I shrugged off his comment. "I thought I'd get here early. We've been too busy for me to waste any more time lying in bed."

He walked in and closed the door. "Now I know something is up. What's wrong?" he asked as he sat down in the chair across the desk from me.

"It's Fran."

His eyes widened. "Is she okay?"

"Your aunt is fine. She just doesn't want Morgan finding Ray. She wants me to handle it."

"Fuck," Thomas hissed and dragged his hands through his hair. "He's already tracking him down. What are we supposed to do about it?"

I tapped my pencil against my calendar and thought about her shaking her fine ass in my face. "I promised her I would try to get to him first. Can you help a brother out?"

Thomas leaned back and crossed his arms. "I have Sam working with him on it, but I can reassign him and put you with Morgan. It'll be up to you to get to Ray first."

"That'll work." It would at least give me some control over the situation. Once we found him, I could find a way to sidetrack Morgan and get my hands on Ray before anyone else.

"I'll talk to Sam as soon as he gets here, and you can tell Morgan that you're working with him. He's really pissed at you."

"I know, but he's going to have to get the fuck over it."

Thomas nodded and laughed. "I'm sure he will. Just give him some time."

"Thomas, it's been weeks, and he's still up my ass. I really like Fran, hell, I think I even love her."

It was the first time I'd said those words out loud, and I even shocked myself more than Thomas, even given the look of disbelief on his face. "I'm happy for you, man. Don't let my mother know, or she'll start planning your wedding."

I held my hands up and grimaced. "Let's not get ahead of ourselves." I did love Fran, but marriage was a huge step. I hadn't thought about saying "I do" since Jackie passed.

"You know how my family is. If Maria hears love, she'll have a deposit down on a hall faster that you can blink."

"Well, fuck."

"Just don't be surprised," he said as he made his way to the door. "You'd be my uncle then and Morgan's stepdad. This could be some good shit."

"Shit," I groaned and covered my face when he walked out the door. I could hear him whistling as he walked down the hallway, and all I could do was shake my head.

Unable to sit still after Thomas planted that seed, I headed to Morgan's office to look through his files on Ray. I wanted to get a jump-start before he arrived.

I opened the first folder marked Ray's Record and almost fell off the chair. The man had a rap sheet longer than mine. It read like a timeline of America's Most Wanted. Everything from petty theft, assault, and larceny filled the lines. The man had been busy since walking out on Fran and Morgan.

The second folder was marked FBI Ray. Inside were reports on Ray's activities while he was under surveillance by the FBI about five years ago. They thought he was involved in organized crime in Chicago and kept eyes on him at all times. After a year of coming up empty, they pulled the team from him and dropped their investigation.

Even with my bullshit, I don't think the FBI had a file on me. That was usually only reserved for the lowest of the low or those whose crimes that were on the federal level.

Ray wasn't a good man. I knew that from Fran, but as I sat in Morgan's office reading the multiple folders filled with crime after crime and every sordid detail, I knew he was worse than I imagined. Fran was right not to want Morgan to get involved with him, and I'd do everything in my power to make sure it didn't happen.

"What are you doing?" Morgan asked from the doorway.

I didn't bother to look up. "Just doing some reading."

"In my office?"

"Yeah. I didn't want to take the files back to mine. I figured I'd wait here for you and catch up."

"Catch up?"

I finally looked at him and closed the manila folder in my hand. "Thomas had to reassign Sam, so I'm your new partner."

His nostrils flared. "You're my new partner?"

"Glad to know you can still hear," I grumbled and readied myself for a fight.

"Old man, I can do this on my own."

"Kid," I said in response to his dig about my age and made my way around the desk. "I know you could do it on your own, but with someone like Ray, you could use some backup. I wouldn't let anyone in this office go after him alone, and neither would you. So put aside your pride and hate for a little while, and let's find him together."

"Fine," he said a little too quickly.

I tilted my head, moving my ear closer because I was sure I'd heard him wrong. "Fine?"

"You deaf now too?" He smirked.

He pushed past me. "Little fucker."

"I talked to my mom already today," he said as he sat down and pulled his chair up to the desk.

"Yeah?" I asked and took a seat across from him.

This could be good or bad. I wasn't going to pretend I hadn't been with her. I didn't know what Fran said to him, though, and I didn't want to start the day with a lie after he already had an issue with me being in his office.

"She said you spent the night." I couldn't read his facial expression, so I sat there and waited for him to say more. "She seems…" His voice trailed off.

"Happy," I said, finishing the statement for him.

"Well, yeah." He scratched his head and pursed his lips. "I don't remember the last time I really saw her happy. But for some reason, when she's with you, she's glowing."

I didn't have the heart to tell the kid I banged her brains out to the point that she had so many endorphins running through her system, happy was the only way she could feel. "I really like her, Morgan. I know I went about it all wrong, and I should've talked to you first, but—"

He held his hand up and stopped me. "You didn't have to ask permission. She's my mother and I love her dearly, but I can't control her and whom she falls in love with."

My head jerked backward. Who was this man sitting across from me? Morgan would never just give in so easily.

"Plus, she hasn't been up my ass like she usually is since you entered the picture. My phone only rings once a day instead of five. It's a win for both of us."

I narrowed my eyes. "So you're okay with me dating her?"

"I guess, as long as you don't hurt her."

"You've met her, right? I think I'll need protection from Fran if I fuck it up, not the other way around."

"If you fuck up, you'll have more to worry about than just me. You'll have an entire family coming after you."

"Ah, this puts me at ease—nothing like threatening a man to keep him happy in a relationship. You know… Your mom could break my heart first."

"Anything's possible."

We stared at each other for a minute, silently wondering what this meant for us as friends before I spoke first.

"I've always respected you, Morgan. You're a good kid with a solid head on your shoulders. You're a family man and a good son. I don't want this to change our friendship. I promise to be good to your mother for as long as she'll have me."

"Bear, you've been through more shit with my family and every guy in this office. We've always been able to depend on you and always know you have our backs. I know in my heart you'll never do anything to hurt us or our families. I know you'll be good to my mom. If you aren't, she'll let it be known."

I nodded and started to laugh. "Are we done professing our love to each other? We do have work to do, and I'm a little uncomfortable with all these kind words we're throwing at each other."

"I'm over it." He shrugged and opened the folder that I had been reading when he walked in. "So what do you think of my father?"

"He's a real piece of shit."

There was no nice way to say it. Based on everything I'd read and the way Fran acted, he wasn't a nice guy. How she ended up with him and stayed for so long was beyond me.

"He always has been."

"How did Fran stay with him for so long?"

He leaned back, placing his fingers together in an arch in front of him. "He's not a good man. She claims it was because times were different, but I think my mom was always scared to leave him."

My grip tightened on my leg. It was the only thing I could do to keep myself in my seat. "Did he hit her?"

He grimaced. "No. He'd just become a different person when he drank. He'd say the meanest shit to her and I always worried he'd eventually hit her. I stepped in between them once when he grabbed her by the arms, and I knocked him out. That was the end of him ever laying a hand on her."

Every muscle in my body tensed. "Goddamn it. You two shouldn't have had to deal with a fucker like that."

His arms relaxed on the armrests, and his hands curled around with a tight grip. "I told him the night before I graduated that if he didn't leave of his own accord, I'd remove him from the house myself. I wasn't going to leave her there with him."

"You're the reason he left your mom?" My mouth hung open.

He nodded with a smug smile. "Yep. Mom doesn't know, though, so I'd appreciate it if you didn't tell her, Bear."

"Lips are sealed."

"I gave him twenty-four hours to clear out before I had my uncle Santino deal with him."

"Santino?" I'd never heard the name uttered from any of the Gallos. "Is he on your father's side?"

"No, he's the black sheep on my mother's side. She has two brothers—Santino and Salvatore. But Santino was the only one still in Chicago, and I knew he wouldn't have a problem handling Ray for me."

"I can't believe I've never heard him mentioned." Not even City had mentioned the name, and I'd known him for over ten years.

"Well, you'd have to meet him to understand. He's not like my uncle Sal. Santino just got out of prison recently too."

"Sounds like an interesting character."

"He's different, but I knew he'd have no problem kicking my father's ass and making sure he never went back to see my mother again."

Morgan surprised me with his confession. All these years had passed, but he'd never told his mother the real reason Ray had left. She'd gone through so much heartache when it happened.

Not only did her husband leave, even if he was a piece of shit, but her son joined the military. She went from a full house to silence in a hurry, just like I did.

"Your mom is worried you're going to get wrapped up in your father's bullshit. She wanted me to help you find him."

Morgan laughed. "I found him about eight years go. An old friend emailed me to tell me Ray was sniffing around the neighborhood. So when I came home on leave, I made sure to find him. I wanted to make sure he stayed the fuck away from Mom. He got the message."

I hadn't realized my muscles were still rigid as I hung on his every word, learning something new about him and Fran that I hadn't known before. "Do you think he had something to do with Johnny?"

He rubbed his forehead and winced. "I wouldn't be surprised. He's a total piece of shit and will find any way to get his hands on some money."

I mashed my hands together, squeezing them as tightly as I wanted to squeeze the man's neck. "Then we'd better find him before something else happens. It's time to make Ray go away forever."

"You takin' him out?"

"That's too simple. We'll figure it out once we have confirmation that he's involved."

"I'm going to make some phone calls. I have a few friends in Chicago, and maybe you should call Santino too."

He grabbed his cell phone from his pocket and turned it over in his hand. "I don't know if Ma or Uncle Sal will be so happy about it, but he'd know if Ray was back in town."

"This isn't about making people happy, it's about getting to the bottom of this entire mess."

"I want to hand him over to the cops when we find him, Bear. It's the right thing to do. They have the letter from Johnny, and we have the evidence from his office."

"Sure," I said, but I planned on getting a few punches in first.

"We'll kick his ass, of course, but let the cops deal with the rest." He smirked.

I laughed. "I thought you went soft on me for a second."

"I'm happy my mom has you by her side, man. Seriously."

Although I didn't need his blessing, it meant more to me than he probably knew. "Thanks, kid. I appreciate that," I told him as I stood and made my way to the door.

"Now get back to work. We have an asshole to catch."

I nodded and walked into the hallway. There was more than one asshole at stake in this mission. I wasn't about to come up empty this time. But I knew I wouldn't make Fran pay up on our deal. It wasn't something to be bartered for, but something to be earned and given in trust. Morgan had every right to find his father and deal with him as he saw fit. I didn't have the right to take that away and neither did Fran.

20

FRAN

“Thanks for coming over. Your brother was about to make me drown myself in the pool.” Maria yanked on my arm and pulled me into her house. “I swear to God he’s making me crazy.”

I kicked off my shoes because her house was too clean to keep them on. She was a bigger clean freak than I was, and that was saying something. “What’s going on?”

“Fucking Santino!”

My entire body rocked backward as if someone shoved me. “What?”

She blew past me and headed to the kitchen, grabbing two wineglasses off the counter. “Santino called, and Sal has his panties in a bunch.” She held up the bottle of wine, and naturally, I nodded. It may have only been only noon, but anytime someone mentioned, Tino it was a reason to drink.

"What the hell did he want?" I slid into the chair and tried to keep my body still. The thought of my brother made my stomach turn.

"Morgan called him," she said quickly as she filled our glasses.

My hands landed on the table with a thud, causing the wine-filled glasses to bounce. "What?" I asked through clenched teeth. "You can't be serious."

"As a fuckin' heart attack. You know I never joke when it comes to that man."

"What would Morgan want with Tino?" I gulped down half my glass in one fell swoop because the entire situation called for liquor and lots of it.

"I guess he wanted to know if Tino knew where Ray was. Sal has talked to him a bit lately. I guess he's trying to get his shit together up there after he finally got released from prison. It wasn't Santino that set Sal off, it was the mention of Ray."

"Huh." I leaned back and took a deep breath.

"Sal will never forgive Ray for leaving you the way he did."

"It was best, Mar. You know how Ray was, and I was actually happy the day he disappeared from my life."

"I know, but Sal doesn't know everything that happened. I never told him, even after all these years."

I stared at her in complete shock. "You better not tell him now. He's going to be pissed at both of us for the rest of our lives."

Mar had never been one to keep secrets. The fact that she held on to the one about Ray and his temper for that long was astonishing. Impressive, even. She had always been known as the blabbermouth. An adorable and caring one, but still she wasn't the one you wanted with you when you buried a body. She would sing like a canary before the cops would even have a chance to question her.

"I know," she groaned and laid her head on her hands. "But now Tino's involved. This is going to be a clusterfuck of epic proportions."

I grabbed the bottle of wine and refilled my glass and Maria's too. "It is what it is now. We have to let the chips fall where they may, Mar. I still can't believe Morgan would call him. Tino back in the game?"

And by game, I meant organized crime. We always used the neighborhood lingo because it sounded more pleasant than the reality. Even prison had a different name too—college. Half the time I didn't know if someone was in school or prison, but I rolled with it.

"He claims he's on the up-and-up, but who the hell knows. Why Betty stayed with him, I'll never know."

"You know they were always explosive, but they had that thing…"

"Insanity?" Maria laughed.

"You know who I feel bad for? His kids."

"I haven't seen them since they were little. It's a shame I have two nephews and a niece that I've lost touch with."

"They're all grown-up now, Mar. Vinnie, the youngest, is in college."

"Shit. I feel even worse. Thanks for the pick-me-up, Fran."

"I'm a people pleaser." I smiled into my glass. "Where is my brother, anyway?"

"He went golfing. He felt the need to beat the shit out of something, so he decided an innocent white ball was the best outlet for his anger."

"Seems normal."

We both started laughing. My brother was a pill. He had that wild mix of Italian temper and gentleness. One thing he wasn't…was an abuser. He and Ray had nothing in common. How I ended up with that worthless dirtbag was beyond me. I knew people always thought the same thing but never asked. Thank God, because I wouldn't have had an answer.

"Feel like cooking?" She raised an eyebrow.

I nodded. "What are you thinking?"

"Everyone has been traveling so much. Let's do an impromptu family dinner tonight."

"Sure," I said, but I needed to see Bear.

"Invite him too," she replied like she'd read my mind.

"Let's do this."

Maria headed to the refrigerator and started to pull out all kinds of things that we could make. Instead of trying to decide on one thing, we started prepping everything. Cavatelli, meatballs, sausage, eggplant, chicken, and a boatload of other family dishes.

No one was going to walk out of this house hungry.

***

"You and Morgan seem chummy," I told Bear as I stood on my tiptoes and kissed his cheek just above the spot where his beard met a clearing of skin.

He wrapped his arm around my back. "Sweetheart, did you ever doubt we could get along?"

Snaking my arm around his neck, I stared into his eyes and smiled. "You two are both hardheaded, baby."

"We both care for you and would do anything to make you happy."

I raised an eyebrow and rubbed my nose against his. "You know what would make me happy?"

"What?" he whispered with his lips barely touching mine.

My fist connected with his stomach. "Making sure Morgan doesn't get my crazy-ass brother in Chicago involved in this shit too."

He barely flinched at the impact and tightened his hold on me so I couldn't get another punch in. "Why?"

"He's no good. He's been involved in organized crime most of his life. I don't want Morgan getting close to him."

"Morgan's a grown man, Fran. I can't make him do anything."

"You're right."

"I like the sound of that." He smiled against my mouth.

"Don't get too used to me saying that," I murmured before he crushed his lips against mine and stole anything else I was about to say.

"You two are gross," Mike said, walking by us in the hallway as he made a gagging noise in the back of his throat.

Bear pulled away and stared into my eyes with the biggest smile I'd ever seen. "It's nice to finally have someone to kiss." I bit my lip and smiled back.

It had been forever since I'd had this feeling. Butterflies still flooded my stomach when he walked into a room, and my mind buzzed with possibilities every time he was near. Bear had that ability to make everything better.

"Where are you guys in the investigation?" Race asked, pushing back from the dinner table and gathering up the dirty plates that everyone had left behind when they headed into the living room.

"Let me get those." Morgan grabbed the stack of plates from Race's hand. "We have some solid leads, babe."

I looked at them, still in Bear's arms, with pride and accomplishment. The man had manners, and I had no one else to thank for that but myself.

"Think we'll get the money back?" She followed him into the kitchen with the half-eaten bowl of cavatelli—why we made five pounds, I'll never know.

"Poor kid," Bear whispered when I glanced up at him with my lips twisted.

"I know. That's a lot of money for a new business to lose."

"We'll figure something out," he said in the sweetest voice and pressed his lips into my hair.

"Wanna get out of here?" I asked and waggled my eyebrows.

"Fuck yeah!" He smirked and licked his lips. "I've been dying to taste you all day." Releasing me, he grabbed my hand, and we started to tiptoe toward the front door.

"Where are you two sneaking off to?" Sal asked just as Bear's hand touched the doorknob.

"Fuck," I hissed and closed my eyes. Even after fifty years, my brother was still a complete cockblock. "We were just going for some fresh air." I sighed, staring up at Bear with my teeth clenched.

He squeezed my hand before he spoke. "I forgot something outside, and we were just going to grab it, Sal. We'll be right back." Bear glanced down at me and winked.

Sal's eyes grew into little slits before he gave us a quick nod. "Don't be too long. We have things to talk about."

"Give us five," I called as Bear pulled me out the front door.

"Five? I mean, I'm all for a quickie, but I need more than five minutes to get my fill, Franny."

"We can't now." I looked around the treelined street in the darkness. "Not here. Someone could be watching."

"Like fuck. Don't be a cocktease, woman. There isn't anyone out here. We're in the sticks, for God's sake." He wrapped his arm around my back and guided me down the front steps.

My feet touched the driveway and my stomach rumbled, but not out of fear. "What if someone looks out the window?" My body tingled, and the thought of getting caught sent a tremor of excitement through my body.

He looked down at me with a smug smile. "No windows on the side of the garage, sweetheart."

"Oh," I whispered and walked a little faster so no one would see where we went.

We were barely around the corner of the garage, hidden from the moonlight by the shadows of the trees, when Bear dropped to his knees and started to yank at my pants. "This is where track pants would be an asset. No buttons." His face was hidden in the darkness, but his fingers worked quickly.

"Can't have it both ways," I teased, placing my palms against the garage and bracing myself for what was coming next.

His hands worked fast, pulling my jeans down to my knees before his lips came crashing down against my skin. I couldn't move my legs. I tried to make my stance wider and give him better access, but I couldn't. My pants were too tight, but it didn't stop Bear.

He dug his fingers into my ass and held me in place as his lips caressed my clit with precision. My eyes sealed shut, the sensation so overwhelming I could barely breathe. Thank God I didn't have any air in my lungs, or I would've been moaning like a whore and drawing attention to us.

When my eyes fluttered open and I was finally able to catch my breath, Bear was already on his feet. He was licking his lips and staring at me like I was the dessert and he was ready for another helping. I bent over and pulled my jeans up, almost falling over because my body hadn't recovered yet.

"How am I supposed to face everyone now?" I asked, sucking in my stomach so I could button the tight jeans that had become my new go-to pants instead of my comfy track pants. Times like these—I missed them.

"Just act natural." He chuckled softly as the moonlight glimmered on his hair when his body moved out of the shadows.

"Yeah, I'm sure that'll be easy." I rolled my eyes and finally got the top button to close. "How do I look?" I asked as I shimmied down the side of the garage to stand under the light.

"Like you just came." He smiled.

"Fuck," I hissed and bit my lip.

"But no one will catch on. I know what I just did to you, so it's easy for me to see it. Your family won't think a thing."

I poked him in the chest as he slid his arms around my back and stared at me sweetly. "You better hope they don't."

"Whatcha gonna do to me if they do?" He quirked a bushy eyebrow, and his eyes twinkled in the dim light.

"I'll think of something. I'm pretty damn good at paybacks." I smirked, still pushing my finger into his chest.

"I look forward to whatever wicked plan you have in mind."

"Don't be so sure, big boy."

I laughed quietly as I followed him, hand in hand, back to the house. The man was thinking sexual payback, but that wasn't my style. I was more the type to get you in a way I thought you needed but would never do yourself. I already had a few ways churning in my head and none of them that he'd like.

"That was fast," Maria said before I even had two feet in the house. "I figured he would take a bit longer." She winked.

I turned around and glared at him. "Paybacks," I mouthed before looking back at Maria. "He just forgot something outside."

"Uh-huh." She walked toward the kitchen and kept laughing loud enough that it annoyed me.

"You're so paying," I said without looking over my shoulder. He laughed with Maria, but little did he know, his laughter wouldn't last for long.

BEAR

"I found him," Morgan said, crashing through my office door without knocking. "Finally found the old bastard."

I pointed toward the chair because his spazzy ass was too much to deal with this early in the morning. "Well, come on in."

He took the hint, planting his ass in the chair, and started to shake his leg so fast I wanted to jump over the desk and nail his foot to the floor. "Santino called this morning. He found him."

I winced and shook my head. "Don't tell your mom that."

"Yeah, she and Tino aren't the best of friends."

"I had to hear about you calling him for twenty minutes last night."

He laughed loudly. "Ha, I have you beat. Try an hour after Aunt Maria spilled the beans."

"Fuck, that woman can sure talk."

"You mean nag."

I pointed at him with a serious expression. "Your words, not mine."

He saluted me. "Anyway, he's in Chicago. Santino has him."

I raised an eyebrow. "Has him?"

"He's keeping him…" His voice drifted off as he smiled. "Company."

"Well, I'll book us a flight."

Cupping his hands, he stroked his cheeks. "I want to get there today before Ray finds a way to…" He wanted to say escape, but he couldn't bring himself to do it.

"Me too." I opened up my browser and searched for flights to Chicago. To my surprise, there were a lot of them. "We can go and come back in one day. Think it's enough time?"

He peered down at his watch. "Let's stay one night. I don't want to rush our talk with Ray."

"Anything you want, kid."

He rubbed his hands together and sprang to his feet. "Let me know what time we're leaving. I'll let Race know I won't be home tonight. I'll handle a place for us to stay tonight too."

"I'm not sharing a bed with you," I teased.

He stood in the doorway, holding the frame in his hands, and glanced back at me. "You're not my type, Bear."

"Hey," I said before he could walk away.

"Yeah?"

"Let's not tell your mom where we're going, 'kay?"

"I have no problem with that. I won't even tell Race. I'll just tell her that we're following a lead. Work for you?"

"Works for me." I rubbed my forehead, thinking about the headache I'd have if Franny found out that we were going to see Santino, along with Ray. My ears would ring for hours by the time she got done chewing my ass out.

I booked us two tickets for noon, and that would put us in Chicago a little after one with the time difference. We'd have plenty of time to deal with Ray and be back by lunch the following day.

"Where are you going?" Fran asked after I told her I was heading out of town but didn't say where.

"Up north."

"As in?"

"Indiana," I lied, but I kept my voice firm so she wouldn't pick up on it.

"Okay. Just be careful. Ray isn't a nice guy. Don't buy his act."

"I'm aware, sweetheart."

"You taking Morgan too?"

"He's insisting."

"Just protect him, Bear. Make sure Ray doesn't fuck with his head."

"It won't be a problem," I told her because Morgan had Ray all figured out and knew exactly how to handle him.

"He's all I've got left. If Ray hurts one hair on his head…"

"Franny, I'll be with him. I'll keep him safe. You know I'd step in front of a bullet if it meant I'd save Morgan's life."

"Don't do anything dumb, babe. I want you both to come back to me."

"I love you," I said to her for the first time because it felt right.

She sucked in a breath loud enough for me to hear it clear as day over the phone. “I love you too, Murray.”

“I’ll call you when we have any information. Just sit tight and don’t worry.”

“That’s easy for you to say. I’m going to worry until I hear from you that you’re both safe.”

“We’ll be fine. Talk soon.”

“Not soon enough,” she said in almost a whisper.

“Bye, sweetheart.”

“Bye, Bear.”

I stared at the phone, almost in shock that I had told her I loved her. I hadn’t spoken those words to another woman since Jackie. My stupid ass had to say them over the phone to Fran the first time. I wasn’t sure how she’d respond, and I wasn’t ready for the reaction face-to-face. It felt right telling her then, just before I was going to board a plane to beat the shit out of her ex-husband.

“Ready?” Morgan asked from the hallway.

“Ready.” I nodded and grabbed my phone and wallet from the desk, sliding them in my pockets. “Let’s do this.”

***

“Tino should be around here somewhere,” Morgan said when we stepped outside the airport near baggage claim.

“What’s he look like?” I peered around like I knew who I was looking for.

“Me only older and probably more gray.”

“Morgan!” a man called out, waving his arms frantically from about fifty feet away. “Down here.” He motioned to a waiting black sedan that was parked at the curb.

"That him?" I pointed to a man who looked like he had stepped out of a GQ cover shoot. His salt-and-pepper hair was perfect, without a strand out of place.

"Yep."

I followed behind Morgan, making our way through the crowd to Santino. I could definitely see the family resemblance. The features in the Gallo family were strong and unmistakable.

"It's so good to see you, son." Santino hugged Morgan tightly and kept his eyes glued to me.

"You too, Uncle."

When he released Morgan, his dark eyes narrowed. "Is this your mom's new friend?"

"Yeah, we work together too. This is Bear."

"Bear." He held out his hand, and I slid my palm against his. "It's nice to meet you." He tightened his fingers around my hand.

"You too." I squeezed tighter, not wanting to be outdone.

We stared each other down. I could see bits of Fran and Sal in Santino's face. Their connection was undeniable. His olive skin was perfectly tanned but completely natural. His eyebrows hung low—almost covering his eyes if he wasn't looking directly at me. It gave him that shifty appearance.

"You two done?" Morgan asked, watching us in a virtual pissing match via handshake, just like one I'd been in with Morgan at some time in the past.

"Yeah," Santino said, finally releasing his hold as I did the same. "Let's go."

Santino walked around the car, glancing over his shoulder as if he was expecting to find someone or something. "Can never be too careful around here. There are cops everywhere."

"Yeah," Morgan said, glancing back at me and rolling his eyes.

Morgan had filled me in on Santino on the plane. He'd spent time in prison for racketeering and had been part of organized crime for as long as Morgan has been alive. It was one reason why Fran and Sal had distanced themselves from him. Santino's family ran a bar on the city's south side called the Hook & Hustle. He had three children with his longtime partner, Betty. Even though they'd been together longer than Morgan had been alive, Betty and Santino never married.

After we got in the car, Morgan in the front and me in the back, Santino said, "Let's stop at the bar first, and then I'll make sure Ray is ready to see us."

"Where is he?"

"At a warehouse a buddy of mine owns. He owed me a favor, and I called it in."

"I'm sure a lot of people owe you favors, Uncle."

"I spent five years of my life locked away for keeping their secrets… They owe me more than a simple favor, Morgan."

Morgan looked over at him, his eyes appraising his uncle. "You keeping your nose clean?"

"Always," Santino replied quickly and without so much as a flinch.

I knew a lot of men like him. It was hard to change after you'd been in the life as long as men like Santino. You didn't run a racket for over twenty years and then turn into an upstanding citizen overnight.

"Why don't I believe you?"

"I'm smarter now. Five years in the joint will do that to a man."

I sat in the backseat, letting them talk as I stared at the city coming into view through the front window. The tall skyscrapers dotted the sky like giant walls of solid rain falling from the clouds. Tampa had nothing on Chicago. The high-rises were minuscule in comparison.

After weaving our way through countless side streets, so many that I'd never find my way out without GPS, Santino pulled in front of his family's bar.

"We're here," he said and turned the car off.

Peering through the passenger window, I took in the Hook & Hustle. The exterior was painted in red and white with a glossy black front door. The sign spanned half the building with its modern, red-block lettering and black background. The windows lining the front had the blinds drawn, keeping prying eyes from seeing inside.

"Be ready for Betty, kid. She's excited to see her nephew."

"It's been a while since I've seen her." Morgan stared out the window too, his forehead almost touching the glass.

"Let's have a drink, and then we'll get out of here."

A small section in the blinds opened, and a set of blue eyes peered out at us.

"Betty's waiting. We better go inside before she comes out and makes a scene in public," Santino said before climbing out.

The crisp Chicago air swirled the leaves that lined the sidewalk as we stepped inside. Like something out of a movie, every person in the bar turned to look at us when the door closed bchind mc.

People were everywhere. The counter around the bar was filled, and the tables were packed too. How in the hell did so many people have time to shoot the shit at a bar on a weekday afternoon?

"Morgan!" a woman—Betty, I presumed—screeched and came running toward him with her arms open.

"Aunt Betty," Morgan laughed with his face growing a deep shade of red.

"You look so good." She wrapped her arms around his lower waist and put her head on his chest. Betty was a tiny thing, barely coming up to the middle of Morgan's chest. "Hard as a rock too." She giggled.

"It's good to see you, Auntie."

I felt a bit awkward as I watched them. Being an outsider wasn't something I was used to feeling, but in the Hook & Hustle, surrounded by Morgan's family, I did.

Betty took a step back and took him in. "I've missed you."

"You too," Morgan told her before leaning over and kissing her round cheek.

She glanced at me over her shoulder. Maybe she felt the way I'd been staring at them. "And who's this?" She eyed me warily.

"This is Bear. He's my friend and Ma's new guy." They talked about me like I wasn't here.

She spun around to face me, and her eyes widened. "This is your ma's guy?"

"Bear, ma'am." I held out my hand as her eyes roamed over me.

"Give me a hug," she said and came at me with her arms ready to wrap around me.

The name Betty fit her perfectly. She reminded me of Betty Boop but with fire-engine red hair and blue eyes. The woman was drop-dead gorgeous. Why Santino had never married her, I'd never understand.

She wrapped her arms around my middle, her hands moving

a little too low to be completely friendly. "They build them big down south," she said into my shirt as her face was buried against my middle. "Fran must have some fun with you."

I'd never been a blusher, but Betty made my skin heat and my cheeks turn a rosy shade of pink. "It's nice to meet you, Betty."

Santino stood to the side, watching everything, and I stayed a complete gentleman. Even if Fran didn't talk with this part of her family, I still had to be respectful.

"You want something?" Betty asked, staring up at me with her soft blue eyes and her hands resting just above my ass. "A drink?"

"That would be great." I tried to untangle myself from her hold, but she kept her grip tight with her arms locked.

"How is Fran? It's been ages since I've seen her."

"She's great." I smiled down at the beautiful Betty because she had that quality that just brought happiness.

"I should give her a call sometime. I've missed her."

"Aunt Betty," Morgan said, coming to my rescue.

"We'd appreciate it if Ma didn't know we were here."

Betty's eyes sliced to Morgan. "Why?"

"We're here on business, and she can't know about it."

"Kid," Betty said, finally releasing me. "I can keep a secret like nobody's business. Just ask your uncle." She pursed her lips when she glanced over at Santino.

"Thanks, Auntie." Morgan kissed the top of her head and looked at me.

Hopefully, she was true to her word, because Fran would rip me a new asshole and then probably kick me straight in the balls for lying to her.

"Sit here, and I'll get you some drinks." Betty scurried off toward the bar.

"She seems…nice." I laughed.

"They're good people," Morgan said and followed Betty with his eyes. "Well, shit. There's my cousin. Let me go say hello, and I'll be right back."

I nodded, and he was off the barstool within seconds. I watched as he went to the bar, shook a man's hand, and then sat down and started to chat.

"That's my son, Angelo," Santino said to me as he took the empty seat across from me. "He's my oldest."

"Looks just like you."

Angelo was the spitting image of Santino but with darker and more suspicious eyes. He was a Gallo for sure. I'd be happy to have him by my side during any barroom fight.

"My youngest, Vinnie, is away at college."

"Like college or college?" I asked because they were two completely different things. I knew enough guys to know that, in some places, they referred to prison as college because it sounded nicer if people were to overhear.

"Notre Dame. He's a football star there."

"Ah." I nodded. I don't know what else to say. I hadn't heard much about Santino and didn't want to bring up his illustrious past.

"So, Fran still hate me?"

Santino's statement caught me off guard, but I mustered a laugh. "Hate's a pretty strong word."

"The woman can hold a grudge forever, Bear. Better watch

yourself."

"I know how to handle her."

"Famous last words," he said and wrapped his arm around Betty when she set down three beers on the table. "Thanks, babe."

"I'll let you guys talk. Maybe I can make dinner for everyone tonight." Betty smiled.

"They're going to be busy, love. Maybe next time."

Her lips twisted, and she sighed. "It's okay. I understand."

"Thank you for the offer, though," I told her and pulled a beer in front of me. I'd rather sit and have dinner with Betty than what was about to happen.

Spending the night with Ray DeLuca wasn't going to be a party, but I was sure we'd find a way to make it fun. Well, as much fun as you could have beating the fuck out of an abusive asshole.

I missed Fran.

Her calmness.

Her body.

Everything about the woman made me happy.

As I sat there, surrounded by her family, I realized how much I loved having her in my life.

Ever since I first kissed her, I hadn't thought about the emptiness that had filled my world since Jackie passed. All I could focus on was the fullness Fran brought into my life.

22

FRAN

I sat there, staring at the tiny piece of paper for twenty minutes and debating if I should dial the phone. After seeing how well the reunion went with Janice, I felt the need to make things right between Bear and his son, Ret.

But that was dangerous territory. Janice and Bear had been cordial for years, keeping in contact but never growing close. There was so much hurt to get over, but with her pregnancy and the passage of time, it happened. Plus, I didn't give them much of a choice.

But his relationship with Ret was different. It weighed on Bear more than he would ever let on. He always said he lived life with no regrets, but I knew that was bullshit. Ret was his biggest regret, and the way Bear had handled the aftermath of Jackie's death was his biggest mistake.

Too much time had passed for them to reunite without a

force bringing them together, and I thought it should be me.

I loved the man, and I wanted only the best for him. I knew people said I was a busybody, but it was always with a purpose. I didn't stick my nose in places it didn't belong unless I had a damn good reason.

After I convinced myself that what I was doing was right, I finally dialed the phone. Janice had given me Ret's number and wished me good luck.

"Hello," a man said, his voice gravelly yet smooth. He sounded so much like Bear that, for a minute, I wondered if I had dialed right.

"Hello, Ret?" I asked before I started in on my spiel.

"Yes."

"I'm Fran, and I got your number from your sister, Janice."

There was a scratching sound and a muffled cough. "Hi, Fran. How can I help you?"

"Well," I said and paused because I wanted to craft my words very carefully. "I'm a friend of your father's, and I wanted to reach out to you."

"My dad put you up to this?" he asked quickly before I could continue.

"No, sir. He has no idea I'm calling."

"Is he okay?"

"Yes." I smiled because Ret cared. No one asked that unless there was a tiny piece that wanted to hear that the person was okay.

"How can I help you, Fran?" he repeated the question again, cutting straight to the point.

"I was hoping you were up to a trip to Florida. Your old man would love to see you." I winced and waited for him to hang up.

"Why didn't he call me himself?"

"He's out of town. I thought you could be here when he got back as a surprise."

"I don't mean to be rude, ma'am, but I don't like surprises, and I imagine neither does my father."

"It's not a surprise to you, and who cares if your father doesn't like them? He'll get over it."

He laughed. "I imagine so."

"Your father talks about you often, Ret. Sometimes adults are assholes, and as we grow older and more time passes, it's hard for us to admit our mistakes. But one thing I know about your dad is that you're his biggest regret."

"I'm sure I am."

I winced. That didn't come out right. "He regrets not raising you and for all the time he missed out on being with you. I know it hurts him, and he knows that he's hurt you. I'm asking as a mother, for you to give him a chance."

There was silence, but he hadn't hung up.

"I'm sure your mother wouldn't want you two to be estranged. I think that weighs heaviest on him… Jackie was his world, Ret. There's no loss like losing the only person in the world who made you feel worthy. He fucked up. He knows he did, but he wants to make amends with you before it's too late."

"He's going to be pissed."

"I know," I said, smiling to myself because he didn't say no.

"I'll do it for my mom, Fran. Not for Murray, but for her. He still near Tampa?"

"Yes, we're about forty-five minutes north."

"I'm in Miami, so I can be there tomorrow morning if that's okay?"

I bounced in my seat, pumping my fist in the air, and tried not to scream out my excitement. "That's perfect."

"What's the address?"

I rattled mine off, figuring it was better if everything went down here. I could control it easier. We chatted for a few more minutes before he finally said good-bye.

I did a quick happy dance, followed by the worst impression of the running man before I sobered.

Bear was going to be pissed.

I was going to owe him something.

And there was only one thing left he wanted.

My ass clenched at the thought, but I quickly pushed it out of my mind. There was so much to do before Ret arrived and Bear came back home. I'd make dinner. Food was always a good way to break the ice and fill the uncomfortable silence. Of course, my cooking left something to be desired.

I picked up the phone and called the only person I knew who could rescue me. "Maria, I need you."

"I'll be right over."

When she walked through the door twenty minutes later, I was on my hands and knees, scrubbing the kitchen tile.

"What did you do now?" She had her hands on her hips as she stared down at me.

Falling backward on my ass, I threw the dirty rag on the floor and wiped my brow. "I invited Bear's estranged son over."

Her perfectly plucked eyebrows shot up. "Does Bear know?"

Hanging my head, I shook it but didn't speak.

"He's going to freak out."

"I know," I whispered. "But I did it for the right reasons."

"Franny," she said and sat down next to me. "Your heart is always in the right place." She rubbed my arm. "It'll be fine."

"You think?"

"Sure. What do you need me to do?"

I finally looked up. "I want to make them dinner."

"Good thing you called me," she said and laughed.

"I'm nosy, not stupid." I chuckled. "Will you help me get everything together and started so tomorrow I can finish it on my own?"

"Babe, I'll do anything you need."

I lunged forward and wrapped her in the biggest bear hug. "Thanks, Maria. I don't know what I'd do without you."

She rubbed my back, soothing away my stress. "Serve shitty food and burn everything, probably."

"Very funny, but probably true."

"Let's get off this floor and start making a plan. I want you to wow them both."

"I don't know what I was thinking." I rolled my eyes, shaking my head as I stood.

"You were being you. Look how great everything went with Janice."

"It went better than I thought."

"See," she said as she brushed off her butt after crawling off the floor. "Everything will be fine."

23

BEAR

After a long talk, Morgan agreed that he'd wait outside and let me talk to Ray first. We both, along with Santino, felt that Ray might be more willing to speak without his son around. Really I just wanted to get in a few licks before anyone else and make him feel a small amount of what Fran must have felt when they were together.

Whether he was involved with Johnny hadn't been determined yet. But…he still deserved a beating. I knew it wasn't civilized, but I didn't give a fuck. Men who hit women—even once—deserved all the bad shit that happened to them.

"Who are you?" Ray asked before spitting blood next to my feet.

"Your worst nightmare." I smiled and flexed my knuckles.

"You're a pussy if you have to beat me with my hands tied

up."

Ray DeLuca was probably a decent-looking guy back in the day, but sitting before me, bound to the chair, he looked frail. His face was littered with wrinkles and covered in hair that wasn't neat or groomed.

"Kinda like a guy who hits women?" I asked and took a step forward, ready to hit him again.

"What the hell are you talking about?" He turned his face to the side, reducing the impact of my fist against his face.

The crunching sound of bone on bone echoed in the abandoned warehouse. Ray's cries of agony continued after the echo died out. "Ready to talk?"

I pretended I was going to hit him again, and he flinched.

Ray licked the corner of his lip, drawing the blood into his mouth from the previous punch. "I'll talk. I'll talk. What do you want to know?"

I pulled over a seat, glancing around the dimly lit building. Instead of calling Morgan in like I'd promised, I prodded Ray further.

"Tell me what happened with Johnny." I crossed my arms over my chest and glared at him.

"That piece of shit," he muttered. "I knew he wouldn't be able to keep his mouth shut."

"I'm going to give you thirty seconds to explain to me what happened, and then I'm going to beat you until you're unconscious. Lie, and I'll make sure you're never found."

I wouldn't have done it, but he didn't know that. All he knew was how my fists felt against his face and that he didn't want any more.

"Johnny worked for my kid. I've been keeping track of

him for years—checking in on him and my ex-wife. Well, I got in deep with a bookie and needed some cash. I went down to Florida a few times and thought about asking for a loan, but then I knew neither of them would give me one. So I went to the track and hung out for a few races. I watched carefully and saw that Johnny was close with the family. I thought I could get him to do what I wanted. He looked like an easy mark, and I used it to my advantage."

"Go on," I said, keeping my eyes pinned to his and straightening my back.

"I did some digging and found out Johnny has a kid. I told him that if he didn't find a way to get me $50,000, I would go after his kid and then I'd start on Fran and Morgan."

"So you threatened him to get what you wanted?" Just needed to be sure I didn't hear him wrong. Plus, the confirmation would be good since we were recording the entire thing.

"Yeah, man. Johnny made it too easy. He was too worried about everyone else that he caved quickly."

"How did he get you the money?"

"I met him in some shitty-ass motel room in Alabama. He brought the cash and fulfilled his end of the deal."

"And what was your end?"

"I promised never to bother anyone else again."

Fucking thief and liar.

The thing about thieves was that a promise was never kept. Once you caved to their demands, they knew they had you for life. I'm sure Johnny knew it too. It was a mistake that too many people made.

Plus, how would Johnny ever be able to face Fran, Race, and Morgan again? He was just trying to keep them safe, but he went about it the wrong way. If he'd only told Morgan, we could've gotten involved and Johnny would still be alive.

"Where's the money now?"

"Joey Two Fingers has it." Ray's shoulders sagged, his torso still secured to the chair.

I rolled my eyes. Damn people with their stupid-ass nicknames.

"Can I go now?"

"The only place you're going is the police station."

"For what? You already beat my ass."

"You'll be safer there. I'm sure Joey will be looking for you once I have a talk with him."

His head snapped up, and his eyes widened. "You can't talk to him. He won't give you shit anyway."

"I have my ways." I smiled and figured Santino probably knew Joey and could help. It wasn't Ray's money to begin with, and once Joey heard the story, I'm sure he wouldn't want the dirty money anywhere near him.

"Bullshit."

I leaned forward and grabbed Ray by the hair on the top of his head, getting in his face. "I'm sure the cops will want to talk to you about Johnny's death too. So between Joey and death row, I'm sure you'll be busy."

He gasped. "What? Johnny's dead?"

"Yep, and he left a note that pointed right at you."

Okay, so I lied a bit, but simple police work could uncover the connection, especially with the recording of him confessing his part. Ray DeLuca was going to pay for what he did.

"Fuck," he grunted and struggled to break free from the

bindings. He gritted his teeth, bloodied spit spewing from his mouth as he pulled at the restraints.

"I have one more visitor for you," I said, unable to hide my smile as I stood. "Come in!"

"What is this shit?" he seethed, still moving around but not going anywhere.

"Hey, Ray," Morgan said as he walked in and let the door slam behind him.

Ray flinched at the impact and squinted in the direction of the voice. "Morgan?"

"Can you leave us?"

"Sure," I told Morgan, but I glared at Ray. "If you need my help breaking his legs, just holler."

Morgan placed his hand on my shoulder when I was about to pass him. "Thanks, Bear."

"You're welcome. I'll go talk to Santino, and you can talk to your father."

"He's not my father. He's just a low-life piece of shit."

I wondered if Ret thought the same way about me. I'd never pulled this shit with him, but I was never in his life for him to have a connection to me. I hoped he didn't feel the same. My heart ached at the very thought.

I gave Morgan a nod before walking toward the door. Turning back, I watched as Morgan pulled the stool closer and said something to Ray that made him break down in tears.

Morgan DeLuca impressed me.

The man had his shit together and stepped up when necessary. Even though Ray was his father, Fran was his world. He made sure Ray walked out of her life over a decade ago, but I'm sure Ray was about to pay the price for coming back and stealing from Morgan's wife too.

"That went well," Santino said as I walked outside and he took off the headphones. "You know, if you ever need a job, I'm sure I can get you one within minutes up here."

"I'm good," I said and held up my hand. "I'm clean, man. I only do this shit when necessary, and usually only for family."

"You're an interesting man, Bear."

"Yeah, yeah. What can we do about this Joey Two Fingers?"

He waved his hand and grinned. "I'll talk to Joey and get the money back. Just like you said. For being clean, you know a whole lot about dirty."

I laughed. "I have a past, but I'm leaving it there, Santino."

"All right." He held his hands up. "All right. I won't push you any further."

"Should I go back in?" I asked and glanced toward the door.

"Nah, Morgan can handle him."

Twenty minutes later, Morgan walked out with Ray handcuffed and a little more bloodied than I left him. Ray's feet dragged on the ground as Morgan pulled him by the wrists.

"Ready?" I asked, looking between Morgan and Santino.

"Where are you taking me?" Ray tried to pull away, but Morgan yanked him forward.

"To the cops with the recording and the evidence."

Ray faltered in his steps and almost fell forward. "They're going to hear you beating me and know I was coerced."

"I took care of it," Santino said. "I'm not worried about them believing your story, Ray. You're about as friendly with the cops as I am."

"This is bullshit."

"Well…" Morgan motioned toward me with his head. "I can let Bear take care of you if you don't want me to turn you over to the authorities."

He eyed me for a moment and grumbled under his breath. "I'll take my chances with the cops," he said before Morgan shoved him in the back of the car.

"Meet me back at the bar after you drop him off. I'll talk to Joey and have an answer for you."

"Thanks, Uncle."

"You're welcome, kid." Santino climbed into his car and drove away.

"You okay with this?"

Morgan nodded and blew out a breath. "I finally feel like everything is going to work out and that Ray will be out of the picture for a very long time."

"He's going to have a hell of a time getting out of this one," I told Morgan as I slid into the car and he did the same.

"Fella, we don't have to do this," Ray pleaded before Morgan started the car and turned up the radio loud enough to drown out Ray's bullshit.

The grittiness of Chicago fit the people I'd met since I stepped off the plane. Santino himself was a product of his surroundings, and Joey Two Fingers, I assumed, wouldn't be any different.

The sky was gray with fluffy clouds that were as dark as those in Florida when a thunderstorm was looming. Rain began to fall as we pulled up at the police station, and when Morgan opened the door, a quick rush of cold air filled the car.

"Don't do this," Ray pleaded when Morgan pulled him from the back seat without any hesitation.

I stayed in my seat, letting the kid handle his father. I

wouldn't want anyone taking that moment away from me, and I sure as hell wasn't going to do it to him.

Ray didn't go like a man. He screamed and tried to break from Morgan's grip as they moved toward the doorway of the police station. When Morgan opened the door and pushed Ray, he kicked him in the ass to give him a final shove inside.

I'd have felt sorry for the guy if he wasn't such a piece of shit.

My phone rang, and it was Fran. I picked it up quickly before she started to call every five minutes until she knew we were safe.

"Hey, sweetheart," I said, watching the door for Morgan. He'd be a few minutes, turning over the evidence and the perpetrator into their custody.

"I wanted to check in on you guys. You two okay?"

"We're great. We'll be home in the morning as scheduled."

"Great, baby," she said and covered the phone, murmuring something. "Maria says hi."

"Tell her hello. So I'll be at your place around noon to give you all the details. I can't really discuss them on a cell."

"I know, Bear. I'm not new." She laughed nervously and a little over the top. "I'll be waiting for you."

"Oh, yeah?" Excitement filled me. "Am I getting my payback for the other night?"

"You are. Don't be mad if it isn't what you expect."

"I'm up for anything you're gonna give me, Franny."

"Remember that. Love you."

"Love you too," I said and hung up as soon as I saw Morgan walking toward the door through the glass.

Fuck. I was so excited to get back to Fran and whatever kinky shit she had planned that I was about ready to catch the next flight out of Chicago and be there before she closed her eyes.

"How did it go?" I asked when he climbed back in.

"They're going to listen to the tape and review the evidence. In the meantime, there was an active warrant out for him, so he's not going anywhere soon."

"For what?"

"Assault and battery." Morgan shrugged. "A leopard never changes its spots."

"Morgan, I need you to know something."

Something had been gnawing at me for a while, and I needed to get it off my chest.

"What's up?" he asked as he turned on the car.

"I'll never lay a hand on your mother. I know sometimes I get carried away when we're dealing with some bad people, but your mother is someone I love. I'd never do anything to hurt her."

He stared at me for a minute before he finally smiled. "One thing I know about you is that you're a good man, Bear. You're not Ray. The thought never crossed my mind."

My face wrinkled. "It hasn't? I've done some pretty fucked-up shit in front of you."

"Each one of them deserved it. I see how you are with my mom and all the women in the family. I never worry about how you're going to treat Ma. Plus, she's not the same woman she was before. Her revenge will be worse than anything any of us could do to you. That much I know."

"Yeah," I laughed. Fuck. He was right. Fran had a wickedness about her sometimes.

If I ever hurt her, I was sure I'd disappear, never to be heard from again. But not before she tortured me in ways I'd never dream possible. I think that's what I loved about her most—her unpredictability.

I sat in silence, thinking of all the ways she'd exact her revenge as we headed toward the bar. By the time we parked the car, my stomach was in knots.

"You're looking a little green," Morgan said as he stared at me.

"Just thinking about Fran. We made a bet, and I lost. Tomorrow, I get my payback."

"I'd be scared if I were you." He laughed and climbed out, slamming the door behind him.

I sighed and waited a minute before following him. "You think I'm in for some shit?" I jogged to keep up.

"I think you should be ready for the unexpected."

My mind wandered to places I never imagined. Hopefully, Fran had planned something sexy. The one place I didn't expect to go was in her beautiful round ass. I wanted it so badly my entire body vibrated at the thought. Maybe I'd done such a good job with Ray that she'd offer it to me as a thank-you.

I shook my head and laughed.

"It ain't that."

My head jerked back just as we approached the door. "What?"

"If it makes you laugh, it isn't what you're hoping. Ma doesn't work like that."

"You're right," I grumbled, and the hard-on that had started to form immediately vanished.

"Morgan!" Angelo waved us over.

Morgan gave him a quick nod. "Hey."

"Shit go alright?" Angelo asked as he leaned over the bartop.

"Hey," I interrupted. "I'm going to go talk to your uncle."

"He's in the back room," Angelo replied and jerked his head toward the hallway behind him.

"Thanks," I said and excused myself.

Not that I was above small talk, I just wanted to get the fuck out of this bar and back to the hotel. I already knew I wasn't going to get much sleep tomorrow when I got home, and I wanted to be ready for whatever Fran was going to throw at me.

24

FRAN

"You have a lovely home," Ret said, sitting on the couch in the living room as I sat across from him.

"Thank you." I smiled, but inside I was slowly dying.

What the fuck was I thinking? There was going to be hell to pay afterward. I was known for pulling some shit, but even this was beyond me. I was sticking my nose in places that I never thought I'd be willing to take a whiff and live with myself.

"I talked to my sister," Ret said, filling the uncomfortable silence.

I smiled at the spitting image of Bear. The tiny lines around Ret's eyes weren't near as deep as Bear's, but everything else about him matched. From his wide shoulders, large arms, gruff voice, and hard face—there was no mistaking that they were father and son.

"How is she?"

"Ready for her pregnancy to be over." He laughed softly, and the faintest lines appeared near his eyes.

"I'm sure." I plucked at the nonexistent lint on my jeans. "She's so beautiful."

"She said nice things about you, ma'am. It's one reason why I came. She said it was time I talked to my father and set shit straight."

"She sounds a lot like me." I chuckled, covering my mouth with the back of my hand.

"She's a bossy thing. When we were little, she'd pretend I was hers. My entire life, she's told me what to do."

"Women," I muttered because I knew we caused more shit out of our need to be helpful.

"When's he getting here?" Ret glanced down at his watch and tapped the glass.

"Any minute now." My voice was shrill, and my stomach was jumping around like I had gymnasts inside.

"What has he said about me?"

Even though a man sat across from me, all I saw was a little boy who wanted to hear that he was loved and wanted. It was the basic need of any child. When Bear left Ret with his sisters, it stripped him of that.

"He told me what happened with your mom and how his sisters raised you and Janice. He's never gotten over the regret from that."

"He could've come back for us."

"Oh honey, your dad went down a dark path. It's hard to come back from how far he fell."

"How far?" He crossed his arms over his wide chest and leaned back into the sofa.

"He was in and out of jail a lot before you were even five. I think he got mixed up in drugs and drank a lot too. He knew he wasn't good for you."

"Fran, I would've taken a fucked-up dad as long as he loved me."

"You say that now, but it's easy to say without living it, Ret."

"I guess," he sighed.

"He loved your mom so much that he didn't think he deserved any happiness. I think he was trying to find a way to join her without actually doing it himself."

"That would've been tragic," he muttered.

"It would've."

"I spent a good portion of my teenage years in therapy, Fran. It's hard to know your mother died when she had you. There's a guilt that comes with that knowledge."

"God," I said and stroked my neck. "I never thought of that."

"Dad could've helped me get over that quicker. His rejection made it easier to believe that I killed her."

My entire body rocked back at the horrific admission he had just made. I'm sure Bear never thought of it that way. He figured he was doing a favor to his kids by leaving them with his sisters, giving them the love of a woman over his.

"Your father never blamed you. He blamed himself, sweetie. I think you've both been feeling the same pain for far too long."

His eyebrows drew down over his eyes. "Why would he feel that way?"

"Men are supposed to protect their women, and your father

wasn't able to do that for Jackie. Naturally, he's going to feel like he messed up somehow. You're a man. You should understand the need to fix everything."

He smiled and it was genuine. "I know the feeling well."

I stared at him, lost in his eyes when I heard Bear's bike outside. I froze, my body going rigid and my stomach kicking back into action.

"Well," Ret said, standing up and taking a deep breath. "I guess it's now or never."

"It'll be fine. Your dad is easygoing," I lied and walked toward the door, clutching my stomach and praying that Bear didn't walk back out as soon as he saw I'd ambushed him again.

Instead of walking up to the door, he stood outside, staring at Ret's truck. Slowly, I opened the door and waved with the biggest smile on my face.

"Hey, baby. I'm so happy you're back."

He looked at me and then back to the truck and scratched his beard, silent.

Well, fuck. This isn't going exactly as I'd planned.

"Who's inside, Franny?" His eyebrow was cocked. That wasn't a look that instilled a warm and fuzzy feeling in my already shaking body.

"Just a friend. Come on." I waved him inside, holding the door open but not moving.

"You come here." He pointed toward the ground, his eyes still going back and forth between the truck and me like a pinball in a machine.

"It's too hot outside." I was grasping at straws, and just like the man he was—seeing right through me—he knew the type of woman I was—a trick up every sleeve.

"Fran. Out here now," he demanded and snapped his fingers.

Instead of running, I crossed my arms and glared at him. "I don't know who you think you're snapping those meat sticks at, buddy, but it sure as fuck isn't me."

"Fran," he started to plead, but I kept talking.

"You don't want to come in? Fine. I'll meet you halfway, but you ever snap your fingers at me like I'm an animal again, and I'll break them in your sleep."

Ret laughed, and I turned to face him, giving him a sweet smile. "Just letting him know who's boss."

"Remind me never to cross you, Fran. You'd do mighty fine with a whip in your hands."

I laughed nervously. "Thanks."

"Fine, sweetheart. I'm coming up," Bear said, finally coming to his senses.

I don't know what came over me. Usually, I'm not quite so stern, but goddamn it, he was ruining my fabulous surprise.

"I'm coming down," I told him, glancing back at Ret and holding up a finger. "Be right back."

"I can go," he offered.

"Sit your ass down," I told him and closed the door behind me before marching my skinny-jean-covered ass down the stairway to Bear.

I huffed the entire walk down to him. My knees were still a little wobbly, but I was too pissed off to really pay much attention to them. "Why won't you come in?" I asked, trying to use my sweetest voice.

"Oh, now you're sweet. You're talking about breaking my… What did you call them?" He tapped his chin and smiled. "Meat sticks. And now you're acting like June Cleaver."

"I have a surprise for you. An old friend stopped over. You're going to want to see them."

"Them?" he asked, his finger stopped on his lip.

"Him." I smiled so big my cheeks hurt.

He sighed. "Fran, you've got to stop with the surprises. They aren't my favorite thing in the world, but you insist on doing it."

"This is your payback, but trust me, you're going to like it." I grabbed his hand and started yanking him toward the house.

He dug his heels into the cement, and his feet didn't move—like there was glue on the bottom, holding him to the ground. "Who's inside?"

Intertwining my fingers with his, I gave them a soft squeeze. "Promise you won't be mad?"

"Fran."

"Well." I swallowed and took a deep breath. "Ret's inside."

"My son, Ret?"

"No, Bear." I rolled my eyes. "Ret, the pool guy."

His eyes widened, and his body rocked back. "My son is here?" He pointed toward the ground.

"No, in there." I pitched my thumb over my back. "Waiting for you and watching your reaction very carefully."

His eyes went to the window and back to mine. "He's here."

I nodded. "In there."

"Shit," he said, releasing my hand and running toward the door without any more nudging from me.

I turned around, but I didn't move as he flung open the door and walked inside. Through the large bay window in the front of the house, I could see them both clear as day.

Bear stared at Ret for a moment, and Ret stood from the couch. A few words were muttered, and I wish I could've heard them. Bear stalked toward Ret and scooped him into his arms. At first, Ret didn't return the gesture, but a few seconds later, he wrapped his arms around his father.

Tears began to well in my eyes, and I wanted to go inside and listen to the reunion, but instead, I just watched.

I had eavesdropped on his talk with Janice, but I knew this one would be different—more important and more personal.

Bear kept hold of Ret, pulling back every so often for a moment to look at his younger reflection before cocooning him in another hug.

Tears streamed down my face from the beauty of the moment. It was better than I imagined when I concocted my little plan.

My knees were shaking as I leaned against the truck, my nerves still frazzled from earlier. Shaking out my hands, I tried to calm myself, but I needed something more. Spotting the fake flowerpot where I stored an extra key and a pack of cigarettes, I glanced around the yard before making a beeline for my hiding spot.

My fingers shook as I opened the hidden compartment around the back and pulled out the pack and lighter. I could barely light the cigarette through my tears and shakes.

"Jesus," I muttered with the filter in my mouth, struggling to steady my hand.

"Fran!"

Naturally, the moment I was going to give myself chemical solace, Bear walked outside to find me. That was exactly how shit had been going down. Tucking the pack, including my unlit cigarette, and lighter back inside, I took a few deep breaths and tried to calm myself before I started to walk toward him.

"Hey," I said, peeking around the corner and catching a glimpse of him standing near the doorway.

As soon as he saw me, he jogged down to meet me. "Hey, sweetheart." He brushed the tears from his cheeks. "I don't even know what to say."

Placing my hand on his chest, I stood on my tiptoes and kissed his lips. "Don't say a thing."

He wrapped his hands around my upper arms, gripping me tightly as he stared down at me. "I'm just so…so…"

"I know, Bear." I smiled.

"Why didn't you come inside?"

"I wanted to give you time alone."

"He's so much like me, Franny. It's like looking in a mirror." He looked like a little kid, so excited and full of wonder. "He's me, but not. You know?"

"He's very handsome."

"Let's go in, babe. I don't want you to feel like an outsider. This is your house."

I nodded, staying tucked under his arm as we walked toward the front door. "So you're not mad at me?"

"Fran, I'm never mad at you. But you do pull some big shit."

"That's what makes me great." I chuckled.

He kissed the top of my head. "It's what makes you mine," he said into my hair as we walked through the door.

BEAR

Part of me was still in shock. Even after spending two hours with Ret, it was hard for me to wrap my head around the reality that my boy was sitting right in front of me.

"I pulled up your rap sheet years ago."

My eyebrows shot up. "Jesus," I muttered. This wasn't going to be good. The damn thing was as long as I was tall.

"Interesting life you've led." He smiled.

"I'm clean and living on the straight and narrow. I have been for years, Ret."

"You really went off the rails after Mom died." He frowned, but he hid it quickly behind the glass of beer he'd been nursing for an hour.

"I did. I didn't handle her death well. I wanted to die too. I was so angry about what happened that I did everything in my power to let the world know just how pissed I was."

"Lucky for me, you didn't get your wish. But based on what I read, you came pretty damn close."

"She'd be so disappointed in me if she knew what happened, son." I hung my head and rubbed my eyebrows. "She'd beat the hell out of me for acting like a fool."

"What's happened, happened, and we can't change it. I'm not angry with you. I was hurt for a long time. I couldn't understand how you could abandon Janice and me without a backward glance."

Lifting my head, I choked back the tears that were threatening to come. "I did come back. I visited for the first three years. I'd come and hold you in my arms and tell you stories. I still remember the way you smelled and the sound of your voice when you cried. You were so damn little, and I was scared that I might break you."

"I didn't know that. No one ever told me you came." His eyes darkened. "Why didn't anyone tell me?"

"I don't know. My sisters can be bitches and probably thought it was best if you didn't know.

"When you started to talk, Caroline asked me not to come back. She said that you would start to remember me, and if I wasn't able to take you and Janice that I should keep my distance. I believed her and wasn't in the right place to take you with me, so I did as she asked."

"I wish you would've fought for us."

"Ret, I couldn't even fight for me," I admitted. "I hope someday you'll forgive me and let me make it up to you. As I've grown older, I've come to realize nothing else matters except for family and friends. I surround myself with good people and lead my life like I should've. Like your mother would've wanted me to. She'd want us to have a relationship, and it's the only thing in my life that I want right now. There's nothing more important."

"We'll see, Dad. I have a lot to think about." Ret smiled softly. "I have to head back soon."

"Already?" I wasn't ready to say good-bye. We'd spent enough time away from each other. Too long, and it was entirely my fault.

Ret rubbed his hands together as he leaned forward, placing his elbows on his knees. "Alese is waiting for me at the hotel."

"Why didn't you bring her?"

"I didn't know what was going to happen, and I didn't want to stress her."

"I'm sorry." The amount of guilt and shame I felt were almost overwhelming. No child should ever have to worry about their parent being an asshole, but I did that to my kid.

"Why don't you get her and bring her to my place tonight? You two can spend some time with me."

"I don't know," he said and peered around the room, looking for Fran, but she was in the kitchen washing the dishes. "We don't lead a regular lifestyle."

"What's that mean?"

"I don't know how to explain it to someone like you." He sighed.

I placed my hand on my chest and laughed. "Someone like me? Ret, I'm not a normal person. Nothing really shocks me anymore."

"She's my submissive." He stared me straight in the eyes and waited.

Maybe he thought I'd be shocked or horrified, but I wasn't. "Janice told me. Is she your sub or slave?" I asked, trying to sound like I knew the lingo, and he gave me a confused look. "I'm not new."

"She's just my submissive, and we keep it only in the bedroom when we're around other people."

I laughed and shook my head. "One of the owners of my company does the same with his wife. I wish I could get Franny to be mine, but she'd just kick me in the balls and tell me to go fuck myself if I ever bossed her around."

"Yeah," he said, laughing with me. "She doesn't seem like the lifestyle would work for her."

"I heard you!" she yelled from the kitchen, and Ret and I laughed louder.

I sobered at the thought that it might be a while before I saw him again, and I had to do something to not keep that from happening. "Will you at least stick around for a few days? I'm not ready to let you go already."

"I can stay for a bit. I'm in between jobs, so I don't have anywhere to be."

"Why don't you find a job around here? You can be close to Janice, and we could get to know each other better."

"Let's see how the next few days go together before I start setting down roots here. I told myself I'd never move back to Florida when I left years ago."

"Your aunts are here, I'm here, your sister's here. What other reasons do you need? It's time to come back home, son. It's time for me to make up for all the time I've thrown away."

"I'm not saying no, but I have to talk to Alese. She gets a say in where we live too. I'll think about it."

"I'll give you all the time you need."

He stood and rubbed his palms against his jeans. "I'll see

you tomorrow, then?"

"Meet me at my office, and we can talk some more. I'll take you to lunch."

"That would be great."

I wanted him to see ALFA PI. He'd fit right in with those guys, and we could use a bounty hunter. He could use our resources, which were vast, and our manpower to track down his cases. I couldn't think of anything more perfect. I'd have to talk with James and Thomas, but I couldn't see them saying no. I'd just have to get him in the door to make shit happen.

Franny walked out from the kitchen, wiping her hands on a dish towel. "Leaving so soon?"

He nodded and walked toward her. "I have to get back to my girl, but I'll be around this week."

She smiled and tossed the towel over her shoulder. "That makes me happy, Ret. Thanks for doing this," she said, grabbing hold of his arms. "I hope it turned out as you'd hoped."

"Better than, actually, Fran." He leaned in and kissed her cheeks, whispering something in her ear.

She laughed softly, her eyes darting to mine for a moment. "I'll see you tomorrow?"

"You will." He hugged her properly as her hands roamed around his back. She was feeling him up, letting his muscles skate across her fingertips. I knew the moves; she did it to me often.

"Dad," Ret said as he walked toward me, and it sounded like music to my ears. He stuck out his hand, but I didn't want a handshake.

"Come here." I pulled him into my arms for the tenth time since I'd laid eyes on him. "I'll see you at the office tomorrow.

Don't leave without saying good-bye. You hear me?"

"I'll be there. Don't worry," he said, gripping my bicep with his fully grown hands.

As I watched him walk out the front door, my heart ached. I longed for the years I'd lost. The days. The hours. The minutes. The seconds. There wasn't a milestone in his life that I had been there for. I didn't cheer him on as he took his first step, learned to ride a bike, or threw his first football.

I'd missed them all.

Everything.

I wasn't willing to miss another moment either.

I had been selfish, and the ones who'd suffered were my kids. While I was out trying to chase down the grim reaper and drowning myself in booze and pussy, my kids grew up without me.

What kind of self-absorbed prick does that?

I did.

Jackie would've been so disappointed in me. I knew that. There wasn't a morning I'd woken up over the last thirty years that I didn't think that. But the guilt never drove me to seek them out and make shit right.

So much time had passed that I didn't think there was a way to repair the damage I'd done. I didn't even know how to make the first move. People knew me as a tough guy. The one who would kick anyone's ass if they were acting like a fool or deserved a beatdown, but when it came to my kids…

I was the biggest pussy on earth.

It was time I paid my penance and made up for everything I'd missed. If I had my way, both kids would stay close, and I'd spend as much time as possible with them.

I wouldn't be up in their shit like Franny is with Morgan, but I'd like to develop a relationship and get to know my future grandchildren.

There was still time, and Fran made it possible.

26

FRAN

"Hey, Ma." Morgan stood outside my front door, but he hadn't called before he'd showed up.

"Hey, baby. What's up?" I asked with the door open only a little bit while Bear gathered up his clothes and ran down the hallway.

His eyebrows were drawn as he tried to peek inside. "You going to bed?"

"No, just relaxing." I smiled and glanced behind me. "What's up?"

He placed his hand against the door and gave it a little shove, but I had my foot against the back, stopping it from moving. "Can I come in?"

I looked over my shoulder, seeing Bear's naked ass as he streaked out of the room. When the bedroom door finally closed, I said, "Sure."

His eyes roamed around the room as he walked inside, taking in the pillows strewn all over the floor. "Bear here with you?"

"He's in the bedroom," I said, clearing my throat. "He wanted to wash up after being on the road."

"Uh-huh," he muttered as he kicked off his boots, placing them next to Bear's boots. "It doesn't matter."

"You don't care that he's here…naked?" I smiled, waiting to see if he'd flinch, but he didn't.

"Nah. We already had a talk. I'm cool with whatever makes you happy. When he stops making you happy, then we have a problem."

"Want something to drink?" I asked as he followed me into the kitchen.

"I'm good, Ma. Come sit with me." He pulled out the chair next to him and patted the seat. "We gotta talk."

"Oh," I said, my voice almost shrill. Pulling my robe tighter, I sat down and braced myself for whatever Morgan was about to tell me.

"We got the money back for the track."

My hand flew to my mouth, and I gasped. "That's great."

His eyes drifted to the window, focusing on a spot in the distance. "We hit a few snags getting it, though. I wanted to tell you before you heard about it from someone else."

My eyes narrowed. "What type of snags, Morgan?"

His fingers started to tap against the table as he brought his eyes back to mine. "Promise me you won't freak out."

"You're making it worse." I crossed my arms. We'd played this game a thousand times, and he already knew that I was going to freak, no matter what I promised.

"Well, um…" He stopped tapping and began to rub the palm of his hand against the table, making the most obnoxious noise. "Ray was involved, for sure."

"Ugh," I groaned and straightened my back, knowing this wasn't the part I needed not to freak out about.

"So we found Ray. He's with the cops now. They're dealing with him. But…" His voice drifted off.

I tilted my head, thinking I heard him wrong. He didn't just mutter what I think he did. My son wouldn't be so stupid to get Tino and Joey Two Fingers involved. "Repeat that again."

"Uncle Santino helped us get the money back. Ray had given it to Joey to pay back a debt. When Joey heard about the theft and that Ray was with the cops, he wanted no part of the money. I guess even criminals have their limits." He laughed nervously, thinking I was going to laugh too, but I didn't.

Grimacing, I dug my fingers into the soft corners of my eyes. "I can't believe you got Joey involved. What a clusterfuck."

"It was the only way, Ma. I swear. Everything is fine."

"Morgan. Baby." I opened my eyes, letting my hands drop to the table like a ton of bricks. "Nothing is fine when Joey is involved. Not only did both of you lie to me about going to Chicago, you went against my wishes when it comes to your uncle and his kind."

"Don't be ridiculous. Ray is one of his kind too. It's the only way Race would've been made whole again. Would you rather the track go broke and Race lose her dream?"

Guilt.

He used my own weapon against me. I'd perfected it over the last thirty years. It's something that mothers passed on to each other because it fucking worked like a charm. But Morgan became hip to my shit a long time ago and had been known to use the trick on me a time or two.

Pulling it out during our conversation was beautiful—almost poetic. "Naturally, I wouldn't want that."

He gave me a tilted smile. "Didn't think so."

"So now we owe Joey Two Fingers."

"We do not," he corrected me, the one side of his mouth rising farther. "He owed Santino a favor. So now they're even, and we're free and clear."

It was done, and no matter the consequences, I couldn't change anything. Tino, Bear, and Morgan made the decision without me and against my wishes, but at least everything was settled. "What did Ray say?"

"I let Bear talk with him mostly."

"What's mostly?" I raised an eyebrow.

He averted his gaze. "I only spent a few minutes with him and had a little trip down memory lane."

My nose wrinkled because there wasn't anything in the past I wanted to relive except for the moments with Morgan. "Remembering all the good times?"

"Just reminded him of a promise I made him a long time ago."

I crossed my arms, leaning back in my chair. "What promise would that be?"

"It's not important. He broke the promise, and that's all the matters."

"It matters to me. Spill it, Morgan Salvatore, or else."

He laughed softly and waved his hand at me. "You going to spank me, Ma? I'm a little old."

"I have all the time in the world to plot my revenge." I smiled while he continued laughing.

"You're a cream puff."

I always liked when someone underestimated me, especially him. You'd think after thirty years, he'd know better. "You know that pretty pink house for sale on your street?"

His smug little face wasn't laughing anymore. "You mean the one next door?"

"That's the one." I laughed. "I think I want to buy it."

"Ma," he said in a stern tone. "Don't kid like that."

"I'm looking for a change. Why not move right next door to my baby?"

"Fuck," he muttered and scrubbed his hand down his face. "You wouldn't do that to me."

"I would, especially if you're keeping secrets. I think I need to keep a better eye on you."

There was no way in hell I'd actually move there. Although I liked being close to Morgan, I didn't want to be within walking distance. Before Bear, I probably would've done it, but now I liked to have my privacy.

"Fine." He rested both hands on the table and reclined back in the chair. "I promised Dad on graduation day that if he came anywhere near you, or me for that matter, that there'd be hell to pay."

My head jerked forward, my ear moving closer to him. "Wait, what?"

"I'm the reason he left, Ma."

"You made him leave?" My mouth hung open, and I blinked repeatedly because I still didn't understand.

"Yeah. I didn't want him beating on you when he drank after

I left. I figured it would go back to the way it was when I was a kid when I wasn't there to protect you."

How did I not know? I couldn't believe he'd kept the secret for this long. I always assumed Ray left because he wanted to, not because Morgan made him. The revelation that Morgan forced him out rocked me to the core.

"Why didn't you tell me?"

"I knew you'd be mad and give me the whole song and dance about how you could take care of yourself."

"Well, I could." I shrugged.

"Ma, don't shit yourself. That guy was like a disease. He wouldn't have left if I didn't make him."

"I wish you would've told me about this a long time ago, Morgan."

"I did what I felt was best for both of us. I couldn't go away knowing he was there alone with you."

It was really unfair of Morgan to grow up in such a volatile household. No child should have to worry about a parent's safety or to step in to protect one from the other. Morgan did that, though. He did more than any kid should have had to do. He wasn't bitter about his past, and neither was I—every second I lived led me to this moment and place.

Without Ray, the alcoholic low-life asshole, in my life, I wouldn't be with Bear. He was the best thing that'd happened to me since the day Morgan was born. Finally, I felt like I had someone who was my partner.

"Hey," Bear said as he walked into the kitchen, giving Morgan a casual chin lift.

"Hey," Morgan replied with the same motion.

I looked at Bear and back to Morgan, my hands following

my eyes. "So this is fine?"

"Yep." Morgan smiled, and Bear nodded.

Coming to stand next to me, Bear put his hands on my shoulders and gave them a light squeeze. "Everything is great," he said as he leaned down and kissed my hair.

"Huh," I muttered, nodding my head as I worked through the fact that Morgan and Bear had finally figured their shit out. "I'm glad to hear you two have made peace."

"I never doubted we would."

"I just needed a little time with the fact that my friend, someone I trust, was trying to date—" Morgan coughed and shifted his eyes "—my mom."

Reaching back, I placed my hand over Bear's. "I'm happier than I've ever been."

"That's all that matters," Morgan said and smiled, bringing his eyes back to mine. "I better get back to Race." He leaned over and kissed my cheek before holding his hand out to Bear. "See you tomorrow, buddy."

"I'll be there. "

After Morgan walked out the front door, Bear grabbed me and stalked off toward the bedroom with me in his arms. "It's time to pay up, sweetheart."

"Not my ass!" I giggled. "Not my ass."

He stopped in the hallway just before the door. "Franny, babe. I'm not taking it unless you're willing to give it. So stop freaking out."

"Okay." I blew out a breath and sagged against him.

"But eventually, you're going to beg me to stick it in your ass."

"Said no woman ever," I mumbled softly.

"What?"

"Nothing." I smiled up at him.

"Liar," he whispered as he leaned forward and kissed my lips as he carried me inside the bedroom.

Every ounce of stress from the day melted away with his lips pressed against mine. It was only us, a man and a woman, together as one, without anything else interfering. Bear made everything feel…possible.

27 BEAR

"James!" Thomas yelled as James walked by his office.

Thomas and I had spent the last thirty minutes talking about the possibility of them hiring Ret as a bounty hunter and private investigator at ALFA. We always had too many cases and often juggled more than we should. An extra body, and one who knew how to find people, would be an asset.

James walked backward, sticking his face in the doorway. "What's up?"

Thomas motioned toward the seat next to me. "We gotta talk. Have a minute?"

He slapped his hand against the doorframe. "I'm not doing anything," he said sarcastically as he walked inside.

Thomas rolled his eyes. "So Bear found us a possible lead on a new hire."

James looked at me and then to Thomas. “Who?”

“Dude’s a bounty hunter and is looking to settle down.”

James rubbed his chin and smiled. “Interesting. Could be a great match for our company.”

“That’s what I think too. We could use another set of hands around here.”

“So then it’s a yes?” I asked, fidgeting in my chair because I wanted this so badly I could almost taste it.

“How do you know him?” James asked.

“He’s my kid.” It felt weird to say that. I didn’t really talk about either of my children with the guys.

James smiled. “Ah, that makes it even better.”

“He’s stopping in today to see me, and I thought I’d see what you guys thought before I introduced him. He’s looking to relocate, and I thought we’d be a perfect fit.”

“Way to be a team player for once.” Thomas laughed, and James joined him.

“If it weren’t for wanting to keep my kid close, I’d tell you both to fuck off.”

Thomas cleared his throat. “Bring him to my office when he gets here.”

I pushed myself up from the chair, too excited to let them annoy me. “I’ll do that.”

“Close the door behind you. James and I need to talk in private.”

I nodded, closing the door and heading straight to my office. Getting work done while I waited was impossible. All I could think about was that my son could be working in the same building as me and I’d never miss another day with him.

"Bear." Angel's sultry voice came through the intercom as I was digging through a pile of papers.

"Yeah."

"A Mr. Ret North is here to see you."

"Send him back," I said in a strangled voice.

My stomach started to flip over, and I jumped from my seat, smoothing down my clothes and combing my beard with my fingers like I was about to go on a date instead of seeing my son again.

Ret strolled into my office in a pair of dark blue jeans, a tight black T-shirt, and black Harley boots like he'd just walked off the set of the Fast & Furious. He definitely looked like he'd fit right in with the other guys here at ALFA. Lord knows I never did.

"Hey, Pop," he said like no separation had ever happened. It flowed easily from his lips and brought the biggest smile to my face.

"Glad you made it." I rounded my desk and pulled him into my arms before he even tried to shake my hand. I'd never been a hugger, but for my kid, I'd hug him every chance I got.

"Impressive setup you have here."

"I wish I could take the credit, but it's my buddies' business."

"Still," he said, pulling out of my arms. "You've done well for yourself."

"It helps to surround yourself with good people. Their family changed my life."

"I talked with Alese," he said and smiled.

"Sit. Let's talk." I motioned toward the chair and leaned against the desk while he sat. "What did she say?"

"She said she's fine moving anywhere as long as we're together."

"And what do you think?" I crossed my fingers under my arm.

"I like the idea of being closer to family and getting to know you and Franny better."

"Her son works here too."

"Oh. How does that work?"

"Now?" I laughed and shook my head. "It's fine, but it was a bit touch and go when Fran and I hooked up."

"Uh, yeah. I can imagine."

"You'll like Morgan. He's former military and a good kid. His wife owns a racetrack not far from here."

"Sounds like my kind of people. And the other guys?"

"Well, there's Sam—he's ex-FBI. Thomas and James are ex-DEA and also brothers-in-law. Thomas is Fran's nephew."

"So this is mainly a family operation?"

I shook my head. "No, but it's friends and family. They only surround themselves with people they know they can trust."

"If they want another employee, then I'm game."

I tried to hold in my excitement, but I failed. "Yes!" Fist-pumping the air, I did a little dance with my upper body.

"Don't do that again."

"What?" My head rocked back.

He waved his hands in the air between us. "Whatever that was. Just don't."

I glared at him. "My moves always impressed the ladies."

"You're lucky your ass is old, Pop. That shit don't work

today."

"Little fucker." I laughed. "You're going to fit in here like a glove."

Thomas and James walked past my door and backed up and pointed toward Ret. I nodded, letting them know that he was indeed my son.

"Hey," Thomas said, walking in very casually. "I'm Thomas, part owner of ALFA. This is James." He pitched a thumb over his shoulder. "My partner in the business."

"Nice to meet you. I'm Ret," he said, holding out his hand and shaking Thomas's hand very calmly.

"So we heard you might be interested in a job."

"Yes, sir." Ret smiled, glancing over his shoulder at me.

"Have a few minutes to talk?" James asked.

"I sure do."

"Bear, we're going to steal him for a bit. Is that okay with you?" Thomas asked out of respect.

"It's fine. We'll catch up when you're done," I told them, but the three of them were already in the hallway.

Thomas pulled the door closed behind him, and I broke out into my dance again. The same one Ret told me never to perform again. But now the audience was just me, and nothing made me want to dance more than the thought of having Ret near.

***

"So how'd it go today?" Fran asked before I had the chance to kick off my shoes.

"Fucking perfect. Ret starts in two weeks. He just needs to go back to Miami and pack up his things."

She ran across the room and jumped into my arms. "That's

amazing."

"It is," I said into her neck, taking in her scent and closing my eyes.

She tipped her head back, giving me access to the entire side of her neck. "We should celebrate."

"Am I getting anal tonight?" I murmured.

"No," she said in a breathy tone.

"Not even if I eat your pussy for an hour?" I smiled against her skin.

"Hmm." She laughed. "That's a tempting offer."

My fingers dug into her ass cheeks. "I want you so bad, Franny." I growled when her ass clenched in my palms. "Do this for me."

"What do I get out of this?" she asked, digging her fingernails into my shoulders.

"A killer orgasm that'll make you black out."

"Uh, I have those without you sticking it in my ass, babe."

"Sweetheart." I pulled away so she could see the need in my eyes. "It was worth a shot."

"My ass is the tightest thing I have on this old body. I'd prefer for it to stay intact."

"You're the boss, Franny. You're the boss." I laughed.

One thing Jackie taught me is that the women run the show. Hell, I'd watched the Gallo family closely over the years too, and Fran and Maria had that shit running like a well-oiled machine.

Men did not rule the world.

Men did not make the decisions.

It's just how shit was, and I knew it was how Fran planned

on being. She couldn't hand over the reins to me. It went against her nature and probably her genetics.

"But," I said, moving my hands from her ass to her beautiful face. "I want you to make me a promise."

"What, Bear?"

"No more talkin' bad about yourself. Your body is beautiful, your face is stunning, but the thing I love about you most is your heart." I rubbed my nose against hers. "Even if you are a nosy little thing sometimes."

"But I brought your kids back." She smiled.

"You did." I kissed her lips softly. "And for that, I'll always love you."

I never expected there to be another woman on this planet who got me. But Fran DeLuca did. I needed her in my life, and she needed me. We were the perfect mix together.

Her nosiness came from a place of love. She knew that I wanted my kids in my life but didn't have the balls to do it myself.

She made it happen.

And for that, I'd always be by her side.

Eventually, maybe I'd get in her ass too.

28

FRAN

Morgan grabbed my leg. “Ma, get down!”

“Oh, honey. I’m having too much fun,” I said, looking down at him and laughing at the look on his face. My beautiful son was stressed out and embarrassed, but you know what? I didn’t give a shit.

“People are looking at you,” he begged.

I twirled in a circle, breaking free from his grip. The table moved with me, making it more like dancing on top of a pogo stick than a tabletop. “It’s my wedding day, goddamn it.”

“Leave her alone,” Maria said as she pulled out a chair and used Morgan’s shoulder as leverage to dance on the table with me. She grabbed my hands and started to jump up and down when Aretha Franklin’s “Respect” began to play.

“Old people,” Morgan muttered and rolled his eyes.

"Go find that pretty wife of yours!" I yelled over the music, holding on to Maria tightly so neither of us would fall off the wobbly table.

We danced like teenagers, pretending our almost arthritic knees didn't ache. It didn't hurt that we'd consumed a good percentage of our body weight in alcohol before we cut loose.

"I freaking love this song," she said with the biggest smile.

"R-E-S-P-E-C-T!" we screamed together, making moves like we used to in the old days when we'd go to the discos.

Half the room was on their feet dancing and singing along. If I weren't so hammered, I'd have tears in my eyes. Surrounded by my entire family, I felt so much love—more than I'd ever felt in my entire life.

The day Bear asked me to marry him, I thought my mind was playing tricks on me. Never did I expect that man, the one who said he'd never settle down, to ask me that question. I mean, he always asked for anal sex, but I told him he hadn't earned it yet. Maybe it was his way of staking his claim and earning the right to conquer all of me.

He was really kind of old-fashioned about some things. He even talked to Sal to ask for my hand in marriage because he was officially the patriarch of the family since our father wasn't here to ask. I found it endearing and sweet, but Bear swore me to secrecy. He didn't want his credibility as a badass to be ruined.

Not even Morgan knew how Bear popped the question. Hell, I didn't even tell Maria because then everyone would know. I might as well have published it on the front page of the newspaper. We kept it our little secret and told the family that he asked me over dinner.

But the truth of it was much different. He took me to Honeymoon Island to watch the sunset, bringing a blanket and cooler filled with champagne, cheese, and fruit. He held me in his arms, whispering sweet things in my ear as we watched the sun fall below the edge of the ocean.

When the sky turned the most brilliant shades of red and orange, he said four magical words that stole my breath. I turned in his arms and straddled him before I said yes. I'd be lying if I said we didn't get a bit frisky in public. It wasn't something I'd done before, but Bear brought out that side of me—he made me want to do things I never thought I'd do.

"You did it!" Maria yelled, wrapping her arms around my neck when the song ended. "You're Mrs. Fran North."

"That sounds so weird," I said and gripped her waist as the table started to shift underneath us.

"Ladies," Bear, my husband, said from behind me. "You two better get down before that table breaks."

"We got this," Maria said over my shoulder and waved him off.

"I'd like my wife to be in perfect condition tonight for what I have planned."

Maria's eyes slid to mine, and her eyebrows shot up. "Is he talking about what I think he's talking about?"

My lips twisted and I nodded, closing one eye as I thought about the pain and the promise I never should've made.

"Well, shit," Maria said in my ear and laughed. "We better have more to drink."

"Fucking hell," I groaned.

When I turned around, Bear held out his hand—the one with the shiny new shiny gold wedding ring—and helped me down.

"Are my two favorite ladies having fun?" he asked when he reached for Maria and helped her down with just as much care as he did with me.

"I have a feeling you're going to have more fun later." Maria winked, and I wanted to crawl under the table out of embarrassment.

He just laughed and whisked me into his arms, placing his lips against my neck. "I won't do anything you don't want."

My belly flipped as his words skidded across my skin. "I'm yours now, Bear. There's nothing I want more than to give you a piece of me that I've never given to anyone." Clearly, the alcohol made me answer him in that way.

That was Bear. My husband didn't often show it, but when it came to family and friends, he had a soft spot.

If I were younger, I'd have little baby Bears running around the house. If he were given the chance to really be a father, I could almost imagine what he'd be like.

I'd been able to catch glimpses of it since Janice had her baby. When Bear walked into the room and saw the little girl for the first time, I thought he was going to turn into a puddle of goo. The man lost it and started to cry when Janice told him she had named her Jackie.

In all my life, I'd never seen a more involved grandfather. I thought Sal was bad, but Bear is a complete sucker for that little girl. He was probably overdoing it because of the time he lost with his kids, but it didn't matter. After seeing him with a baby in his arms, it had me longing for the days of having a little one in the house.

"Well, I better go find Sal. I'm sure he's getting into trouble somewhere." Maria kissed Bear on the cheek before wrapping me in the biggest hug. "Use lots of lube and do at least three more shots before you go upstairs."

"But I'll black out," I whispered in her ear.

"You want to be half unconscious your first time. Trust me. Or your ass is going to pucker up like no one's business. Thank me tomorrow."

I started to giggle, covering my mouth, and glanced back at my husband.

"I don't know what you two are talking about, but are you ready to say good-bye to everyone?"

"Remember… Do more shots," she called out over her shoulder as she started to walk away.

He quirked an eyebrow at me. "Sage advice from a pro?"

I nodded, still laughing as I looped my arm around his back. "Let's have a drink with our boys, and then we can say good-bye to everyone else."

"Just one?" He smiled and pushed on the small of my back, leading me through the crowd.

I shrugged. "However many it takes."

"Are you sure about this? Before you get too shit-faced, Franny, I need to know this is what you want." He looked so cute when he had that super serious, concerned face going on.

I nodded quickly as my hand slid lower before giving him a quick ass squeeze. "I'm completely sure." I smiled up at him and sighed. "Bring on the tequila, baby!"

Morgan saw us first and nudged Ret with his elbow. They were handsome devils, especially dressed in tuxedos. "Hey, guys." I smiled and looked back and forth between them.

"Ma," Morgan said, leaning forward and kissing me on the cheek before shaking my husband's hand. "Bear."

"Morgan," Bear replied, pulling him into a hug and lifting Morgan off his feet. Instead of being a stick in the mud, Morgan hugged him back.

As soon as his feet were back on the ground, Morgan punched Bear in the shoulder. “I’m so fuckin’ happy for you.”

“Fran, you’re a beautiful bride.” Ret kissed my cheek, making my toes curl a bit.

Down, girl. He’s your husband’s kid. Every time I saw Ret, I imagined a young Murray. Even in his fifties, Murray was sexy as sin, but in his youth… Meow.

“Thanks, Ret. I’m happy to have the entire family here,” I said as Janice approached from the other side of the bar.

“I brought a bottle,” she said, waving the tequila bottle in the air. “Who wants a shot? Jackie’s with a sitter all night, and I’m not letting this opportunity pass.”

“Well, damn. Let’s drink, mama,” I said, rubbing my hands together as I winked at Bear.

“Don’t drink too much, Franny.”

“Oh, shush it, buddy. Just two for the road.” I smiled and pressed my hand against his chest and motioned with my fingers for him to give me his ear. “You want ass, I get shots.”

“Mom!”

My head snapped to Morgan. “What?”

His eyes bulged out of his head. “You may not realize it, but you most certainly did not whisper that.”

I chuckled, feeling my cheeks turning pink. “Sorry.” I grimaced. “Let’s just drink until you all forget what you just heard.”

“Not enough liquor in the world for that,” Morgan muttered, looking like he was about to vomit while Ret and Janice laughed.

Bear poured the drinks and handed them out. We formed a tight circle, Morgan to my left and Bear along with his kids to the right. “To family,” Bear said and held his glass high in the air.

"That's all ya got?" I asked.

"Does anything else matter?" he asked, peering down at me with an adorable smile.

"Not really. To our kids and the future," I said, raising my glass too.

"Salute," Morgan said, followed by Janice and Ret.

My entire body tingled as the tequila slid down my throat. Not just from the warmth of the liquor, but at being surrounded by my family. Our family. Over the last year, I'd grown to love Bear's kids as much as I loved the man himself.

After years of loneliness, my life had become full.

"One more," I said and held my glass in front of Bear, shaking it.

He just laughed and refilled all the glasses.

"To Fran and Bear," Ret said and clinked his tequila to his father's.

I quickly clinked my glass before downing the shot. My legs felt a little wobbly, and I knew I needed to get off my feet. "Love you, baby," I said to Morgan before he put down his shot glass. "I'll see you tomorrow."

"Not if I have anything to say about it." Bear wrapped his arm around my waist from behind.

Morgan narrowed his eyes. "I can still knock you out, old man."

"Now, Morgan, let your mother enjoy herself and her new husband," I told him.

He scrubbed his hands down his face. "Go. Have fun."

"Bye," I said, quickly hugging Ret and Janice.

Bear waved to everyone as we walked away. His arm was

still looped behind my back, which I needed to give me support with my liquor-induced sway. I giggled most of the way up to the room—over what, I'm not sure.

Bear couldn't wipe the smile off his face, kissing my neck and groping me as the elevator dinged with each floor.

The door to the honeymoon suite wasn't even closed before Bear had me against the wall, hiking my dress up my body and feasting on me like a starving man.

"Bear," I moaned and dug my fingers into his hair.

He didn't stop. His hands slid down my body and groped my bare ass in his hands before lifting me off the floor. My feet dangled for a moment and then instinctively wrapped around his waist.

Sometimes, I wanted to pinch myself because I didn't believe he was mine… But feeling our bodies pressed against each other reminded me that we were forever part of each other.

"You sure about this, Franny?" he asked as he paused in front of the bed and I climbed down his body.

"I'm sure," I said, or at least, I think I did. It's what I meant to say if I didn't. My brain started to get fuzzy from the mass amounts of alcohol I'd consumed.

I stood still while Bear undressed me, kissing the skin he'd exposed until he knelt down in front of me as the dress hit the floor.

He pulled my body closer and leaned forward, placing his fur-covered lips against me. My body jolted from the warmth. I gripped his hair again, but this time to keep myself from falling backward. I closed my eyes and savored the feel of his mouth on my clit.

"I'm so close," I said within minutes. When his mouth pulled away, I gasped. "What are you doing?"

"Just getting warmed up, sweetheart." He smirked.

I blinked slowly, my lopsided grin growing wider. "Ravage me," I proclaimed like I was part of some trashy romance novel.

His hands gripped the sides of my waist and held me tightly before tossing me onto the bed.

"You're lucky I didn't break a hip," I said in the worst, slurred, drunk-off-my-ass tone.

He moved quickly, ripping off his tux in record time. "I wanna break you, Fran," he said as he climbed on top of me. "But only in the most sinful way."

I gasped when his huge erection settled between my legs. "I don't think it'll fit." I wiggled underneath him.

"Baby, it'll fit. I'll go nice and slow. You've taken my fingers like a champ. My cock will be nothing." There wasn't a man on the planet who hadn't used that line in some form to try to get into their girl's ass.

I wasn't stupid, but lucky for him, I was inebriated enough to say, "Yeah." To which I got a smirk before he went down on me again.

My eyes grew heavy and even blinking became a struggle, but every time I started to feel the weight of sleep begin to pull me under, Bear would dig in harder or fuck me deeper.

But when he flipped me onto my stomach, I immediately woke up. "Oh, God," I moaned. "This is going to hurt."

I glanced over my shoulder, using one eye to try to focus as he lifted a bottle of lube in the air. He was nestled between my legs as he squeezed the bottle, letting the lube trickle down my ass crack.

When his finger touched my hole, I puckered, along with every muscle in my body going rigid. "You want this, sweetheart?" he asked as the tip of his finger glided across me.

Fuck, it felt amazing once I let myself relax. Bear had magical fingers, and he knew exactly what to do to get me going.

"Keep going," I said, sealing my eyes shut. "Don't stop."

He growled and dipped the tip of one finger inside. My body melted into the bed, except my abdomen which stayed high from the pillow he'd placed underneath my belly.

Slowly, he worked his finger in and out, and once I adjusted, he added a second. "So good," I moaned. With two fingers buried inside me, coldness slid down my ass. More lube…thank God. "You better lube that giant dick of yours," I told him because Maria's advice still played on repeat in my mind.

"I gotcha," he whispered.

I could hear the mass amounts of lube he was coating his cock with. The sound of wetness filled the air along with my gasps as his other hand never stopped working me—driving me closer to climax.

When he pulled his fingers out, I grabbed on to the comforter as if my life depended on it and closed my eyes.

"Breathe, Fran. It'll feel so good."

Bullshit. I grunted as the tip of his cock pushed against my opening. At first, it felt like his finger when he'd rim my ass, looking for permission.

"Bear down," he told me, and I did.

The first inch was the hardest and felt different than I'd imagined. I felt full. Not just a little full either. If he put any more inside of me, I thought my body might split in two.

"So fuckin' tight," he growled behind me and pushed in deeper. "Jesus, I'm not going to last."

Bear had the most stamina out of any man I'd ever know.

Maybe my list was short, but the man could fuck like a champ. He wasn't known as a manwhore for no reason.

My mind grew fuzzy.

The darkness began to take me until he reached around and started to tweak my clit between his thumb and index finger. He'd spent at least an hour working me up, always denying me the orgasm I wanted, until now.

But my hand to God—he wasn't inside of me for twenty-five seconds when he cried out. "I can't stop it! You're just too tight."

I gasped for air. My mouth was open like a guppy, but nothing was getting in. It was like his cock had been jammed so far inside me that it punctured my lung, making it impossible for me to breathe.

Within seconds, my body started to tighten, even my ass around his cock clamped down, and I tumbled into the most wonderful darkness. Suddenly, explosions of colors filled the void as my body twitched through the most spectacular orgasm of my entire life.

"Franny," I heard him say, but I couldn't move. My body and mind were paralyzed from the aftershocks.

"Franny," he said again.

I mumbled something, but I didn't know what the fuck I said. When he pulled out, my body jolted—partly missing the fullness and the other part shocked by his size. My eyes were still closed, and I concentrated on my breathing after going so long without air.

The bed dipped, and his footsteps softened. "Here, baby," he said before touching my bottom with a warm, wet washcloth and cleaning me up.

I'd never had a man who cared for me afterward. The first one…the one who shall not be named…was more of a wham, bam, thank you, ma'am kind of guy.

But my husband knew just how I wanted to be treated. "I love you," I murmured into the plush comforter.

"I love you too, Fran." The bed dipped again, but this time, he pulled me into his arms and pressed my back to his front. "Sleep, wife," he whispered in my ear.

As I drifted off, I thought about how much my life had changed. I was no longer a divorced, tracksuit-wearing woman who sat home and played bridge. I was the wife of a badass biker man who looked more like a lumberjack than a private investigator. I felt loved, protected, and content for the first time in my entire life.

It was funny how things worked out. Sometimes good things happened when we least expected it. Especially when the person who came to my rescue was a sexy hunk of man who always kept me on my toes with his smart mouth—and satisfied in the bedroom with his glorious cock and talented tongue.

Tucked against his body and feeling like the sexual beast I knew I was—I slept in my husband's arms for the first night after saying I do.

29

BEAR

Fran almost pushed me out of the house and ordered me to meet the guys at the Neon Cowboy. She muttered something about cleaning out the spare bedroom. I guess my extra things were cluttering the garage—and maybe we needed our alone time.

Going from bachelor living to being married had been an adjustment, but one I'd actually enjoyed. I'd spent most of my life single and bed-hopping that it was nice to finally settle down and live like the other half did.

"The ol' ball and chain let you out to play?" Tank asked with a chuckle as I sat down and grabbed a beer from the middle of the table.

"I wanted to stay home with my wife and enjoy my birthday, but she insisted I come spend the night with you miserable bastards."

"Smart lady," Ret said and slapped me on the shoulder.

Ret had fit in better than I ever could've imagined. He'd only been at ALFA PI for a short time, but I almost couldn't remember a time without him.

"Where's Morgan?" I asked.

Everyone looked at each other, waiting for someone to respond, but no one said anything.

"Is he okay?" They were acting weirder than usual. None of them were "normal," but usually they answered simple questions.

"Yeah, he's fine. He'll be here in a few. He's just handling a few things," Tank said, but he didn't put my mind at ease.

After being friends for as many years as we had, it was easy to read him, and there was definitely something he wasn't saying.

"Haven't seen you much lately. My aunt keepin' you busy?" City asked.

"She has been dragging me to some classes and shit," I muttered, trying to make it seem like I was still the same miserable, brooding bastard.

"Basket weaving?" He raised an eyebrow and smirked.

"That isn't Franny's style." I laughed, turning the beer bottle in my hand.

Mike leaned forward with a serious look on his face. "You can't just drop that knowledge in our laps and not tell us what you're learning, old man."

"Well…" I shrugged. Fran would absolutely murder me if I told them the truth.

"Just drop the shit," City said, narrowing his eyes. "You're learning to knit. Just admit it."

"Fucker. It's a dance class," I lied. It was a white lie. There was dance, but it involved a pole and very little clothing.

She'd seen an ad online about staying fit and learning new moves, and she'd begged me to go with her. Never in my life did I think I would go to a stripper-pole dance class. It sounded like bullshit. But I didn't expect there to be benefits like a sex-charged wife by the time the sessions were over.

Tank laughed first, and then the others followed suit. "I can't fucking believe it. We have Fred Astaire sitting at our table." Tank shook his head in disappointment. "I never thought I'd see the day you'd be a twinkle toes."

"It ain't that kind of class, dumbass."

"Oh?" he asked, challenging me to answer.

"What kind of class is it, Uncle?" City asked. It was his new way to annoy me. Technically, I was his uncle, but he used every opportunity to remind me just how much older I was than him.

"I can't say." I bit down on my tongue and imagined Franny's face if I spilled the beans.

"I know," Anthony teased with a sinister smile that I wanted to smack right off his face.

"Shut the fuck up," I growled.

"Auntie Fran tells Mom everything." Anthony stuck out his tongue and gagged. "Trust me, I know too much."

Thomas looked from Anthony to me with a scowl and threw up his hands. "I don't want to hear it."

"Now I gotta know. Spill the beans, kid," Tank said to Anthony, rubbing his hands together and peering at me out of the corner of his eye.

"Assholes," I grumbled before taking a swig of my beer.

Anthony put his hands up and laughed, tipping back in his

chair. The cocky little fucker. “All I’m going to say is that there’s a pole involved.”

One by one, each set of eyes looked over at me with their mouths hanging open. I shrugged. “I can’t help if I have a girl who likes to mix shit up.”

City started to rub his face and groaned. “I shouldn’t know this shit about my aunt, man.”

“You asked, he told.” I smirked.

Mike sat there, still looking a little green around the gills. Thomas laughed his ass off and grabbed another beer like we weren’t talking about his aunt.

“Fran’s a wild woman,” Ret said and shook his head. “She’s perfect for you.” He nudged me with his elbow.

“Best woman I’ve ever known besides your mom.” I gave him a bittersweet smile. He nodded, knowing exactly how I felt. “I’m having one more drink, and then I’m outta here.”

“Oh, no, you don’t,” James, the bossiest SOB in the group, said. “We have plans tonight.”

“Plans?”

“Yep. So sit your ass there and drink your beer. Fran isn’t expecting you until we’re done with you.”

My entire body rocked backward, taking the chair with me. “Done with me?” These “friends” who sat around the table definitely had something up their sleeves, and they weren’t sharing.

“It’s your birthday, you old fucker.” Tank looked at me like I had three heads.

“Fran doesn’t want me out all night.” I was making excuses, but it didn’t matter. I wanted to be home with my sweetheart. I’d spent too many years in bars and going home to an empty house to want to spend my birthday the same exact way.

"Mom's meeting us at the next stop," Morgan said, walking up from behind me and placing his hands on my shoulders. "So stop the bullshit. Drink your beer and enjoy your seventieth birthday."

"Fifty-second," I corrected him.

"Still old as fuck," Morgan teased before he took a seat across the table. "Everything's in place."

"I don't like surprises."

"Just shut up," Tank sneered. "Always gotta ruin everything."

I crossed my arms in front of me and scowled. "Fine, but I don't gotta like it."

My phone beeped with a text.

Fran: Stop being a pain and follow the program.

I couldn't wipe the stupid grin off my face as I typed back.

Me: Fine, but only because I love that fine ass.

"Where are we headed for my extra special celebration?"

"The Pink Panther." Tank smiled.

"Eh, I've seen enough tits and ass in strip clubs to last a lifetime." I slammed back the rest of my beer and grabbed another because if I was going to the titty bar for the night, I sure as fuck needed to be drunk.

"So, Ret, how are you settling in at ALFA?" City asked, ignoring my unhappiness about the itinerary for the evening.

"Fucking great, man." Ret leaned forward and gripped the beer bottle in both hands. "Never worked any place where I actually liked the people."

"Smart thing to say since everyone is here."

"Not Sam. Where is that prick anyway?" I asked.

"He's getting something important," City replied and exhaled in annoyance.

"Getting something?"

City nodded. "Stop trying to find a way out of it, Bear. Your ass is ours tonight." He turned back to Ret. "What case are you working on now?"

When there weren't any active PI cases for Ret, he was given free rein to track down wanted criminals. He was a bounty hunter, after all, and the rewards brought in big cash for ALFA. Since he used their resources, he split the money with the company, but he kept the bulk of it.

"Tracking this asshole on the FBI Most Wanted list. He killed his family and took off about fifteen years ago. I'm going to find him and put him exactly where he belongs."

Anthony finally put his phone down to join the conversation. "How much does something like that pay?"

"Hundred grand."

Anthony's eyes lit up. "Fuck, I need to change professions."

"It's risky as fuck, man," Ret told him. "It isn't something you can do without accepting the possibility that they will kill you to keep their freedom."

"Eh, I don't have to worry about that at the shop."

"Smart man, Anth." Mike elbowed him. "Plus, where else can you work where you see tits and ass all day besides a strip club?"

"Dude." Anthony winced. "Some of those tits and ass should never see the light of day, let alone be exposed in front of me."

"You're a real tool," City told him before turning to Ret. "You don't go after guys like that alone, do you?"

"Sometimes. But he's going to be a pain in the ass, so I'll probably rope someone at ALFA to go with me once I get a lock on his location."

"I'll go," I offered because I took every opportunity I could get to spend more time with my son.

He glanced over at me and nodded slowly. "I'd have you at my back anytime, Dad."

Man. It never got old hearing him call me Dad. No sweeter word in the English language. Every day, I felt less guilty about my past and the way I'd left my kids. They seemed to accept me and forgive me for what I'd done, but it'd taken me longer to forgive myself.

"One more round and we're outta here. Sam's on his way," Thomas said.

"Fucking great," I muttered to myself.

***

"Thanks for being the designated driver tonight," James told Sam as we climbed off the party bus.

"Eh, with Fi being pregnant, I try not to drink. She gets jealous that she can't have one."

"You're smarter than you look." I laughed.

"You're still an asshole," he replied with a smirk.

The kid had grown on me. Who the fuck knew? I hated him when I first met him. Thought he was a weasel, but he's not. He's a stand-up guy and has had our backs more times than I could count.

"Happy birthday, old bastard." He smiled.

I straightened my back and rubbed my chest. "You only wish you could look this good at my age."

As I started to walk away, he said, "Too bad you won't be around to see that I look better when I'm as old as you."

I turned quickly, narrowing my eyes. "I'll still be here, fucker. Heaven won't take me, and the Devil's too scared to have me down there. I'd take that shit over."

Sam rolled his eyes. "Yeah, I forgot. You're a badass."

I socked him in the shoulder with my knuckles. "Keep it up, and you'll be there before me."

"You two done with your bullshit?" James asked, holding open the door to the Pink Panther.

We both started to laugh, and I grabbed Sam around the neck, locking him under my arm. "We're coming!" I yelled back and then started to mess up Sam's hair. "Even though you're a dick, I still love you."

He punched my ribs, trying to break free. "Not the hair, man." He grunted, pushing against my ribs.

I released him and laughed when he frantically tried to fix his hair that looked like a bird's nest on top of his head. "You're still like a chick."

"You're lucky it's your birthday."

"Fuck off."

"We're late. Get your asses inside and shut up," City said and shoved me in the back.

We had just been here for my bachelor party, and some things were meant never to be discussed again. Explaining to Fran why I had bite marks on my chest the next day wasn't a pleasant conversation, but she eventually forgave me. She mumbled something about her son and nephews being with me so it couldn't have been as bad as she had imagined. I wasn't saying shit because my big mouth would just get me in more trouble.

"Ah, the smell of pussy and desperation," I said when the door closed behind us. "Nothing like it."

"It's a smell you know well," Mike laughed, holding his stomach and thinking he was the funniest fucker ever.

"I do," I admitted.

James walked ahead of the group, motioning for us to follow. "Let's get a table up front."

"Bossy bastard," I mumbled.

The Pink Panther was one of the seediest strip clubs in the area, but it was centrally located between our houses. Keeping with the name, the lights shining on the stage were pink, casting a hue that made each of the dancers appear to be sunburned.

Epic fail.

Instead of licensing the logo for the Pink Panther, Crater, the owner of the joint, created his own version with a cracked-out pink cat and stuck it on the wall. Whoever was his designer for the logo should be shot.

"I hate this place," I groaned as I sat on a weirdly sticky stadium chair in the front row between Ret and City.

"I've been in worse," City said and eased back in the chair.

The speakers squealed, and I covered my ears. "Next up, we have the divinely delicious Cupcake. Are you ready to sink your teeth into her, gentlemen?"

Hoots and hollers could be heard from the back of the room as the music started to play and the lights lowered. First, a leg appeared, lit up by a spotlight, before the rest of "Cupcake" emerged, covered in a faux fur coat and high heels. I could barely look at her—she was so young, I wondered if she was even really legal.

Ever since spending more time with my daughter, I couldn't look at younger women the same way. They no longer did anything for me. Janice fucked that shit up.

Ret leaned over. "Cupcake lookin' a little young, or is it me?"

"Yup. Just thinking the same thing."

"Either I'm getting old, or she's way underage."

Cupcake showed a shoulder first, shimmying up and down the pole in rhythm with the music. I squirmed in my seat because the entire thing made me uncomfortable. I could almost be her grandfather, and it creeped me out.

"Lap dance?"

I looked up to see Carly, the same girl who gave me all those pretty chest decorations at my bachelor party.

"No thanks." I waved my hands.

"Come on," she said, grabbing my hands and pulling me forward. "It's already been paid for." She grinned. "I promise I won't bite you this time."

"I'll pass." I didn't feel like going home to a pissed off wife. She'd told me to go out, not come home smelling of pussy and covered in more shit that I didn't want to explain.

"Go, dumbass," City said and pushed my shoulder. "Trust me, you want to go."

I gave him the stink eye. Why would my supposed best friend push me to go with Carly? It didn't make sense.

"Come on, Dad. Man up." Ret challenged me and joined City's side.

Carly yanked on my hand again. "I have something special planned for you."

"Oh, goodie."

"Pussy," City coughed.

"Fine," I said and finally stood up to follow Carly, pointing at City. "But if Fran gives me any shit, I'm sending her straight to you, and then she's coming for Carly."

Everyone laughed. They didn't know what it was like to love Franny. She had balls bigger than me, and that was pretty hard to do.

"Let's go in a different room," Carly yelled when we passed by the speakers blaring "Cherry Pie" by Warrant.

I shrugged because I didn't care where we went; I was not going to enjoy this. Well, I would enjoy it, but not the aftermath it caused.

She opened the door at the end of the hallway and stepped aside. "Sit down, and I'm going to turn off the lights. I want to try a new routine out on you."

"I don't know if I'm the best judge, Carly."

"You're perfect, Bear." She smiled up at me. "Now, in you go."

I did as she asked and sat down on the chair in the middle of the room before she switched the lights off and closed the door. I could hear her heels click against the tile as she approached, and I held my breath.

One of my favorite songs started to play—"Addicted" by Saving Abel—and I couldn't help but think of Fran and smile.

When the lights turned on, my mouth fell open.

I was dumbfounded.

Standing before me in fuck-me pumps, a lacy G-string, and nothing else was my girl.

"Franny?" I mouthed, but the music was too loud for either of us to hear.

She shook her head, placing her index finger over my lips. Her body started to move with the beat, circling around my chair and touching my body as she walked.

Fuck, my wife is hot.

Still in shock, I stared at her, watching as she danced around me and put into use all the moves she'd learned at our dance class.

She backed up, straddling my legs and hovering over my cock as she ground her body against me. Jesus. My cock had already perked up when I'd seen her, but now she was about to give me a hard-on that wouldn't go away without fucking her.

My hands slid around her body, gliding up her stomach, and just when I was about to touch her tits, she slapped my hand away. "No touching," she said with a shitty smirk.

"Come on!" I yelled, trying to grope her again, but I ended up getting my hands smacked.

The entire thing made me laugh, but I wasn't laughing at her. I couldn't believe that Fran would do this for me. Her dark hair swayed with her shoulders as her hips moved the other way. I kept reaching out to touch her every time she got close, but she made sure I didn't make contact.

Before the music ended, she sat in my lap with the biggest smile, her body sweaty and glistening. "Did you like your birthday gift?"

I wrapped my arms around her body and pulled her closer. "Best fucking present ever, sweetheart."

"I'm not done yet." She giggled and slithered off my lap to the floor.

Her fingers worked quickly, unfastening my button and pulling my stiff cock free. My belly fluttered, and my cock waved in anticipation as her tiny hand wrapped around the shaft.

She licked her lips, blowing gently on the tip. "You want me to suck your cock?" she asked, sending chills down my spine.

I freaking loved when she talked dirty. "Fuckin' A."

Her lips slid over the head of my dick, and my hips jumped from the chair, trying to shove myself deeper. She placed her hands on my legs and pushed me back down without missing a single stroke against her tongue.

In the short time we'd been together, she learned every trick to make me come apart at the seams. I said it was to make me come faster so she had to work less, but she claimed it was just to drive me wild with lust. I ain't buying what she was selling.

Her hands twisted back and forth, resting against her lips as she moved up and down. Her tongue flicked the spot that gave me goose bumps, and every time I moaned, she sucked harder.

I dug my fingers into her hair, needing to ground myself to something as my mind became fuzzy. I looked down at her, and there wasn't a sexier sight in the world than seeing your woman with her cheeks caved in, working your cock like a pro. Every time she pulled away, my body went with her.

I needed this.

I wanted this.

I wanted her.

I loved Fran's unpredictability. Sometimes it was a bit much and verged on sticking her nose where it didn't belong, but it always revolved around love.

"Franny," I called out as my body shook through the orgasm. My toes curled inside my boots, and my head tipped backward as I gasped for air.

When I came back to my senses and finally glanced back down to her, she dabbed the corners of her mouth and licked the remnants of me off her lips. Before I could catch my breath, she tucked my cock back into my pants and zipped me up before climbing into my lap. Planting a giant kiss against my mouth, she whispered, “I love you, baby.”

“I love you, sweetheart.” I gave her a lazy smile.

“Ready to go out there?”

“In a minute. I need to get my legs back.”

She tipped her head back and giggled. “I’m excited to finally be at a strip club. You know, I’ve never been to one?”

My eyes widened. “What?”

“Yep. Never stepped inside.”

“We’re getting you a lap dance.”

“Why?”

“It’ll be fun.” I’d never share Fran with anyone, but it would still be hot to see another woman rubbing against my wife.

“Then what are we waiting for?” She smiled and rubbed her nose against mine. “Let’s get out there.”

I chuckled and lifted her off me before standing on wobbly legs. “Didn’t you see them dancing when you came in earlier?”

“Nope. I came in through the back door.”

“We’re going to talk about how you pulled this off later.”

“Shh, baby. It’s all good.” She bit her lip.

“Uh-huh.” I knew Fran had tricks, but she didn’t know Crater. But Morgan did, and he probably helped her. I trusted her, and that was all that mattered.

We walked down the corridor, the music growing louder the closer we came to the main room.

She whistled, and her eyes bulged when she got her first

look. Carly was dancing, half dressed and hanging upside down from the pole. "I want to do that."

I glanced up at the ceiling. I could already envision a trip to the emergency room in our near future. "I'll teach you," I told her and wrapped my arm around her shoulders.

"You?" She smacked my chest. "I'll talk to my girl, Carly."

I didn't need Carly and Franny becoming best friends. "We'll talk about it later."

City was making a beeline for us, and he didn't look happy.

"What's up?"

"Ret left."

"Where?" I looked around, even though I knew he wasn't anywhere in here.

"He got a tip on that dude he was talking about earlier. I begged him to wait for you or let one of us come, but he wasn't having any of it."

"He just left?"

City ran his hand through his hair and grimaced. "Yep. You better call him."

"Fuck!" I pulled out my phone and dialed. I stared at City as it rang and flipped over to voice mail. "He's not answering."

"Call him back," Fran said, gripping my sides tightly.

I pressed redial and waited.

He answered on the third ring. "I know what you're going to say."

"What the fuck are you doing?"

"I'll be fine, Dad. I had to go tonight. You stay with everyone and enjoy your birthday party. I got this."

"Not alone, Ret. You need backup."

"I've done this a hundred times, Dad. Don't worry about me."

"Ret," I started to say, but he hung up.

I pulled the phone away and stared down at it. "He hung up." My mouth gaped open at the audacity of my kid.

"What did he say?" City's eyebrows were drawn down.

"He said he had it and not to worry."

"That fucker," City growled. "Thomas and James are going to be pissed."

"Let me break the news," I told him and placed my hand on his shoulder. "I'll handle everything."

"I have a bad feeling about this, Bear. A really bad feeling."

"Me too, buddy. Me too."

Ret was too much like me—hardheaded and too macho to ask or wait for help. He shouldn't be out there on his own, tracking a killer who had been on the run for over a decade. There was too much that could go wrong.

"If you gotta go tonight," Franny said, resting her head on my chest, "I understand. You can't let him be out there alone."

"I can't sit here and worry. I'll go talk to the guys, and we'll head out."

James and Thomas must've figured out what was going on because they were jogging toward me. "We heard. You ready?" James asked.

"Let's go." I looked toward my best friend. "Can you take Franny home?"

"Sam will get us all home. Don't worry. Go get Ret."

"Baby, I'm sorry I have to leave," I said, wrapping my hand

behind her neck and pulling her lips to mine.

"I love you, Bear. Be careful and keep your boy safe."

"I will," I told her and kissed her. "Thanks for the best birthday ever. I love you too." I smiled, staring into her dark eyes.

"Let's hit it," Thomas said and yanked on my T-shirt.

"On it," I said and followed behind him as he pushed open the exit doors.

My night of calm relaxation had gone out the window hours ago, but I never thought I'd be chasing after my kid who seemed to have a death wish by going after a murderer on his own.

Surrounded by my friends and leaving my wife behind, we headed to the office to get a fix on where Ret was headed.

"Let's fuck shit up," James said with a wicked smile as we climbed into a waiting taxi.

"I'm all about it." I wanted to smile, but since my kid's life was on the line, I couldn't. If anything happened to Ret, I didn't know what I'd do with myself.

The End...

THROTTLE ME

SNEAK PEEK - NOW AVAILABLE

CHAPTER 1

The Darkness

Suzy

The moonlight filtered through the pine trees lining the fields, leaving shadows on the pavement. The crisp air that had been missing for months caressed my skin. Cranking up the radio, I sang along to Justin Timberlake's "Rock Your Body." It was just the cool breeze, JT, and me. I couldn't wait to crawl in my bed and close my eyes, getting lost in a dream world that had nothing to do with my current reality.

The night had been perfect. I'd had dinner and drinks with my best friend, Sophia, and although I was exhausted from a long workday, I felt a sense of serenity. Spending time with Sophia always made me happy. She was like a sister to me, especially when she had lived with me for over a year. I felt like part of me had been missing since the day she moved out, leaving me behind.

Dancing in the seat, screaming out the lyrics, I thought about how I wanted someone that would do everything the song described. No one had ever made me feel the way that JT sang about women. The steering wheel shook in my hands and a screeching sound pulled me out of my JT trance.

"Damn it," I said, hitting the steering wheel with my palm.

The orange flash from my hazards blinked against the dark pavement as I pulled off the road and my car sputtered to a stop. Bad luck seemed to follow me. I squeezed the steering wheel, trying to calm my frazzled nerves. I knew the day would come, the day my car would die, but I prayed it would happen after my next paycheck…no such luck.

Resting my head on the wheel, I closed my eyes, taking a deep breath. "Great, just fucking great." I rocked back and forth, feeling sorry for myself, hitting my head on the cool plastic. I thought about whom to call or where to walk. I hadn't passed a gas station or even a damn streetlight in miles. Without picking up my head, I reached for my phone, bringing it to my eyes.

"Shit." The screen wouldn't power on after I hit every button I could think to press. It was useless. It was dead and now I was totally stranded. What else could possibly go wrong? Sighing, I sat up and glanced in the rearview mirror, but only the shadows from the trees filled my view. No cars, neon signs, or streetlights. Fuck.

I placed my hand on my chest to feel the beat of my heart, which was so hard I swear it was audible. Visions from slasher movies flooded my mind. Girl deserted on the side of the road until she's found by a handsome stranger that ends up being a serial killer.

Should I start walking to God knows where? Do I just sit there and wait for a stranger to offer me help? I never liked feeling helpless—I was too smart to be helpless, but it was the only thing I felt in this moment. It could be hours before someone found me in my car.

I grabbed my purse, dead phone, and keys, and climbed out of the car. My feet ached in the extra-high heels I wore. Leaning against the car, I gave my feet a moment to adjust, as I looked in both directions. Neither of my options were good and I was exhausted. My feet fucking screamed from standing still. Thank God I could sleep in tomorrow after the way this evening was ending. There was a gas station a couple miles back—better to go with what I knew than to walk into an uncertain future. I tapped the lock button on my key chain one more time, helping relieve my OCD need to double-check everything, before I started walking away.

Barely clearing the trunk, a single light came over a small hill in the distance, hurting my eyes with the brightness. The roar of the engine grew louder as the distance closed. I waved my arms as a figure came into view, but the asshole biker drove right passed me as I screamed, "Hey! Hey!" The wind from his bike caused the dust on the road to kick up and fill my mouth.

I turned around, coughing, and screamed toward the bike. I knew it was pointless. There was no way in hell he'd heard me yelling above the roar of his bike, but he had to see me. The red taillight lit up the road as he turned the bike in my direction. I swallowed hard, unsure if this was my best idea of the night—but I'd already made too many mistakes to dwell on that. He was my only hope of getting home.

I stood there like a deer in headlights, unable to move, as I gaped at him. My hands trembled as the figure on the bike came to a stop. The engine was almost deafening, as I took in the sight of him on the machine. The bike was a Harley, a Fat Boy, with no windshield, chrome handlebars, and a dark body. He wore black boots, dark jeans, and a dark t-shirt. He was large and muscular, and I sucked in a breath as my eyes reached his handsome and rugged face. A playful grin danced on his lips as he watched me ogle him. Fucking hell.

"Need some help, lady?" he asked, removing his helmet, running his fingers through his disheveled hair. The dark peaks stood up on the top, the sides were short and clipped, and the color matched the sky—dark. I couldn't see his eyes; a pair of tinted glasses hid them. Could serial killers be so sexy?

"Um, do you have a cell phone I could use to call for a ride?" I asked without taking a step in his direction. Don't get too close—leave room to run. Who the fuck was I kidding? I couldn't make it five feet in these damn shoes.

"Sure." As he leaned back on his bike, I studied his body as he dug in his pocket. The skintight jeans showed his muscles through the denim fabric. Everything clung to him. I wanted to poke him to see if he felt as hard as he looked. What the fuck was wrong with me?

I was too busy staring to notice what he was holding out for me. "Lady, you wanted my phone?"

Snapping back to reality with the sound of his deep voice, I took a step toward him, reaching for the phone. "Oh, sorry."

My fingertips grazed his palm, and a tiny shock passed between us. His fingers closed on my hand as I pulled away. My heartbeat, which had calmed, now began to pound feverishly in my chest. It had to be my hormones. I hadn't had sex in God knows how long—I stopped counting after three months. The man in front of me wasn't my type, but his sex appeal wasn't lost on me. He looked like a whole lot of trouble, and I didn't need that in my life.

I stepped back, keeping my eyes trained on him, as I dialed the only person close enough to help—Sophia. The phone rang and his eyes traveled up and down the length of my body—with each ring, my stomach began to turn. I didn't have anyone else to call.

Tapping the end button, I sighed. "There's no answer. Thanks." I gave him a sheepish smile as I handed him the phone.

"Let me take a look and see if there's anything I can do. Okay?" he asked, as he began angling the bike to shine the headlights on the hood.

"Sure." I hit the unlock button on my car key before climbing in. I put the key in the ignition, but stayed aware of his proximity. No one would hear me scream if he tried to kill me. I couldn't let my guard down.

He put the kickstand down, climbed off the bike, and placed the helmet on the seat. Pulling the hood latch next to my seat, I watched him from the relative darkness of my car, my face hidden by shadows.

He was large, larger than he looked sitting on the Harley. He had to be more than a foot taller than me, and looked more solid with the bike illuminating his body. I stared at him, mouth open slightly, my breathing shallow as I looked at him like a piece of meat through the gap between the hood. He oozed masculinity and ruggedness, and I tried to picture him without all the skintight clothes. The muscles in his arm rippled as he touched the parts under the hood.

What would it be like to be with a man like him? Every man I'd dated just didn't work out. They were nice guys, but the spark I wanted was always missing. People think I'm a good girl, and I am, but my mind is filled with dirty thoughts that I could never share with a mate. I'd shared them with Sophia, but she doesn't count. No one had ever done anything fantasy-worthy with me. I can barely speak the words that are needed to describe the things I want done to me, or that I'd want to do to another person in this world.

"Ma'am," he said, snapping me out of the evaluation of my sex life, or lack thereof.

"Sorry, yes?"

"Can you try and start it for me, please?" he said, leaning over the hood, his hands placed on either side of the opening. "Now," he said. The car churned and churned. "Stop," I heard him yell over the screeching noise. He moved methodically around the engine. "Try it again." I turned the key, causing the engine to rattle, but not start.

He stood, rubbing the back of his neck as curses spilled from his lips. The only thing I could see was his crotch. I stared, motionless. His t-shirt covered the belt loops and stopped just above his groin. Damn. He filled out those jeans. He had to be big. Everything about him was big—he couldn't, just couldn't, have a small cock, could he?

The last guy that I'd slept with was more the size of a party pickle. It was the most unsatisfying sexual experience of my life. He was a teacher, and I wanted someone who was educated and self-sufficient, but he was boring in and out of the bedroom. I thought I'd found that with Derek, Mr. Pickle, but I was wrong. He was a wreck, and filled with more mental issues than anyone I'd ever know. He was germophobic, which was problematic when having sex. He'd jump right out of bed immediately after sex to shower and wash the dirty off. I sighed to myself, remembering his need to be clean—never mind that he was an asshole, too.

The hood of my car made a loud thump as the man slammed it. "Your car is a little tricky. Foreign cars can be complicated. I can't seem to get it to start," he said, walking toward the driver-side door.

"It's okay. Thanks for trying." I climbed out, not wanting to be trapped inside. What the hell was I going to do now?

"I was heading to the bar up the road. Want to join me?" He smiled and tilted his head as he studied me. "You can call a tow truck from there. It may take them a while for them to get out here."

I couldn't think of any other option. He was my only hope, my saving grace from the dark roadside, and a means to an end. There were worse things than climbing on the back of his motorcycle and wrapping my arms around him. "Okay, but I've never been on a bike."

"Never? How is that even possible?" he asked, shaking his head, a small laugh escaping his lips. His teeth sparkled in the light, straight and white. His jaw was strong, his cheekbones jutted out more when he smiled, and a small dimple formed on the left side of his face.

I looked down at the ground, my cheeks heated. "I don't know. I just never knew anyone that had one and I find them totally scary."

"It's not far from here and there isn't much traffic. I'll keep you safe," he said, holding out his helmet.

My stomach fluttered as I closed the car door and thought about my first motorcycle ride. The black, round helmet felt cool against my fingers as I took it from him. I scrunched my eyebrows together as I studied it. I didn't know if there was a front or a back, or how to put it on.

"Here, let me help you," he said as he reached for the helmet, removing it from my grip. His hand touched mine and I felt the spark again. Not a real spark, but electricity that I felt with every fiber of my being from the slightest touch. My body wanted his touch, but my mind was throwing up the caution flag.

Placing it gently on my head, he ran his rough fingers down the straps, almost caressing my skin, to adjust it to fit my face. I inhaled deeply, trying to fill all my senses with him. He smelled different than any other man I'd smelled. He didn't smell of cheap cologne, but there was a spicy, woodsy scent that reminded me of home. I closed my eyes and relished the feel of his warm skin against mine.

"All done. Are you ready?" he asked.

I opened my eyes, heat creeping up my neck, as I had been lost in his touch. "Yes." I prayed my voice didn't betray me.

He climbed on the bike, sliding forward, making room for me. "Lift your leg and climb on."

Placing my hand on his shoulder to help balance myself, I followed his instructions; my body slid forward, smashing against him. Rock solid. He turned his head, looking me in the eyes. "Put your feet on the pegs and wrap your arms around me. I don't bite—well, unless you want me to." He smirked, and my heart felt like it was doing the tango in my chest as I pressed against his back. He didn't just say that to me, did he? I lifted my feet off the ground, turning over complete control to the stranger I was entrusting with my life. I locked my hands together, completely wrapped around him.

"Ready?"

"Wait! I don't even know your name. I mean, I'm putting my life in your hands and I don't even know who you are." I gripped his body tighter, clinging to him.

I couldn't hear his laughter, but I felt the rumble of it from deep in his chest. "My friends call me City, sugar." He throttled the engine and my heart skipped a beat. Fear gripped me—there was no turning back now.

My grip became viselike, fear overcoming any need to be cool or seem calm in front of him. He patted my hands before the bike began to move, and I couldn't bear to look. I buried my face in his back, avoiding any chance of seeing the road. The wind caressed my skin, causing it to feel like ice compared to the warmth my palms experienced. Did this man have any soft spots? I flexed my fingers against his chest, wanting to feel his hardness, praying like hell I made it seem natural and not like I was molesting him.

The bike picked up speed, and my heart thundered against his back. I gripped him harder, holding on for dear life, the sound of the engine drowning out everything else around me, except the two of us. He leaned into the bike, his ass moving snugly between my legs. I didn't dare move. He was warm, comfortable, and I enjoyed every minute my body touched his. I closed my eyes, trying to not think about the movement of the bike underneath us—the slight shift and unevenness of the road made me feel off balance.

The noise of the engine changed, and I finally peeked over his shoulder. The parking lot of the Neon Cowboy was packed with bikes and was the brightest thing for miles. I'd driven by it dozens of times, but never thought about stopping. This wasn't the type of bar for kids on speedy, foreign-made bikes, but a place for tough bikers to hang out, drink beer, and pick up chicks.

City backed the bike into an empty spot, and I could feel my body begin to tremble from the fear that finally began to seep through my veins. I did it. I rode on a motorcycle, and with a stranger, no less. My breath was harsh as I blinked slowly and tried to calm myself down.

"You can climb off now, sugar." His legs were straddling the bike and he held the handlebars, securing the bike for me. "Enjoy your first ride?"

I released my hands from the security of his body and hoisted myself off on trembling legs. “It was the single most terrifying thing I’ve ever experienced,” I said, thankful when my feet were firmly on the ground. I stood, trying to get my body to stop shaking and my heart to slow down before walking inside the bar with him at my side.

“If that’s the scariest thing you’ve ever experienced, you need to get out more, sugar. I took it slow with you.” He grinned, and my stomach plummeted from his sinful smile. I wanted to see him above me naked and moving in and out of my body slowly, almost at a torturous pace. Everything about him made my body convulse and scream for attention. He wasn’t my type. I preferred a bookworm and a man that liked to spend an evening inside watching a movie or playing Scrabble, not riding like a bat out of hell on a Fat Boy to hang out at a bar. I wasn’t a barfly and never would be.

The outdoor lights gave me a full view of the man that called himself City. His hair was darker than I originally thought, almost jet black, and an inch long on the top, brushing against his forehead as he shook it out. It was a mess from the wind, with the front hanging over his forehead. I couldn’t tell the color of his eyes; they were still hidden behind the tinted lenses of his glasses.

“Yeah, lucky me.” I chuckled and tried to play it cool, even though my body shook. If that was slow, I didn’t think I wanted to know what his idea of fast and hard were—or did I? Fuck me. He had my brain all jumbled.

After removing the helmet, I ran my fingers through my hair, trying to straighten it after the wild ride. He laughed as he crawled off the bike, taking the helmet from my hands, and placed it on the seat. I watched, mesmerized, as he removed his glasses and put them inside a small bag hanging from the side of the bike. I wanted to see his eyes, and the entire man without a mask or veil.

“Ready, babe?” He motioned toward the door.

I wanted to scream no, but I didn’t have a choice. I could never walk into this sort of place on my own.

“Yeah, ready as I’ll ever be.” I started walking toward the door and felt a hand on my arm, stopping me in my tracks. I looked at his fingers wrapped around my arm and turned toward him. “What are you doing?”

“You can’t just walk into a place like this. You’re an outsider. They’ll eat you alive in there. I don’t want anyone giving you shit. We have to make them believe you’re with me so they leave you the fuck alone. Unless you want the attention?” he asked with a crooked eyebrow.

“I don’t.” I didn’t mind the idea of making everyone in the bar think we were together. City was hot and seemed like a nice guy; he did stop to help me when he could've driven right by me.

"Just stay by my side and follow my lead. I know these people and I don't want them sniffing around you. They look for easy prey," he said, giving me a smile that made my body tingle and my sex convulse.

"Okay, I'll stick to you like glue and follow your lead." Jesus, I sounded like a dork. I've always been a bookworm. I was national honor society member, and when all my friends were partying, I stayed in my dorm to study.

City nestled me against his side, tucking me between his body and arm. I moved with him, trying to keep up with his fluid movements, but my legs were so short I felt like I almost had to jog to keep time with him. He opened the door and I was immediately hit with a smoky smell, loud, twangy music, and a dozen set of eyes looking directly at us.

Randomly people yelled out "City" throughout the bar, giving me a clue that he was a regular. I felt like I'd entered a seedy version of Cheers and City was Norm, only sexy and muscular. He leaned down, placing his mouth next to my ear. I felt his hot breath before I could hear his words.

"Stick close and show no fear," he whispered, causing goose bumps to break out across my skin. "Let's say hello then we'll call a tow for you."

City looked big enough to handle any man in this place, but I didn't want to take that chance. I concentrated on breathing, keeping my chin up, and watching where I walked. The floor was filled with peanut shells and dust, and it made the walk in the stilettos even more treacherous than normal. I could barely walk when I bought them, but they looked too sexy to pass up.

We walked to a table filled with men all wearing their leather vests, covered in patches. They were unshaven, as dangerously sexy as City, with mischievous smiles on their faces. "Who's this lovely lady, City?" one man asked. His eyes raked up my body, stopping at my breasts before he looked at my face.

"This is Sunshine. Don't even fucking think about it, Tank, she's with me," City said with a smile on his face as he pulled me closer.

Sunshine? I'd never told him my name and he never asked. I didn't like the way Tank looked at me. Thank God he wasn't the one driving by while I was stranded. He looked at me like I was a piece of meat, a meal for his enjoyment.

Tank put his hands up in surrender. "Dude, I'd never. Chill the fuck out. I'm just enjoying the view," he said, his eyes moving from

City to me, and not being coy about his visual molestation.

City squeezed my waist. "Sunshine, this is Tank, the asshole. This is Hog, Frisco, and Bear," he said, pointing to each of the men.

The nicknames didn't seem to fit any of the men, except Bear. His arms were hairy and he was big, huge, in fact, with dark hair and a fuzzy face. He looked huggable and kind, with soft hazel eyes.

"Hi," I said, looking at each of them quickly, but I didn't try to memorize their names.

"I didn't know you were bringing a woman tonight, City," Bear said.

"Wilder shit has happened, Bear," City said, pulling me closer, leaving no space between us.

"She doesn't look like your usual taste, my friend." Bear smirked. "I don't mean that shitty, girl, I just mean you're one fine piece of ass and too good for that low-life motherfucker. You should be sitting on my lap." He patted his leg, and I wanted to find an exit. I looked down and studied my clothes. I didn't wear the trashy clothes some of the women in here wore, but I looked classy, sexy even, with not a hint of nerd to be found.

City moved toward Bear, and my heart sank as he began to speak. "Show some respect, you asshole. That's not how you talk to a lady." City stood inches from Bear's face. "Apologize to the lady. Now." City towered over him as Bear stayed rooted in his chair.

Bear looked at me, and I could see him swallow hard before he spoke. "I'm sorry, Sunshine. I was just kidding around. I really am an asshole. Forgive me, please."

"No harm done, Bear," I said with a fake smile, hoping to calm the situation.

"We're going to sit at the bar." City looked at Bear, not moving his eyes.

"Come on, dude, sit with us. Don't mind Bear. He's a total dick. Make his ass go sit at the bar," Frisco said.

"Sunshine and I want to be alone. I'll catch you guys another night," City said, pressing his hand against my back, guiding me away from the table and the large bar area.

"I'm sorry. They can be childish dicks. Bear doesn't have a filter," he said as he pulled out a chair for me. City had manners. Not many of the men I dated did something as simple as pull out a chair for a lady—it was a lost art. "He's a good guy, but sometimes his mouth runs and he doesn't think before he speaks."

"It's okay, really…it is. Thanks for sticking up for me," I said to him as I sat down, pulling my stool closer to the bar. "Why did you call me Sunshine?"

"Well, I don't know your name and you remind me of sunshine—your hair is golden and your smile glows. Just sounded right. I had to come up with something on the fly," he said. "I hope you didn't mind." He shrugged and grabbed the menu lying nearby.

"I didn't mind, but my name is Suzy."

"What would you like, Suzy?"

I wanted to say "you," because somehow this man made me lose my grip on reality. "Virgin daiquiri, please."

"Virgin? Really?" His brows shot up and the corner of his mouth twitched.

"I already had a drink tonight. I just want something sweet, no liquor."

"Do you want something to eat?" he asked. "You a vegetarian too?" He laughed.

"Shut up." I smacked him on the arm. "I'm good. I just want to call a tow truck."

"Gotcha." He pulled out his phone and placed it on the bar. "Hey, darlin', can you put in an order for a cheeseburger, a beer, and a virgin daiquiri?" he asked the bartender.

"Sure thing, handsome," she said, walking away, slowly swaying her hips to grab attention. I turned to City to see if he was watching her, but he was staring at me instead, and my mouth felt dry and scratchy.

"You want to call Triple A or someone else?" he asked without taking his eyes off me. They were an amazing shade of blue, and I couldn't look away. I'd always loved my blue eyes, but his were almost turquoise. I felt like he was staring through me, into me, seeing everything I hid under the surface. I wanted him, but I didn't want to admit my attraction. I couldn't admit it.

"Triple A is good," I said, reaching for my purse to find my membership card. I fumbled with my wallet, finding the card behind everything else inside. I could feel his eyes on me; he studied me and it made me nervous. What was he thinking? I dialed the number as I swiveled away from him, needing to avert his stare.

"Hello, Triple A, how can I help you?"

I could barely hear the tiny female voice above the loud classic rock that pulsed throughout the smoky bar. City chatted with the bartender as I tried to drown them out and give my location and details about my car. They wouldn't be able to make it out to my car until morning. Fuck. I thanked her for helping me before hitting the end button.

"What'd they say?" City asked with a sincere look as the bartender sashayed away from us.

"They won't make it out here until morning because they're busy and we're in the middle of nowhere. I'm to leave it unlocked so they can get in and put it in neutral or something. I don't know how it works. I've never had my car towed before." Now what the hell was I going to do? I was stranded at the Neon Cowboy with Mr. Sexalicious and my dirty thoughts.

"I'll bring you back to your car when I'm done eating. I guess you'll need a lift home too?" he asked, sipping his drink as he eyed me.

I smiled at him. Though I hated the thought of him going out of his way, and I wasn't that comfortable with a stranger knowing where I lived, I couldn't say no. "I'd appreciate it, if you don't mind."

"Not at all, Suzy. I can't just leave you here and walk out the door. I got ya, babe." He turned his stool toward me and leaned into my space. "Where do you want me to take you after we leave? Home?" He quirked an eyebrow, waiting for my response, and held me in place with his hard stare.

Home? Whose home was he referring to? City looked to be the type that had different women falling out of his bed every morning… or maybe he kicked them out before he fell asleep. His fingers brushed against the top of my hand and my internal dialogue evaporated.

"Where. Do. You. Live?" The laughter he tried to hide behind his hand made it clear that I'd sat there longer in thought than I had realized.

I cleared my throat. "I need to unlock my car then I need a lift home. I live about fifteen minutes north. Is that okay? I mean, I don't want to—" He put his finger over my lips and stopped me mid-sentence.

"Doesn't matter, I'll take you anywhere," he said with a sly grin that made my pulse race and my body heat. He licked his lips, and I stared like an idiot. My sex convulsed at the thought of his lips on my skin. What the fuck was wrong with me? Every movement he made and word he spoke turned sexual, as if permeating my brain. I needed to get laid; this man was not hitting on me, was he?

"You want some? I can't eat it all," he said as the plate was placed in front of him.

I shook my head and picked up my drink, trying to cool my body off from the internal fire caused by City. The cool, sweet strawberry slush danced across my tongue and slid down my throat.

I swirled the red straw in my mouth, trying to occupy my mind. His arms flexed as he lifted the burger to his mouth, forearms covered with tattoos. The left arm had various designs woven together—a koi fish, a tiger, and a couple of other nature-themed pieces that seemed to move across his skin, and his right arm had a city skyline. I wanted to touch his arms and run my fingers across his ink. He looked big everywhere, and my gaze drifted down his body and lingered at his crotch. I wondered if his motorcycle and tattoos made up for shortcomings elsewhere, but I couldn't believe a man like him was tiny. There was no way in hell he had a party…

"Pickle?"

I blinked and moved my eyes away from his crotch to his eyes. Pickle? He held it and motioned for me to take it.

"No. Thanks, though. You eat it," I said, feeling like he was reading my mind. God, I hoped he didn't see me staring at his crotch. I sucked down the rest of my drink, wishing now that it did have alcohol in it. Maybe then I wouldn't feel so embarrassed. "I noticed your tattoos. What's the one on your right arm?"

"That's the Chicago skyline," he said, as he took another bite.

"You from there?"

"Born and bred, baby." He grunted and continued to chew. I couldn't take my eyes off his mouth. Watching him eat was erotic to me; his lips moved as he chewed, and he sucked each finger in his mouth to clean off the juices that flowed from the sandwich. Damn. It had been too long since I'd had sex—when eating becomes sexual. Houston, we have a problem.

ABOUT THE AUTHOR

Chelle Bliss, USA Today Bestselling author, currently lives near the Gulf of Mexico, but hates sand. She's a full-time writer, time-waster extraordinaire, social media addict, and coffee fiend. She loves spending her free time with her 2 cats, hamster, and her alpha male boyfriend.

Sign up for Chelle's newsletter to keep up to date on her newest releases and other news at

chellebliss.com/newsletter

To learn more about Chelle's book visit chellebliss.com

BOOKS BY CHELLE BLISS

~MEN OF INKED SERIES~

THROTTLE ME (CITY & SUZY) Book 1, 2014
HOOK ME (MIKE & MIA) Book 2, 2014
RESIST ME (JAMES & IZZY) Book 3, 2014
UNCOVER ME (THOMAS & ANGEL) Book 4, 2015
WITHOUT ME (ANTHONY & MAX) Book 5, 2015
HONOR ME (CITY & SUZY) Book 6, 2016

~ALFA PI SERIES~

SINFUL INTENT, Book 1, 2015
UNLAWFUL DESIRE, Book 2, 2016
WICKED IMPULSE, Book 3, 2016 (COMING IN FALL)

~STANDALONE BOOKS~

REBOUND NOVELLA (FLASH AKA SAM), 2015
ENSHRINE (BRUNO & CALLIE), 2016
TOP BOTTOM SWITCH (RET & ALESE), 2016
DIRTY WORK (JUDE & REAGAN), 2016
MANEUVER, 2016

To learn more about Chelle's book visit chellebliss.com

ACKNOWLEDGEMENTS

I never know whom to thank first. There are so many moving parts and people involved when creating a new novel. I'm sure I'll leave out about a dozen individuals that should be given credit, but please understand… I verge on the cusp of having Old Timer's disease.

Lisa A. Hollett of Silently Correcting Your Grammar has been a Godsend. She puts up with my crazy like a champ. I can send her ten versions of the same thing and she doesn't bat an eye. Well, I'm not there so she's probably cursing me behind the computer screen and reaching for another glass of wine. But I like to believe that she's smiling like a loon and enjoying re-editing the same thing she did minutes before I tweaked it again.

Fiona Wilson of Fiona's Dreaming Proofreading has my loyalty and I'll forever be grateful to her. She's quick and efficient but always lets me know when she loves something. She was a fan of my work before she I hired her. She always catches the small things I miss before publication.

I adore Cat Mason and her daily comments and funnies to keep me going. She loved Bear since the first time she met him in Throttle Me and was more than happy to dive into Wicked Impulse. Her words of encouragement and enthusiasm made it easier for me to continue writing during the darkest times.

To my lovely agent, Kimberly Brower of Brower Literary Agency, thanks for putting up with my special kind of crazy. I know I'm not easy to deal with, but your words of wisdom help more than I can ever explain. Thank you for always being there for me.

Mo Mabie and Aly Martinez keep me grounded. I can't

explain how much their support and friendship has meant to me over the last few months in particularly. They're my girls. I'll always have their backs and will cut anybody that messes with them. I don't have a sister and they're the closest things I have to being one. They're wackier than me and I think that's why I love them most.

Meredith Wild, you my friend are always a pillar of strength. Thanks for always being there when I want to whine or if I have a question. Even with your amazing success, you haven't changed a bit. You always make time for me and for that I'll be eternally grateful.

I have so many betas, but it's because I love them so much I keep them close. They're my private cheering section and the cold slap of reality when I need it. I couldn't release a book without them. Special thanks to: Renita M., Malia A., Ashley H., Patti C., Mandee M., Kathy L., Maggie L., Kelly S., Stefanie L., Michelle E., and Michelle F.

And a giant wet sloppy kiss to my readers. Thank you for your understanding the last few months. Writing Wicked Impulse was a slower process than I planned, but no one complained about it. Your love and friendship amazes me.

The last few months have been the hardest of my life since the death of my brother. It was hard to form a thought let alone remember anything I'd written. I lost my words for a while, but eventually found the strength to finish Wicked Impulse. He would've wanted me to - he was my biggest fan. He always made me feel special and told everyone he knew that his sister was a writer. He was proud and I knew it. Without him, I'm lost, but I'll soldier on and find a way to make him even more proud of his little sister. I'll always love you, Kevin.

CPSIA information can be obtained
at www.ICGtesting.com
Printed in the USA
LVOW11s1611100517
534023LV00002B/397/P